MAFIOSA PRINCESS OMERTÀ

MAFIOSA PRINCESS
BOOK FIVE

LIZA MALLOY

NOTE

Omertà is a code of silence followed by men in the Sicilian mafia. Those who value omertà honor secrecy about their own criminal conduct (and that of their family), but traditionally, omertà extends even to one's enemies. Under that view of omertà, honorable men should seek their own justice and never speak to the police.

CHAPTER 1

Luca

I shuffled my feet in the gravel, grimacing at the dust already coating my leather shoes. I'd left the apartment in a hurry that morning, and even though I realized my mistake with the shoes right as I reached the car, the risk of seeing Giada outweighed my need to change into tennis shoes.

I nudged my sunglasses on top of my head, squinting at the wooden crates perched atop the forklift. I hadn't read the bill of lading, but I trusted my mental picture of the contents of the entire shipment. I didn't doubt the delivery included precisely what had been promised, but I certainly couldn't admit that to the inspector currently grimacing at Alessio.

"None of this is right," Alessio insisted, gesturing wildly at the sole crate he'd pried open earlier. That container held hundreds of silver bookends, as did the other parcels we'd unloaded. According to the bill of lading, the crate should've contained silver candlesticks. Of course, we had no more interest in the candlesticks than the bookends, but we needed the inspectors to find an innocuous but erroneous item in the containers.

"How do you know the entire shipment is wrong?" I asked my second-in-command. "Maybe the other crates are correct."

Alessio scowled, as if my mere question undermined his competency. "It'll take days to pry open every carton in this shipment. We pulled half a dozen at random, and they're all wrong."

It wasn't random, of course. The crates he randomly selected all had a faint yellow mark on the bottom left corner. If we opened the remaining cartons, we'd find their contents to be exactly what we expected, which wasn't candlesticks. This particular shipment was chock full of fine Italian leathers, watches, and jewels. Alessio and I had long since perfected our performance for the various inspectors, though, so neither of us worried.

The inspector shook his head, dismissing the suggestion of opening every crate. "If you're returning the entire shipment, you don't need to open everything. I can just make a notation that it was all rejected."

Alessio maintained his disgruntled expression, but so far, the entire discussion had gone according to our unwritten script. I nodded and let my Gucci sunglasses drop back over my eyes.

"Thanks, Joe," I said, offering the inspector my hand. I hadn't met him before, hence the tension creeping its way up my lower back. "If you want to check out anything else, we'll both be here all day. Let me know if you need anything from us."

The man pursed his lips and cast one last glance towards the container ship. "Well, I suppose to be thorough I should have the dogs do a quick search. It's just so odd that the entire shipment is wrong..." He scratched his head as his voice trailed off.

Alessio rolled his eyes.

"Of course. Take your time," I said, motioning towards the dock where a few of the armed guards stood.

There were no drugs aboard the ship, no contraband of any sort that dogs were trained to sniff, actually, so I didn't mind the search. Still, Alessio made no attempt to hide his annoyance as we walked off.

"It's fine," I reminded him. Even with the delay from the dogs, the inspectors would still be long gone by nightfall, when our guys would come in and empty the crates and replace their contents with stones before "returning" the shipment.

"It's a pain in the ass," he replied. "If your buddy Joe wants to be a fucking boy scout, he shouldn't have taken that Christmas bonus."

I blew out a sigh. "Honestly, this bullshit is the least of my problems at the moment."

Alessio quirked an eyebrow. "Rough morning?" he asked.

I shuddered, hating that my emotions were so transparent. Although, the morning had been fine, really. The problem was that I barely slept the previous night. I'd watched TV for more than an hour before Giada came in, apologized for accusing me of assaulting a stripper, and then stretched out beside me. We'd changed the channel to one of those upbeat design shows she loves to critique, and we made it through three episodes before she fell asleep, mid-show.

I felt guilty for snapping at her, but really—did I *hurt* Carla? How did Giada even think that? And Carla…Jesus. Bringing that fucking kid over as if I'd buy her sob story. She and I had hooked up once years ago. I didn't remember the date, but it was long before Giada and I were together. I'd guess it was more than four years ago, but absolutely had not been within the last two years.

Unless Carla had the gestational period of an elephant, that kid wasn't mine. Not. A. Chance.

How stupid did Carla think I was? Like I'd just fork over money to support some other guy's kid? Nope. Not gonna happen.

Still, I couldn't get the kid's stupid face out of my mind that night. Every time I started to drift off, I saw those dark brown eyes staring at me, mirroring my own.

But that meant nothing. Lots of kids had brown eyes. Babies rarely actually looked like their fathers that young.

I couldn't concentrate on anything. I felt guilty for evading my fiancée that morning, pissed off by Carla's claims, and frankly, confused by the timing of it all.

"Do you remember Carla, who used to work at Rize?" I asked Alessio.

"Candy?"

I shook my head.

"Kylie?"

"No."

"Carolyn?"

I glared.

"Okay, I guess not. Was she not that hot? I tend to have a pretty good memory when they're…good at their jobs."

I shrugged. "She's tall. And a redhead. I thought she was pretty cute."

Recognition washed over his face. "Ahh, yes. I remember Carla. The one you hooked up with."

"I did not!"

Alessio raised an eyebrow. *God*, I really did tell him everything.

"Okay, I did, but years ago. Anyway, do you think we still have a number for her at the club?"

His lips parted. "Everything okay with Giada?"

"I don't want to fuck Carla. I just need to talk to her."

Skepticism colored Alessio's eyes, but he reached for his phone. "Yeah, I'll get you the number."

I waited impatiently by the ship while two officers approached. One of them gripped the lead of a German Shepherd who looked like the type of animal who mauled mail carriers for sport. I knew the drill well enough to not have to watch the drug search too closely. All that mattered was that the canine approached each container with a similar level of disinterest.

I zipped my jacket a few inches higher, shivering. The sun was shining, but with the wind whipping between the shipping crates, it was freezing. It couldn't have been more than a couple of minutes when Alessio returned. He recited the number to me, and I dialed, then walked away for privacy.

A woman answered.

"Carla?"

"Yeah, who's this?" she sounded impatient.

"Luca."

"Oh. Hi."

Suddenly, all the anger I'd felt the previous night rushed back, and I couldn't even talk yet.

"Look, I'm sorry I came by when your girlfriend was there. I didn't realize…"

"She's my fiancée," I interrupted. "And if you fuck things up with her, you will regret it."

Carla took her time answering. "I don't want to mess anything up for you. I don't even want to ever see you again."

"Then why did you show up to my apartment?"

The skank blew out a sigh like *I* was exasperating *her*. "I just want what I'm owed. He's your son, and it isn't right that he doesn't get anything from you. I could go through the court system and make you pay child support, but I thought you'd rather handle this privately."

"We slept together once, at least two years before he was born."

"Yeah, we did. But we also slept together once about nine months before he was born." She paused. "Look, I'm not surprised you don't remember. You were drunk and…you didn't exactly take your time with me or call after."

"You've got the wrong guy. I was with Giada then. I wouldn't have cheated on her."

Carla sighed. "I don't know what you want me to say. I was there, and obviously, we did have sex. And the fact that you got me pregnant makes it pretty hard for you to dispute it. Look, I don't want to ruin your life. I just need money."

"He's not my kid."

"Did you even look at him, Luca? You can't deny he looks like you."

I chewed the inside of my lip. Nothing she said was convincing me.

"If you don't believe me, we can do a paternity test."

Now that was something I could work with, except it would have to be done in a way where she couldn't tamper with the results. "How?"

"You go to a lab. They take a swab from your son's cheek and a swab from you. Then you get the results."

I considered that. It didn't seem too complicated. I opened my mouth to agree, but then it hit me. There was no point in testing anything. I wasn't the father. I did not have sex with Carla nine months before her kid was born.

"He's not my kid," I said, hanging up.

I turned back to the ship, just in time to see Alessio smile and shake hands with the officers as they walked away with their dogs.

At least one problem was solved this morning.

~

Giada

I'd struggled to sleep the previous night, the silence between Luca and me settling over us like an interminable fog. I had so many questions for him, but I wasn't sure I wanted the answers. And besides, he should be the one talking. Luca owed me explanations without me having to ask. When I finally had drifted off, I was still pouting over the fact that everything had gone to shit so quickly. Luca and I had been happy, undefeatable, and now, we were inches away from each other, both of us pretending to sleep simply to avoid facing the truth.

When I woke the next morning, Luca was still asleep, stretched out on the far side of the bed. I tried to recall the last time we'd shared a bed and hadn't slept entangled in each other's limbs, or at least touching in some way, but I came up empty. It had been ages since we'd fought about anything although the more I thought about it, we actually hadn't even had a fight. Whatever we had now was almost worse, though.

I could handle arguing with Luca. Our loud, passionate fights led to loud, passionate sex—and that always compensated for whatever dumb issue had caused the disagreement in the first place.

But this — the silence, the avoidance — this I didn't know how to resolve. How could I fix a problem no one would even acknowledge?

I didn't have the heart to wake Luca in the morning, so I'd headed to the gym to sweat out my frustrations. I hoped to have a clearer head when I returned, and then, I assumed we'd talk over breakfast. But instead, the apartment was empty by the time I'd returned.

Luca had scribbled on a sticky note beside the coffee maker. "At the docks w AR today. Sorry I missed you this AM. Text if you need me. XOXO Luca."

I sighed and wadded the note into a ball before dumping it in the trashcan. I stirred some fresh berries into a cup of yogurt and texted Lorenzo while I ate. He worked for my father and had served as my driver the past several years. Enzo was only a few years older than me and we got along great, when he wasn't acting like an overprotective big brother. I'd harbored a crush on the guy for years before finally acting on my impulses one drunken night when Luca and I weren't together, but thankfully we'd all moved past that awkwardness.

I needed a distraction from everything with Luca, so I wasn't about to sit around the apartment all day even if Enzo wasn't available to drive me. But I also didn't feel like tackling traffic just to get to my new office. Luckily, Enzo said he had some business in that area and could pick me up on his way.

I luxuriated under the hot spray of the shower, then styled my hair and applied my makeup before finally dressing. I chose a pair of black slacks and a matching blazer, but kept the outfit cheery with a bright magenta shell under the jacket. I'd narrowed down my shoe choices to a pair of responsible black heels or obscenely tall magenta heels when the doorbell rang.

Lorenzo's eyes scanned up my body as I swung open the door. He paused his gaze on my face, and smirked.

"What?"

He shrugged, stepping inside further so he could shut the door behind him. "You're actually dressed."

I was tempted to make a crack about the insinuation that I'd invite him over while naked but opted against it. I did have a tendency to run behind schedule. "Which shoes?" I asked.

"Depends on the occasion. Do you want to appear responsible or fun?"

I cringed at his word choice. "Responsible of course, but I don't want to come across as boring either."

"Only a fool would ever mistake you for someone boring," Enzo said, a half grin on his face.

I opted for the black shoes, then followed him to the car. Once at the office, an interior design firm, I busied myself helping out with random projects that arose. I skimmed through a couple of client portfolios and sat in on one meeting, but it wasn't exactly my most productive day. Still, I made it until mid-afternoon before caving and texting Luca.

I asked when he'd be done working and if he'd want to meet up for dinner. At a restaurant, I figured, we could talk without all the pressure—or potential for drama—we could face at home. But Luca replied almost instantly that he would be late. He apologized but said some shipment had gotten screwed up,. He suggested I go out with a coworker instead.

I considered that but called my best friend Gabriella instead. I was craving sushi anyway, and that had never been Luca's favorite. I beat my friend to the restaurant by fifteen minutes though, which gave me ample time to stress about Luca.

Usually, when he was busy, Luca took his time replying to my texts. Today, he'd claimed to be swamped, but he'd responded immediately. What if he wasn't busy at all? What if Luca was just avoiding me?

Gabriella waltzed into the restaurant before I could panic further. I stood to greet her with a hug, then we both complimented each other's outfits before sitting. We each ordered dry champagne, having long since agreed that our typical go-to drinks were too sweet to enjoy with sushi, as the sugar detracted from the flavors of the fish. We perused the menus a moment longer, then Gabby sighed and relaxed into her chair.

"Busy day at work?" I asked, sensing her overwhelm.

She nodded. "Yeah. But what's up with you? You look stressed."

I opened my mouth to speak, then closed it. I certainly couldn't tell her the truth. Less than a month ago, I'd finally convinced Gabby that Luca was the perfect fiancé and would never cheat on me. I didn't want to undo all my hard work by admitting some woman had showed up at my apartment with a kid who looked suspiciously like my faithful fiancé... or that Luca had been avoiding me ever since.

"Giada, come on. What's wrong?" she prompted, pausing before adding, "Where's Luca tonight?"

"He's working. Some mix-up with a shipment kept him late, nothing major."

Gabriella looked relieved at my explanation. "Good. So you're not stressed out about him?"

I shrugged, grateful she'd given me an easy opening to deflect. "No, we're doing great. Wedding planning is more overwhelming than I'd anticipated, but I suppose that's a good kind of stress."

She grinned. "I'm always happy to help with major decisions. Did you bring your notebook?"

"Of course." I rarely left the house without my wedding planner. The small binder contained everything from menus to seating charts and deadlines. Anytime my mother called me, I flipped through the magical little planner until I found a page answering whatever question she had. It was truly a lifesaver.

"Honestly though, I want a break from the wedding stuff tonight," I continued. "Let's talk about you. I want to hear more about your job. And didn't you go on a date Saturday night?"

Luckily, my friend was more than willing to fill the next couple of hours chatting about her life.

When I got home, Luca still wasn't back. I browsed through some bridal magazines to brainstorm ideas, then poured over online images of celebrity weddings for inspiration. A little after eleven, I stopped waiting for Luca and went to bed.

I felt like I'd slept for hours when I was awakened by a series of loud thumps. I sat abruptly, instantly alert. Judging from the continued racket, though, it wasn't a burglar. I grabbed my robe and flipped on the lamp, rubbing my eyes as I went into the main living room.

"Uh oh," Luca said as he saw me, his voice infinitely louder than necessary. Then he laughed and mumbled something in Italian before stumbling.

Alessio caught him by the arm, eying me sheepishly. "Sorry. I didn't realize he'd had quite so much until we got here. He had some trouble getting out of the car, so I figured I'd walk him up."

"He's drunk?"

"Yes," Alessio said.

At the same time, Luca answered. "I'm not drunk. I'm just a po ubriaco."

"That means drunk," Alessio translated.

"I just need some rest," Luca insisted.

"Can you walk him to the bedroom?" I asked. Most likely,

Luca could walk himself, but since Alessio was here, there was no reason to risk Luca falling over when I wouldn't be able to get him up on my own.

"You sure? I'd make him sleep in the guestroom. Or the bathroom," Alessio said.

I shook my head and pointed to the master bedroom. I'd never fall back asleep if Luca was in a different room. I'd spend the rest of the night worrying that he was sick. I followed as Alessio walked him back to our bedroom. Luca kicked his shoes off and started towards the bed.

"Hang on," Alessio said. He reached behind Luca and pulled a gun out of his back waistband, then patted near his ankle. "Is that it?" he asked Luca.

Luca nodded and awkwardly fumbled with his jacket.

"Thanks," I said.

Alessio set the gun on top of the dresser. I wondered if he knew Luca usually kept that one in the nightstand drawer. I wasn't about to mention that because it didn't seem like Luca should have easy access to a gun at the moment.

"No prob. I can lock up," he said.

"You have a key to our apartment?"

Alessio froze as if uncertain whether I was supposed to be privy to that information. *Of course* he had a key. Luca trusted him more than he trusted me.

"Nevermind, it's fine," I said, waving him off and making a mental note to use the chain more often.

I went out into the kitchen for a bottle of water and brought it to Luca. He accepted it, drinking thirstily.

"Are you hungry?"

He shook his head. "Tired."

I unfastened the buckle on his belt then worked on his pants. When I paused before working the pants down his hips, I caught the look he was giving me.

"Not a chance," I clarified. "I just figured you'd be more comfortable without your pants.

"Grazie."

"Prego," I replied.

"Hey! You can speak Italian! When did that happen?"

I shook my head, certain it wasn't actually impressive that I'd picked up on how to say "you're welcome" in a language spoken by most people in my life. "Go to sleep Luca."

He dropped back against the pillow, let me tug the covers up over his legs, then appeared to fall asleep. I nudged him onto his side, then crawled back into bed beside him. I watched him sleep for a while, wondering what could have possibly inspired him to drink so much.

CHAPTER 2

Luca

I awoke to my head throbbing so intensely that it felt like someone was using my skull as a drum. I tried to roll over to read the clock but had to move slowly, fighting back nausea. When I saw it was ten, I panicked. Surely I was late for something. My damn head hurt too much to recall what, though.

I heard the shower running, and a moment later, it shut off. I decided to bide my time until Giada emerged from the bathroom, steamy and clean. It took another ten minutes, but it was worth the wait. She had dried off, applied makeup, and combed her long hair but apparently hadn't brought clothes in the bathroom.

She froze in the doorway as she saw me staring. After a moment, she put her hand on her hip and shook her head, causing her breasts to sway.

"You look like shit," she said.

"You look like an angel," I replied. Silhouetted by the light of the bathroom, her dewy skin glistening with the last drops from her shower, she truly did.

Giada barely cracked a smile. She crossed the room, retrieved panties and a bra, then pulled them both on before heading into the closet. She put on leggings and a long top, then went into the kitchen. Just as I started to question if she was coming back, she did. She handed me a mug of coffee, two slices of toast, and some ibuprofen.

"Thank you," I said.

Giada disappeared into the bathroom again, and this time, I heard the hair dryer. I drank the coffee, slowly at first, then ate a few bites of the toast before swallowing three of the pills. As I finished the coffee, I stood and went into the kitchen to get another cup.

When I returned to our bedroom, I was feeling better, and Giada had finished drying her hair. I tapped on the door, and when she didn't protest, I joined her in the bathroom and brushed my teeth.

"I already worked out," she said, in case I didn't already feel lazy enough.

"Are you going into work today?" I asked her.

She hesitated, as if trying to come up with an excuse to avoid me. "No. And we are supposed to meet with the priest for our last pre-cana meeting."

I couldn't help but grimace. "When is that?"

"One o'clock."

"Okay."

"Are you planning to tell me why you drank yourself into oblivion last night?"

The truth was on the tip of my tongue, but I couldn't say it. As soon as I told Giada what Carla had accused me of, she'd do the math, assume I cheated, and leave me. I couldn't risk that.

"Bad business investment," I said instead. "Really bad. Lost a lot of money."

"Alessio didn't seem bothered."

"He's not as high-strung as me."

She seemed to accept that. "If it's okay with you, I'm going shopping," she said.

I nodded.

"Don't worry. I won't spend any of your money. I'd hate for you to run out altogether."

Ouch.

I made a point to arrive at the church a half hour early, thinking Giada would be there saying her rosary or praying and I could earn some major bonus points, but she wasn't. I sat outside for a bit, catching up on emails, but then went on inside.

Giada arrived just in time for our meeting with the priest. I was disappointed we didn't have time to discuss anything in private ahead of time, but I supposed I didn't know what I would've said anyway. I hadn't been in favor of these pre-marriage classes. I still thought they were pointless in many ways. The priest encouraged us to discuss lots of topics that I figured were pretty important to normal couples. How would we handle finances? What were our rules for arguing? Would we both work? How many kids did we want? Where would we live?

The problem with the majority of the questions was that they weren't things Giada and I had any say in. My job wasn't one I could leave, my duties weren't exactly negotiable, and that job dictated a pretty big portion of our life. And as for the rest, well, I'd let Giada do whatever she chose. I didn't actually care what kind of a house we bought, as long as we were together. I could be happy with one kid or twelve, if that was what Giada wanted. We could spend all of our vacations in Canada if it made her happy.

Besides, Giada and I already knew each other. We'd known each other our whole lives, and that meant we'd long since memorized each other's likes and dislikes, quirks, fears, and dreams. We didn't need some generic one-size fits all class to realize we had differing views on desserts, church attendance, or the frequency of dinners with extended family.

As this was the last class, the priest talked a lot about the actual wedding with us. Again, I had no strong preferences on any of that, but Giada did. Well, mostly she just wanted to be married in the church, surrounded by friends and loved ones. She was hardly bridezilla over it all. Not that I had expected otherwise.

"It's been a pleasure getting to know you both," Father Ben said as our time drew to a close. "I wish you a long, healthy life together and hope you both grow as individuals and a couple during your marriage. Remember, no marriage is without trials or struggles. The key is mutual respect, and everything that entails. Trust each other, be honest with each other, and forgive each other."

I swallowed the lump in my throat.

We held hands as we walked out of the church.

"Can you drive me back to the apartment?" she asked.

"Of course." I frowned, trying to guess how she'd arrived there. "Where's your car?"

"Gabby and I met for lunch and shopping," she explained. "She dropped me off here."

"Oh. How is Gabby doing?" I asked.

"Fine." She paused. "I had dinner with her last night, too."

I nodded, certain that was a dig at my failure to come home at a reasonable hour the previous night. We reached the car, and by the time I started the ignition, guilt was creeping over me. The priest's words kept echoing through my brain. I didn't think I could handle any more meaningless small talk.

Apparently, Giada felt the same, and she beat me to the punch.

"The boy that Carla brought to our apartment the other day," she began, abruptly shattering the awkward silence of the car. "Is he your son?"

"No!" My reply was instantaneous. I gritted my teeth before continuing. "There's no way he could be."

I glanced at my fiancée as her face registered what I was

saying. Not that he wasn't my son and no one was suggesting as much, but essentially admitting Carla had called me the father.

"Why didn't you tell me that sooner, like right when she left?"

"I don't know. Because it's ridiculous, I guess. I wasn't with her then. It isn't possible."

"He looks like you," Giada said, her voice dripping with accusation.

"His eyes," I said. "I know."

She frowned, but seemed calm, which was saying a lot for Giada. "How old is he?"

"Fifteen months."

I waited while she did the math.

"So we were together when he was conceived."

I nodded and rested my hand on top of hers in a comforting way. "I didn't sleep with her then. He isn't my son. There is no question."

I thought I sounded convincing, which made sense since I spoke the truth. But Giada picked up on something else from my response. She yanked her hand out from under mine.

"Then? You didn't sleep with her then?"

Shit. "We were together three or four years ago. One time. For about five minutes."

"Sounds delightful."

"You were in college at the time. You'd just started dating Adrian I think."

"Pregnancy doesn't last that long."

"I know that, and I'm telling you I haven't slept with her since then."

"Then why does she say he's yours?"

"Because she wants money. She probably picked up on the coincidental similarities in our eye color and figured it was worth a chance that I'd fall for it."

Giada was quiet for a few minutes. "If he's not yours, take a paternity test and prove it. Then she'll have to leave you alone."

"I'm Luca Marino. She'll leave me alone either way." I pulled into the parking space and killed the ignition.

Giada rolled her eyes dramatically. "I get that sometimes you can't come up with another way, and you have to intimidate people, but this isn't one of those times. Paternity tests are quick and easy." She waited until I'd walked around to her side of the car to continue. "I'd like to know if you have a child before we get married."

"I already told you I don't. I swear to you I didn't cheat on you. Not with that woman, and not with anyone else. Do you seriously not trust me?"

She turned to me, gazing into my eyes as though the answer to my question was written in my pupils. Or maybe it was the answers to her own questions she sought. Either way, I don't think she found it. After a moment, she wiped a tear from her eye and started towards the apartment.

"Giada, wait," I said. When it became apparent she wouldn't, I jogged to catch up with her. I reached for her hand and waited until she turned to me. "I'll take the test," I said.

She swallowed. "Thank you."

I followed her into the apartment, but neither of us spoke for a minute. Giada seemed desperate to avoid my stare. First, she busied herself refilling her water bottle. Then she wadded up a damp paper towel and began scrubbing at invisible spots on the counter. I decided she needed a distraction, so I started talking about work.

"We got a big shipment in yesterday. We thought there would be some hiccups, but in the end, everything went smoothly. My papà is actually pleased for once."

"That's nice," she mumbled, running a second cloth along the cabinet trim work.

"It's supposed to warm up next week. That'll make the work at the docks nicer."

"Um hmm," she mumbled.

Clearly, small talk wasn't working. I tried a different tactic. "And I was thinking. We should get a dog." I half expected her to simply nod her agreement, but apparently she was, at least, listening to me.

"I don't like dogs," she said as if I didn't already know her disdain for all creatures with fur, feathers, or scales.

I blew out a sigh. "You can't even look at me?"

She finally gazed up, her eyes distant and sad.

"Whatever happened to innocent until proven guilty?" I asked.

Giada exhaled slowly through her nostrils as though willing serenity to wash over her. "I'm sorry. I'm trying. I want to believe you. I do believe you, I think." She paused. "It's just a lot to take in."

"For me, too," I said. "I wasn't exactly expecting to be accused of fathering a child with a woman I haven't seen in years."

I supposed she was still too upset to actually feel any sympathy for me, so I wasn't surprised when she simply repeated her apology.

"I'm glad you told me, and I'm not trying to punish you for something you say you didn't even do. I just feel...I don't know, confused. And it doesn't help that instead of talking to me about it right away, you avoided me for days."

"I'm sorry. I needed time to process it all before I told anyone," I admitted.

"You told Alessio."

"I did not. I haven't said a word to anyone. I planned to tell you, but I was scared you'd react...well, like this. Things were so great with us last week, and now you don't trust me."

"I can't trust you when you're hiding things from me."

"I'm not hiding anything."

Giada sighed. "Look, you said you needed time to process all of this. Well, I do too. Maybe it would help if we spent some time apart."

I actually felt my heart skip a beat. "What?" I gripped her

biceps as if about to shake some sense into her. "Giada, no. That's a terrible idea. I didn't do anything wrong!"

My strong response seemed to have caught her off guard. She winced and shook her arms free.

"Shit. No, I don't mean like that. I mean, like a night or two. Like you go out with Alessio or whoever and have a guy's night tonight, and I'll burn off some steam with Matteo and then crash at home."

"This is your home."

"Luca, come on. You know what I mean. I have a bunch of wedding plans to go over with my mom anyway, and everything is fine with you and my brother now, right?"

I nodded, trying not to focus on the fact that my fiancée wanted time apart.

"So there's no problem if I go to my parents' house just for few days?"

I shook my head. "That's a bad idea. You belong here, with me."

"Luca, this will be good for both of us. I can see it in your eyes that you're mad at me too," she paused. "Although, I have no idea why."

Annoyance hit me like a wall of bricks. "Seriously? We're supposed to be married in a matter of months, and you just admitted you don't trust me or believe anything I'm saying."

"That's not at all what I'm saying. And you can't seriously blame me for having questions. It wasn't that long ago that you told me I was everything to you and then went and made out with Mila."

I rolled my eyes. That stupid date back in Italy had been biting me in the ass for years now. If I could take back one thing I'd done in life, that would be it. But it was ages ago. And I wasn't the only one who'd faltered in the early days of our relationship. "What about Adrian, Giada? How many times were you with him when we were together?"

Her expression turned to ice. "I'm not proud of how I treated Adrian, but I never cheated on *you* with him, and you know it."

My fiancée stormed out of the room. I let her go. I needed time to cool off, too.

I skimmed over some emails, checked in with Thomas and Giovanni, then decided it was time to face the music. I rapped my knuckles on the outside of the bedroom door, prepared to grovel.

Giada swung open the door, a look of fierce determination in her eyes. Gazing past her, I noticed the bags stacked neatly on our bed. I brushed past her to confirm she'd actually packed, and wasn't just cleaning out the closet or something less devastating.

"Giada, you're not seriously leaving," I said, despite all evidence suggesting that was exactly what she was doing. Desperation welled up inside of me, overpowering the crushing anger I'd been feeling for days. "You said you'd stand by my side no matter what. We're supposed to get married," I reminded her.

"And we will," she insisted. "This isn't that sort of a break. You are still my fiancé. I still expect you to call me and text me obnoxiously often. Maybe even pay Enzo to spy on me. I just feel discombobulated. I need a couple of days with my mom."

I felt sick, but plastered a smile to my face. "I don't feel like I have a vote in this."

"Luca, come on. You've been avoiding me the past few days anyway. This will be good for both of us."

I opened my mouth to reply, but the buzzing of her phone cut me off.

"Shit. Wow, that was fast," she mumbled, gazing up to meet my eyes. "Enzo's here."

My chest tightened at the thought of Lorenzo, of all people, being the one to take Giada away from me. But I wasn't about to beg. I lifted her duffel over my shoulder and gripped another in my hands. Giada grabbed her purse and another bag I suspected held all of her hair and makeup. I walked slowly towards the door, searching for anything I could say to fix this before she left.

But Giada had already opened the door, shifting her bags from my arms to Lorenzo's.

"Call me in the morning, okay?" she peered up at me.

I nodded my head once, and she leaned in for a hug. The embrace was more than I'd expect if she were really mad, but less than I'd receive before any separation if she were happy with me. She rose to her toes and pressed a soft kiss to my lips before smoothing her palm along my cheek.

I acknowledged Lorenzo with a quick lift of my eyebrows, then watched him walk off with my fiancée.

~

Giada

The look in Luca's eyes as I left that night wrecked me. For such an arrogant ass, he sure knew how to pull on my heartstrings. And for what? We'd only be apart for a couple of days. I wasn't trying to punish him.

Well, maybe I was. But maybe not. I would've loved to stick around and hash things out. But it was obvious we both needed some time to ourselves. Neither of us was in a place where we could rationally discuss it all, as our argument that night proved.

Besides, hanging around the apartment, walking on tiptoes around Luca, and watching him do the same for me, I felt like I was going to crawl out of my skin. It wasn't right. We'd both said everything there was to say, and somehow, that wasn't enough. Not yet, anyway.

Luca told me he hadn't cheated. The fact that he was willing to take a test to prove it to me should have reassured me. But it didn't. Rationally, I knew that even if he had cheated, it was two years ago. He was a different person then. We were a different couple back then. Regardless of what he'd done then, he wasn't the type to cheat now.

I felt Enzo's eyes on me a moment before he spoke. "Everything okay, Princess?"

I plastered a smile to my face and turned. "Yep."

"Luca okay? He seemed…off."

"Yeah, he's…" I paused. "He's got a lot on his plate with his work at the moment, so I figured it was a good time to head home and hammer out the final wedding details with Mom. I just don't like being away from him."

Enzo turned back to the road, so I couldn't tell if he believed me or not. "Well, that's a good thing, I suppose, seeing as how you're about to chain yourself to him for life."

I hadn't decided how to respond to that when Enzo started speaking again.

"Matteo wanted us to pick up food on the way home. Is that okay? He's planning a long night of reality TV and mixed drinks for the three of us." Enzo paused and glanced at me again, biting back a laugh. "It only seemed fair to warn you, even though he asked me not to."

A natural smile filled my face for the first time that day and my heart squeezed at the thought of seeing my favorite brother again. Not that it had been that long, but ever since I'd moved out, things had been different between Matteo and me. We were no longer the inseparable buddies we'd been as kids. And the more he worked without oldest brother Angelo, the less I felt like it was the two of us versus the world.

Luca

A wiser man would've used the time alone to think, or at least to catch up on sleep. I opted to go a different route, self-flagellation. I slipped into running shoes, then headed to the gym. It wasn't yet closed at this hour, but it wouldn't have mattered if it was. Giovanni's uncle owned the place, and we did a fair amount of work from the office here. I had my own key and twenty-four-hour access.

Eddie, Giovanni's uncle, greeted me as I came in, not bothering to hide the look of surprise on his face at seeing me so late in the day. "Everything okay?" he asked.

"Eh, it will be," I replied. "Nothing a few rounds with the bag won't fix. How's Cara?" Eddy's wife Cara had just undergone knee surgery a few weeks prior. The last time I'd seen her, she was still on crutches.

"Strong as an ox," he replied, grinning. "I don't think a full leg amputation could keep that woman down."

I smiled and moved past him. I dumped my stuff in the office, forgoing the shared locker room, then warmed up with some jump roping before moving to a punching bag. I supposed it was good that I had this outlet— a safe, socially-acceptable way to pound out my anger and frustrations. But I'd be lying if I said it offered as much relief as a real fight. There was something to be said about the adrenaline coursing through my body when I faced off with a live opponent. The potential for injury, pain, or defeat was both unnerving and thrilling.

But fights these days had a lot more at stake than back when I was in high school.

I drove straight home from the gym, torturing myself with a short, icy shower in hopes of ridding myself of the last ounce of angst. But it didn't work. The apartment was too quiet without Giada. I missed seeing the random pieces of jewelry and bottles of nail polish she left lying around, missed the quirky way she'd occasionally talk to herself, missed the smell of her lotions and shampoos wafting through the room as she wandered about. I missed her.

I dialed Alessio. "Are you alone?" I asked.

When he confirmed he was, I said I was on my way.

One stiff drink later, my friend finally worked up the nerve to ask me what was wrong. Surely he already knew it had to do with Giada, but after crashing his evening, I owed him more detail.

"Giada went home to work on wedding plans for a few days," I began. "We had a fight earlier, and she says we both need time to think."

"And do you?"

I shrugged at the loaded question. "I don't know. I still want to marry her, if that's what you mean. But neither of us is budging on our stances, so I see why she doesn't think it's productive to keep arguing."

Alessio snorted. "You are the two most stubborn people I know. Care to share what this fight was about?"

I hesitated. I yearned to tell Alessio the full story, but for some reason, I didn't. I could tell him later, once the whole debacle was behind me. "Giada thinks I did something. I told her I didn't. She won't believe me."

"What kind of something?"

"She's afraid I cheated."

"Did you?"

"No."

Alessio looked surprised but didn't contradict me.

"But now I'm mad that she doesn't believe me, and she's mad because she thinks I cheated. Hence the standstill."

My friend dragged his fingers through his shaggy hair then tipped his glass back, swirling the swig in his mouth before swallowing. "I get it. You're big on trust. But look at it from her perspective. You kind of have a track record of being an asshole."

I flipped him the middle finger.

"Seriously. You haven't exactly been the dream boyfriend. Someone could make a soap opera about all the shit you've put that woman through."

"She hasn't exactly made it easy for me either."

Alessio nodded. "That's why I don't do serious relationships."

I laughed so hard that I spit droplets of my drink across the room. "You don't do relationships because you're a whore with commitment issues."

My friend shrugged. "Yeah, that too. You want my advice?"

"I'm here, aren't I?"

"Give her a day, buy her some expensive crap like you always do, then apologize and agree with whatever she says. Sure, she may not be right, but once you're fucking like rabbits again, I don't think you'll care who won the fight."

I blew out a sigh. Despite his crassness, Alessio did make a valid point.

He paused, making a face like he'd drank sour milk. "So, do you want to vent more, or can I distract you with some work stuff? I'd hoped to wait until you were in a better mood, but it's making me nervous."

"What?" I growled. Few things stressed out Alessio. If he was anxious about something, it had to be bad.

"There's a new player in town. Russian guy, Dmitry Petrov. He's bad news. Weapons dealer, human trafficking, and our intel shows he's trying to knock out the competitors."

As Alessio went on, detailing the reasons he thought Dmitry was encroaching our territory. I wanted to tell him it could wait, but I knew it couldn't. I'd heard this guy's name before—Dmitry Petrov. Evidently, that was one of the most common names in Russia, but here, I knew of only one man with that name, and he was trouble.

Dmitry's reputation preceded him. I'd never met the guy, but I believed the rumors that he was ruthless and that he had no loyalty or love aside from his own greed. He was reportedly involved in the arms trade, drug deals, and human trafficking. Some of the stories of his actions made my stomach churn. He wasn't the type of guy I wanted in my city. Especially if he was coming after me and my family.

"How long have you known about this?"

"A day or two. Iacopo told me last week that Dmtitry was coming into town, but he didn't arrive until this past weekend. I wanted to wait to tell you until you could concentrate. You've seemed distracted lately."

I blew out a sigh. I had been distracted, which was a risk I couldn't take in my line of work.

"Has anyone spoken with my papà about this? Or Marco?"

"Your dad knows. Not sure about Marco. Someone should catch him up to speed."

I thought about it, then nodded. It was the perfect excuse. I'd give Giada a day or two to miss me, then head to the Conti house and talk with her dad. Surely by then, I'd have gotten over Giada's lack of trust.

"There's more," Alessio said.

I waited for him to elaborate.

"Your dad asked me to tell you he wants you back home for a week or two. He wants you to meet with some of his new guys."

I rolled my eyes. My papà was incessant with his plans to build his army. Personally, I thought we had enough men. To him, it wouldn't be enough until he'd conquered the world. Or at least until he had ever Italian American sworn to protect what's his.

"Fine. Figure out a time we can meet with Thomas and Giovanni tomorrow to work out the details." I paused, trying to recall what other pressing matters I needed to attend to in the morning. There was nothing work-related that I couldn't delegate. But there was something else I needed to handle, on a more personal note. I wouldn't be able to focus on the situation with Dmitry until I did.

"I need to pay someone a quick visit tomorrow afternoon, so let's aim for earlier in the day," I said.

"Sure. Who are we visiting?" The corners of Alessio's mouth quirked up in anticipation. He loved toying with people who'd wronged us. He had a special gift for instilling terror without actually harming anyone.

I ticked my head to the side. "I'll deal with this alone."

He frowned. "One of the other guys can go if you don't want me involved."

"It's not that. It's a personal matter, and I won't need backup."

CHAPTER 3

Giada

Sun was already streaming through my blinds when something jostled me awake the next morning.

"Tina, she's up!" called a shrill voice.

I sat slowly, rubbing my eyes. My aunt Sofia perched on the end of my bed.

"We were told we could go dress shopping today," Aunt Bianca said from the corner of my room.

"What?" I stifled a yawn and smoothed a hand over my hair.

"Your mom said that's why you're home, to finish up some wedding plans," Bianca said.

"Yes, but not at…" I paused to glance at the clock, expecting to see it was some ungodly early hour. Instead, I found it was already ten thirty. I reached for my phone, noting two missed calls from Luca. "Shit," I mumbled.

"Giada Francesca!" my mom shrieked, flitting through my room like a hummingbird on a mission. "Language!"

"Sorry, I just…I need a few minutes."

"Her fidanzato called," Aunt Sofia told my mom.

"I didn't mean to sleep in so late," I explained. "It's Matteo's fault."

"Well, he doesn't need his beauty sleep, does he?" Mom said.

"And he's not planning a wedding," Aunt Bianca added, tugging the covers off my bed. "Come on, up you go. Get showered and dressed and you can call your Luca on the way to the first shop."

I hurried into my bathroom, worried my aunts would follow me in and try to dress me if I didn't move quickly. I wasn't in the mood to shop for dresses, but once we were out of the house, surely I could convince them today was a better day for floral arrangements or caterers.

The previous night had been the perfect distraction. My brother Matteo, Enzo, and I had stayed up way too late, watching crappy TV and eating all the foods most brides avoided in the months before the wedding. We laughed, we talked, and my brother told me all about his sordid dating life. I hadn't drunk enough to suffer a hangover, but I was definitely exhausted.

A fist pounded on the bathroom door, reminding me I had limited time. I skipped the shower, certain they'd never leave me alone long enough for that.

"There's some coffee on your nightstand, mia cara," my aunt called through the door.

"Thanks!" I hollered back. I washed my face and brushed my teeth before peeking out the door. Seeing the coast was clear, I grabbed the coffee and my cell phone, heading into my closet to pick out my clothes for the day. I dialed Luca, but the call went to voice mail.

"Hi, sorry I missed your call. Matteo and I were up late, and now my aunts are hassling me to go pick out wedding dresses. I'll talk to you later," I said, disconnecting and cringing at my own awkwardness.

I dressed quickly, pulled my hair into a messy bun, then applied my makeup. As I made my way downstairs, I planned how to tell my aunts I wasn't in the mood for dress shopping. Luckily, no one questioned my logic when I said I was too bloated from all the junk I'd devoured with Matteo.

We spent the day carrying out various other wedding errands instead. We chose the florist, and selected the flowers for my bouquet, as well as those for the general décor during the ceremony and the centerpieces at the reception. I hesitated before selecting the flowers for Luca's boutonniere, but the florist assured me the groom could make changes if he didn't like anything I'd chosen.

We visited the stationary shop next, and my aunts instantly overwhelmed me with the plethora of decisions to be made. I didn't just have to decide the wording on the invitations; I had to choose the color, size, and font of the lettering, the color and weight of the cardstock, and the general design.

Bianca, Sofia, and my mom were all voicing opinions loudly. Meanwhile, I felt like hyperventilating. The saleslady sat us down and offered me a binder of options to select. I flipped through, finding something I liked about nearly all the designs. I was about to tell them I couldn't decide when my phone rang.

"It's Luca," I said, flooded with relief. *Saved by the bell.*

I clicked to answer his call, then scurried out of the shop. "Hey," I gushed, answering.

"Hi." He paused. "Are you…at the gym?"

I breathed a laugh. "Shopping for wedding invitations with my aunts, but it's quite the workout. I had no idea there was so much to decide." I explained the various choices, even though he hadn't asked. I was mostly just venting, not expecting him to have an opinion on stationary or to be able to decide anything over the phone, but I should've known better. Luca was nothing if not decisive.

"Go with a thicker cardstock," he said. "Thin invitations seem cheap."

"That's what my mom said, but won't people just throw them away anyhow?"

"It's the first impression of our wedding the guests will have. You want it to be a good one. And you'll save an invitation forever. Your father has his framed in his home office."

My lips parted in surprise. I had forgotten that fact, but moreover, I was surprised Luca had even noticed.

"Any off-white or cream-colored cardstock will do, and you want a scripted font that is legible," he continued. "As far as color, you can't go wrong with black, but I think something bolder suits your personality. Maybe a bright color to match the bridesmaid's dresses?"

"Yes," I whispered. "All of that sounds…perfect. What about designs?"

"I like elegant and simple. Less is more, you know? Pick your favorites, and I'll help you decide tomorrow."

Everything he said sounded amazing, but I didn't think I'd be done with all the planning by the next day. "Tomorrow?" I repeated.

Luca sighed. "I need to meet with your father tomorrow evening about some business stuff. I'd give you more time to think, but…" His voice trailed off, so I wasn't sure if he just didn't want to give me more time, or if he didn't think it was an option because of the meeting.

"Could you stay the night here after your meeting?" Silence followed my question, so I kept talking. "My family would love to see you, and then we could hammer out some of the final plans together with my mom. There are a few things I don't think I should decide alone."

"I'm not sure your father would want me to spend the night," he finally said.

"You've done it before. He won't mind."

"Will I sleep in the guest room or with you?"

My stomach clenched as I realized the real question he was

asking. Was I willing to let him back into my bed? I dodged the question altogether. "Everyone would expect you to sleep in my room."

My aunts pounded on the window of the shop, motioning for me to wrap up my call. I sighed. "I should go. They need me back inside."

"Okay," he replied.

"Wait, did you need anything? You called me."

"I just wanted to hear your voice," he said. "And to make sure you hadn't forgotten about me yet."

"I could never," I promised.

~

Luca

Fortified by my talk with Giada, I called my papà. He informed me he was just finishing dinner, so thankfully, the call was brief. I updated him on the situation with Dmitry, then went in for the kill.

"I don't think now is a good time for me to leave the country. I should stay here and monitor the situation with him," I said.

"Nonsense. You need to be here in the next week."

"But—" I began, not the slightest bit surprised when he cut me off.

"I need to get back to my associate here. We'll talk soon," he said, hanging up right after I heard a woman's laughter.

I sighed, but I could handle it. Maybe I'd fly out alone, give myself some time to think. I supposed there wasn't any point in asking Giada what her preference was until after we talked. Maybe we'd be on better terms by this time tomorrow. Probably not.

I climbed out of my car then gazed around me. I was at a playground, not too far from one of my clubs. It only took me a moment to spot Carla. She had the kid with her, but I couldn't see his face from this distance.

I approached slowly, not eager to discuss the situation in front of a lot of people, but also not willing to let her and the kid into my car.

She smiled when she spotted me.

Whore, I thought, my stomach churning.

The only other people by the baby swings wandered off right as I approached. That, at least, was a relief. I just needed to get this stupid discussion over with fast, then move on with my life.

Carla started to speak, but I shushed her, stepping right up beside her and keeping my voice low.

"I'm not giving you any money, but I'll do your stupid test just to prove that you're a lying whore." I pulled a scrap of paper from my pocket. I'd written the address of a lab on the front of the paper. "I'll leave a blood sample there. Take the kid, and—"

"Jacob," she interrupted. "His name is Jacob."

I bit back nausea. It wasn't a bad name; I just hadn't wanted to know it. There was no reason for me to know his name. He wasn't my child. "Take him to the lab. Once they have both samples, they can do the test."

She looked like she wanted to protest, but she nodded.

"I'm getting my own test run elsewhere too, though, just to ensure you can't tamper with it," I added. I pulled a small baggie from my pocket and held it open. "I need a hair sample."

"From him?"

"Yes."

Carla frowned but reached for the kid in the baby swing. She slowed the swing, and then, instead of tugging a hair out like I would've, she simply ran her fingers through his dark locks. A few strands were in her palm when she turned back to me.

"Put it in the bag," I said, my voice gruffer than I'd intended.

She did, and I zipped the bag shut, careful to avoid any accidental eye contact with the kid as I did. His stupid face already haunted me whenever I closed my eyes. I didn't need a clearer image.

I turned on my heels and trudged back to my car. I took a moment to steady my breath. Just as I was about to start the ignition, my phone rang. It was Thomas.

"Pronto," I answered, grateful for the distraction.

"Hey, you're going to talk with Marco tomorrow, right?"

"Yes, that's the plan. Alessio thought we should let him know about this new guy in town."

"Yeah, well, I'd say he already knows. One of his guys just called. Looks like one of our shipments was hijacked."

"What?"

"Yeah. None of our guys were injured, but all the shit's gone."

I rubbed my forehead. I wasn't about to ask what exactly had been in that shipment, not over the phone anyway, but it couldn't have been good. "How did Marco's guys know about it before us?"

Thomas breathed a chuckle. "Seems the thieves thought it was his stuff."

"Idiots," I mumbled. Although, it seemed a lot of criminals assumed anything being shipped from Italy to one of Marco's docks belonged to Marco, and that simply wasn't the case.

"Yeah. His guys still seemed to think Marco would expect his cut from the shipment, but since he's about to be your father-in-law…"

"I'll figure that out later," I said. I needed to know what we'd lost and how much it was worth before I could even think about whether we'd try to weasel out of our usual fee that we paid the Contis for use of their shipyard for our less legit enterprises. "Any idea who it was?"

"That's the kicker," Thomas said. "The guys were Russian. They were all tossing Petrov's name about like it was no big deal."

I sighed. "So Dmitry stole our shit and wants everyone to know," I summarized. "Great."

We made plans to meet in another hour, then hung up.

~

Giada

*E*xhausted from wedding planning, I slept great my second night at home. But on Wednesday morning, with the hours until Luca arrived ticking by, I realized I wasn't feeling better about anything with him. I'd just ignored my worries for two days. I needed to talk. And there was only one place I could ensure my conversation was confidential.

"Bless me, Father, for I have sinned. It's been two weeks since my last confession," I paused.

"Still haven't found an English-speaking priest in Palermo?" the priest said with a chuckle.

"You're not supposed to interrupt."

"My apologies," Father Ryan said.

I hesitated. "I haven't been in Italy. I've just been going to the parish by our apartment. It's closer, and since Father Martins is performing the wedding ceremony…"

"Giada, it's fine. You can go to whichever church you choose. I'm not offended, and that certainly isn't a sin."

I squeezed my eyes shut and shook my head, "But lying is." I inhaled slowly through my nose. "I've been avoiding you. I've been so mad and embarrassed and… I don't know."

"Tell me what's on your conscience."

I quickly breezed through the list of minor transgressions I'd committed before pausing and getting to the meat of it all.

"Some woman—a stripper—showed up with a baby and said it's Luca's. The timing of it…he would've been conceived when Luca and I were together. Luca says the baby isn't his, but there's a resemblance…"

"That's not your sin," he said calmly. "If he was unfaithful…"

"I know," I interrupted. "My response to all this hasn't been so holy, I guess." I shifted uncomfortably against the short wooden bench. "Can you give me my penance so we can go talk more in your office?"

Father Ryan agreed and quickly did so.

I left the booth and made my way to his office while he heard one additional confession. When the Father finally joined me, I launched right into my spiel.

"If Luca just admitted he cheated, apologized, and swore he'd changed, I think I could forgive him. But he's just so adamant that he hasn't been unfaithful." I paused, omitting the part about me accusing him of being so promiscuous or so drunk that he just forgot.

"Forgiveness is a gift to yourself, not to the person you feel wronged you. When you forgive, you're allowing yourself to feel joy again."

"What if I want him to see how unhappy he's made me?"

"You don't need me to tell you that isn't helping anything."

"Tell me what I should do then," I said.

"You have to make a choice. Only you can decide if you can forgive him or not." The Father paused. "But you can't enter into a marriage with him if you haven't forgiven him."

I knew all that already, so I wasn't sure what I'd hoped for. Maybe some magic Catholic method of changing the past. Or at least making Luca remorseful for what he'd done.

"I encouraged him to do a paternity test, and that made him mad. He says I don't trust him."

"You don't."

I made a face to show I didn't appreciate his directness. "Luca agreed to do the test."

"So if it shows Luca's not the father, you'll apologize and beg for forgiveness. But if the test indicates… otherwise, then what? Is that a deal-breaker?"

"No," I answered without hesitation.

"What if he still doesn't apologize?"

I considered that. "I still want to marry Luca."

If this response disappointed or surprised the Father, he didn't let it show. "Have you told him that? Sometimes people need to hear that you have faith in them."

"I want to believe him," I said. "But those eyes…they're identical to Luca's. They're Luca's father's eyes. I don't remember much about his uncle, but I'm positive he had those eyes too."

"That isn't the point. If you're going to marry this man, you need to forgive freely, trust implicitly, and love unconditionally. This won't be the last time he disappoints you, but it may be the last chance you have to evaluate if you're really ready for marriage."

"How can it not be the point?" I asked. "It matters whether or not that is his son."

Father Ryan shook his head. "Unconditional means you love your spouse whether or not they're perfect, that you accept him despite his flaws."

I wrinkled my nose. "I'd rather he just not have any flaws."

The bell rang, indicating someone had stepped into the confessional. Father Ryan stood to leave.

"I can come back after if you need to talk more," he offered.

"No, you made your point. I'm a terrible girlfriend and a complete hypocrite."

"I didn't say that. Your feelings of frustration and betrayal are completely normal." He cocked his head to the side. "How are the pre-cana classes going?"

"We're done. Passed with flying colors. Of course, they didn't cover surprise illegitimate children, but…"

Father Ryan chuckled. "Take care, Giada."

I sat in a pew in the back of the church for a bit, working out exactly what I'd say to Luca. When I returned to my parents' house, Luca hadn't arrived yet. I didn't feel like being around other people though, so I brewed a cup of mint tea for myself, grabbed a thick blanket, and made my way outside with a book. Curled up on the sofa closest to the outdoor fireplace, I barely noticed the chill in the early-spring air.

I'd become so engrossed in my book that I startled when I heard the door open as Luca came to join me on the patio. He looked particularly handsome in a dark gray business suit, but his red nose suggested he could've used a hat.

I patted the couch beside me. "It's warm over here," I said.

"It's warmer inside," he countered, joining me despite his words.

"All those sixty-degree days last week fooled me," I said. "Every year that happens. We have a few gorgeous days, and once we get a taste of spring, then it snows again."

"It's not supposed to snow."

"Yeah, but it's going to be in the forties and fifties all week."

Luca made a face. "Are we really discussing the weather?"

My stomach tightened and I bit back a cringe. "How was your day?"

"Fine."

"Were you at the shipyard all day?"

Luca hesitated, probably wondering how I'd known he had been there at all. "No, only for about an hour. Alessio and I checked in on a few businesses, and then I spent most of my day at Rize. Did you enjoy shopping?"

I shrugged. "I guess so. I didn't feel very focused, in light of how everything is with you and me right now."

Luca nodded, then peered into my mug. "Is that tea?"

"Yeah. Mint. I figured I should take a break from the coffee this late in the day." I rearranged the blanket so it covered his lap as well as my own. "Look, I wanted to talk to you."

Expressionless, Luca waited for me to continue. I downed the rest of my tea, then took a deep breath.

"I wanted to say I'm sorry. I've been so upset the past few days that I didn't think about how any of this is affecting you and I haven't been there for you like I should."

Luca frowned, clearly not having expected an apology.

"And I love you. No matter what the test results say, I love you, and I want to marry you."

After a moment, a polite smile appeared on his face, and he squeezed my hand.

"Let's go upstairs," he said.

"That's it?"

Luca winced. "Do we have to get into this here?"

I stood up and folded the blanket on the side of the couch, now pouting like a petulant child.

"Hey," he said, reaching for my arm. "I…appreciate what you're saying. And I love you, too. It just bothers me that you don't believe me."

"But it doesn't matter—"

"It matters to me," he said, carrying my empty mug into the house.

~

Luca

Mr. Conti insisted on meeting after dinner, which meant Giada and I needed to play the part of lovestruck fiancés in front of her entire family. I wished we'd had time to talk in private, since nothing about the home's back patio struck me as secluded. Somehow, I felt more annoyed than before, anyway. I'd told her how much her lack of faith in me bothered me, and still, she wouldn't budge. Was this what our entire marriage would be—her questioning my loyalties every few minutes? Would I have to spend my days with men sworn to follow me only to head home to a wife who assumed the worst of me?

I retreated to Giada's room for a few minutes under the guise of making a phone call, then nearly slammed into her on my way back downstairs. She greeted me stiffly, keeping her distance until we reached the kitchen. Then, she clutched my hand and smiled as though accepting an award she'd never wanted.

Throughout the meal, I caught her watching me multiple times. It was obvious she thought I was the one failing to act convincingly, and perhaps she was right. But for once, I didn't feel like fawning all over her.

After dinner, I joined Marco Conti in his office along with his sons, and three other men he employed. Usually, I'd insist on a few of my men accompanying me in a meeting with so many from a different family, or at least I'd bring Alessio. But this was different. Soon, the Contis would be my family. Not in the blood-relative way, and not in the criminal enterprise sort of way either, but hopefully in a different, meaningful way.

I caught them all up to speed on the latest information we knew about Dmitry, answered their questions, and promised to keep them all apprised of any new developments. Marco gave me similar assurances, then dismissed us all for the evening. Angelo and Matteo made their way to the bar.

"We're going to have a drink on the patio," Matteo said. "Why don't you join us?"

I doubted either of them thought I'd accept the invitation, but I did. Drinking with Giada's brothers seemed infinitely less stressful than being alone with her. And if I dawdled long enough, she'd be asleep before I joined her in bed.

Giada had mentioned spending time with Matteo the night before, so I supposed it was possible she'd told him about my alleged crimes. If she had, though, he didn't say.

When I finally made my way upstairs, Giada's room was dark. I crept in, inching the door shut behind me. I undressed in the bathroom, then tiptoed to the bed. I hadn't made a single noise, but when I approached the bed, she shifted, then sat up.

"Sorry," I mumbled, slipping under the covers beside her.

"I hate that you're mad at me," she said.

I didn't have a response for that.

"I thought the time apart would help," she continued, "but it seems like it made things worse for you."

I supposed it had given me more time to brood on my annoyance, to wallow in my self-pity and dwell on the fact that the one time I hadn't done anything wrong, my fiancée still didn't believe me.

"Luca, I'm sorry," she said, an urgency to her voice.

"It's fine," I said.

"It's obviously not. You're mad, and I hate that."

I didn't respond.

She swung a leg over my lap, straddling me. "You chose to spend your time with Angelo over me," she said. "I thought he was your least favorite person alive, so what does that mean for me?"

Giada tugged her shirt over her head before I could answer. She grabbed my hands and placed them on her breasts, arching her back in a way that forced her flesh further into my hands.

"You play dirty," I said.

"I don't know how else to apologize to you. You've never stayed mad at me this long."

"I don't want your apology. I want your trust."

"I know. But surely this won't hurt my chances of forgiveness," she said, scooting backwards. She fumbled with my boxers, stroking me from within the thin material for a moment before freeing my shaft from the garment. Her lips were warm as they wrapped around my sensitive skin, and I couldn't help but harden and grow at her soft touch.

I couldn't resist Giada even if I'd tried, so instead, I just closed my eyes and focused on the sensations as she worked me further into her mouth. Her tongue traced the vein running along the length of me, and then she sucked harder around the head. My breath came faster, and I struggled to hold my hips still as Giada bobbed back and forth over my lap.

When the pressure became too intense and I was about to fall over the edge, I nearly nudged her back in warning.

Only, then, I didn't.

If she truly wanted to apologize, she could take whatever I had to give, and be grateful for it. I gripped her hair, thrusting deeper as all of my muscles contracted. I groaned as my seed spurted out of me into her mouth. A calm sense of satisfaction filled me as I adjusted my boxers back over myself.

But the moment Giada peered up at me, a hint of sorrow tainting her innocent eyes, the bliss was gone.

"I love you," she said. "And I'm not going to let you stay mad at me forever."

Guilt squeezed at my chest as she snuggled against my side. Somehow, I slept soundly despite my conscience.

That next morning, Giada's Maid of Honor was coming for brunch and wedding planning. Giada told me it was a ladies only brunch and I didn't have to show, but I figured I'd at least make an appearance. I was about to round the corner into the kitchen when I heard my name.

"You're sure Luca will be okay with that?" Mrs. Conti asked.

"Yeah. Luca's been surprisingly easygoing about all of this stuff," Giada replied, making me wonder what, exactly, I was so easygoing about. I would've asked, but then the conversation grew even more interesting.

"Surprisingly?" her mom said. "Why would that be surprising? He's always agreeable."

"Luca?" Giada laughed. "No one would ever describe him as easygoing or agreeable."

Her mom snorted. "Well, he sure isn't too demanding or unforgiving when it comes to you. Just think of all the stuff you've put him through these past few years. The poor man puts up with all of it without complaint."

I smirked to myself. I'd never really gotten the impression I was Tina's first choice for her daughter, so it was nice to hear her taking my side for once.

"What stuff have I put him through?" Giada asked.

"Oh, come on. Everything with you-know-who."

"Omigod, Mom. I'm not even discussing Adrian right now. We're planning my wedding for goodness sake."

I swooped in before they could launch into a full debate. Gabriella looked relieved to have another intermediary, I bent down and pressed a kiss to Giada's forehead.

"What's this I hear about Adrian? He should be on the guest list," I said, retrieving a sparkling water from the refrigerator "He's a friend, plus I think your brothers are pretty close with him."

Giada turned to me, a wry expression on her face as if she thought I was trying to trick her. "You are not serious," she finally replied.

"I am. Why not?" I straddled the backwards chair beside Giada.

Tina slid a lengthy list across the table to me. "This is everyone Marco and I wanted to invite. If you could look over it and just make sure you don't have any objections..."

I picked up the paper and scrolled down the list of names. Most I recognized as members of the Conti family or associates of their family, but a few were unfamiliar. I pointed to those. "I don't recognize these," I said.

"Those are neighbors," Giada chimed in.

"Oh, yes. And that second column is out-of-town relatives," Tina explained. "Did your mom show you everyone she added to the list, Luca?"

"Uh, yeah. I think so."

"Okay, well, if you have no objections, I think this is everyone then."

"That's a long list," Giada said, grimacing.

"That just means more presents," Gabby said, her upbeat tone consistent with what I'd expect from the Maid of Honor.

"It's impossible to cut someone without also cutting other folks or offending someone. I don't know why it matters to you anyway. It's not like you're paying for any of it," Tina said to her daughter.

"It'll be perfect," I told them both, offering my most reassuring smile.

Giada's mother checked her watch and stood. "I have some errands to run before dinner. Don't forget you have the final floral decisions to make, too. And as soon as you get back from Italy, you need to do the cake tastings."

Giada nodded, then turned to me. "You seriously want to invite Adrian?"

"Absolutely. Half the fun of marrying you is making him watch while it happens." I wiggled my eyebrows then kissed her again, pretending I didn't see the horrified expression on her friend's face.

CHAPTER 4

Luca

I flew back to Italy later that week, and for once, I was relieved not to have Giada with me on the flight. She'd stayed behind allegedly for wedding matters, but promised to join me in Rome that weekend. I spent several days in Palermo, meeting with my guys there and checking in on the businesses we oversaw before flying up to Rome. My parents were there, as they rarely left Italy in winter, so I spent a fair amount of time with them when I wasn't working.

I'd expected my mother to have a billion questions about the wedding plans, but she asked none. I supposed that was her way of signaling that she didn't believe this engagement was any more likely to lead anywhere than my last one with Giada. Two weeks ago, I'd have brought up the topic of the wedding to her myself, simply to gloat about how wrong she'd been about Giada and how wrong she'd been about my ability to please a woman like Giada.

Only now, I wasn't so sure my mother had been wrong, so probably it was for the best that we didn't discuss it. By some stroke of good luck, my parents were flying down to Palermo the same day Giada would arrive in Rome. So, we wouldn't even have to endure a single dinner or awkward conversation with my parents during this trip.

Two days before Giada was scheduled to arrive, I received an alert that my DNA test results were ready—the hair follicle test I'd sent on my own. I shut my office door, and logged onto the site, my limbs already tingling with the anticipation of vindication. The security protocols for the website were over the top, taking me longer to actually view my results than I'd like. Even once the results appeared on the screen, I had to scroll down over a page to see the part I was looking for.

But then, there it was, in boldface, right in the middle of the second page.

According to the test, the man whose samples were tested —*i.e.,* me— was "not excluded" as the biological father of the child tested. Scrolling down further, I read where the test claimed that meant there was a ninety-nine percent chance I was the father.

I slammed my laptop shut and went straight for the liquor. Those results didn't make sense. Why would I have slept with Carla when I was with Giada? And how would I have forgotten it?

I wasn't the slightest bit surprised when the results from the blood paternity test came back the next day, similarly identifying me as the father. I suspected I should be focused on the larger issue—the fact that, apparently, I was a father. But I was more concerned with how this would affect Giada. Carla didn't expect anything but money from me, and that, I could provide. Lacking any experience with a good father or even a positive role model, I had no misgivings that I'd be able to contribute anything else to the kid, so that seemed a moot point.

What I needed to figure out was how to apologize to Giada. She'd gone out of her way to tell me she still loved me even after I cheated, and all I'd done was make her feel guilty for not believing me when I swore I'd been faithful. I'd been a self-righteous ass, and I deserved whatever she flung my way. I just hoped I could convince her not to leave me.

~

Giada

*L*uca met me at the Rome-Fiumicino airport, but Giovanni waited outside with the SUV, presumably in case I'd packed too much to fit in the Maserati. I politely greeted Giovanni before turning to Luca. His eyes were bloodshot and puffy, and it was obvious he hadn't slept well in days.

"What happened? You look terrible," I said, wrapping my arms around his neck and hugging him.

"You look gorgeous," Luca replied, stiffly returning the hug then releasing me too soon.

I'd worn yoga pants and an off-the-shoulder long-sleeved tee shirt for the flight and my hair was gathered on top of my head in a messy bun. I'd spritzed my face with water and reapplied my makeup at the end of the flight, then tackled my hair, swished some mouthwash, and swiped on more deodorant in the airport restroom while we waited for my luggage. So, I supposed I didn't look awful, considering the length of the flight. But "gorgeous" was clearly an overstatement.

"Do you have to work today?" I asked.

"Just for a little bit. I'll do it when you nap."

I'd clocked a few hours during my overnight flight but I'd never make it all day without rest. Luca, having traveled back and forth between the two continents his entire life, had mastered the art of beating jetlag. The key, according to him, was to sleep some during the flight, eat upon arrival, take a short nap followed by enough caffeine to last until the local bedtime, then wake up in sync with the correct time zone.

"You look like you could use a nap yourself."

He opened his mouth to say something, then simply shook his head.

When we arrived at the apartment, a box of pastries from my favorite local bakery awaited. I selected one while Luca unloaded my stuff. He didn't say much as he tucked me into bed.

"I'm worried about you," I said.

"I'm fine. I'll be back in time to wake you up," he promised. "We'll talk then."

I was too tired to protest, and I fell asleep before I heard him lock the door.

I awoke to the fragrant smell of strong coffee. As my eyes fluttered open, I felt the steam tickling my nose. I gazed up to the best sight in the world—Luca crouched on the bed holding my favorite drink.

"That was too short," I said, sitting up before accepting the coffee.

"You always say that."

"What time is it?"

"Two o'clock."

"And you're done working?"

He shrugged, which I interpreted as a no. He plopped the box of pastries from earlier on the bed beside me. A small royal blue jewelry box was on top. I glanced up, eyebrow raised, then opened the box. Nestled inside, I found oval earrings with two layers of hoops adorned with sparkling gems.

"They're gorgeous," I said, already trying to decide what I could wear them with. They were definitely too formal for everyday clothes.

"They're fake," he said. "Cubic zirconia. But I thought they'd go nicely with this." He held up a garment bag.

"Luca, you don't have to buy me stuff all the time," I protested.

He unzipped the bag to reveal a strapless floor-length taupe dress with a sweetheart bodice that plunged nearly to the hips in the back. The silky lining had a mesh fabric overlay that was glittery and adorned with sequins.

The gown was stunning. And it was Versace.

I brushed the crumbs off my lap, wiped my fingers on a napkin and rose to my knees so I could touch the material. It reminded me of the type of dress a princess would wear. It probably cost the same.

"They can alter it at the boutique if it doesn't fit," Luca said, abruptly interrupting my admiration of the dress.

I broke my stare away from the breathtaking gown long enough to look up at him. Luca never before questioned whether something would fit; he had always been positive he'd bought the perfect item in the perfect size. So far, he always had. Although, historically, when Luca presented me with extravagant gifts, a cocky grin crossed his face. But today, he appeared uncertain, distraught even.

I draped the dress over the foot of the bed and reached for Luca's hand, tugging him onto the bed beside me. "What's wrong? You couldn't honestly have thought I wouldn't love that dress.."

His eyes drifted shut for a moment. "He's my son. The paternity results came back."

I lost my grip on Luca's hand as his words washed over me and settled in like a thick fog. I knew if there were any chance the results weren't valid, he wouldn't be telling me. Luca wouldn't look so devastated if it weren't true.

Suddenly, I felt painfully tired, like I hadn't slept in weeks.

I reached for the coffee mug and sipped continuously, draining more than half its contents. I sensed Luca was waiting for me to answer, to say anything, but I couldn't.

"I'm so sorry," he said, his voice deeper than usual. "I don't…I don't expect you to believe me, but I swear I don't know why or when I would've slept with her. I have no memory of it. I didn't mean to lie."

I set the mug back on the nightstand before it slipped out of me weakened fingers. I shifted onto my side, facing away from him. "Okay," I mumbled, tugging the covers up to my shoulders.

"You shouldn't sleep anymore," Luca said, his voice gentle.

"I just need a minute alone!" I snapped, startled by the tenor of my own words.

I felt the bed shift as he stood. A moment later, the bedroom door clicked shut.

I lay there for a while, but no coherent thoughts filtered through the noise in my head. Eventually, I crawled out of bed, slipped back into my sweatpants, and grabbed my jacket.

When I emerged from the bedroom, Luca was on the phone. As he saw me, he ended his call, rising from the chair to approach me.

"I need some fresh air. I'm going to take a walk," I said, adding, "Alone." I held up my cell phone so Luca wouldn't worry then started for the door. The fact that he didn't insist on following me raised a huge red flag.

Luca had screwed up before, many times, but never so badly that he stopped being overprotective and controlling. I supposed that should be reassuring, signaling that he truly felt guilty. Honestly, though, I didn't need a sign to tell me that. His guilt was obvious from his red eyes and the uncertainty in his voice.

I believed Luca when he said he didn't remember cheating. But whether or not he recalled the act didn't change the fact that it happened. In some ways, it almost made it worse. What was to stop him from doing it again if he didn't know why he cheated the last time? And what did that mean for us? Could I really marry a man who already had a child with someone else?

I walked to a nearby park, the one with my favorite small pond. I'd discovered the place the first time Luca had brought me to his apartment in Rome, and I'd visited it frequently when I'd been here with Matteo. Usually, it was a good place to think, but today, I couldn't shake the chill in the air. After a few minutes on my favorite bench, I stood and continued walking.

I hadn't realized how far I'd gone until I reached the doors of the church. I'd attended mass here several times, but hadn't found it quite as comforting as the services back home, since the entire mass was in Italian.

Sitting alone in the pew, I could finally collect my thoughts. And the more I thought about it all, the less I understood why I was so upset. Sure, I'd hoped the boy wasn't Luca's, but deep down, I'd known he was from the moment I saw him. Luca had apologized, and I didn't doubt his sincerity or his love for me. What he'd done was awful, but it was in the past. It wasn't *my* Luca who'd cheated; it was the old Luca. So why was I still so upset?

I thought about my discussion with Father Ryan, when I'd told him the whole mess. He'd said the test results didn't matter, that Luca needed to know I loved him unconditionally and wanted to marry him regardless. I'd told Luca as much, but judging from the look on his face when he confessed it to me, the results mattered to him.

I cringed thinking back to every moment of the past week with Luca. He'd been so hurt, so…angry, when I hadn't instantly believed him about the baby. And even after I'd apologized, he was still mad. There wasn't a doubt in my mind that he'd been punishing me that night at my parents' house. He'd never before been rough with me during oral sex and definitely had never failed to at least offer to return the favor.

The worst part of it all was that he'd told me what was upsetting him. Luca was mad that I didn't trust him. And, of course, he was right. I hadn't trusted him, and now, it turned out that I was right not to.

What I hadn't considered was how much Luca valued trust. I knew enough about what he did every day to realize trust was the most important thing to Luca. He'd told me many times that he wouldn't work with someone he didn't trust. He certainly wouldn't be friends with someone he didn't trust. And Luca would never marry someone he didn't trust.

So what if all this time he'd been assuming I felt the same? All of his crazy behavior the past couple of weeks made sense, if I looked at it from his perspective. Luca had been terrified of losing me. And what had I done? Ditched him for a night out with my brother and the guy I'd made out with years before.

A wave of nausea washed over me as I realized how stupid I'd been. Lots of people had babies with someone before meeting their spouse, so this was hardly any different. It didn't mean Luca loved me any less or anything at all about how he would conduct himself as a husband. What it did do was give me a fantastic opportunity to show Luca once and for all that I did trust him and I did love him unconditionally.

I sat there for a few more minutes, then scurried to the vestibule just outside of the sanctuary to call Father Ben. I had an idea, and I needed to know if it could actually work.

∿

Luca

*P*art of me worried Giada had checked herself into a hotel or, worse yet, hopped right onto a return flight for the U.S. I understood her need for time alone to process what I'd told her, but I hadn't expected her solo walk to last for three hours.

I texted to see if she was okay. I wouldn't have blamed her if she was too angry to reply, so relief flooded me when she texted back, apologizing for being out so long and asking me to meet her at a nearby park.

When I arrived at the park, I spotted Giada near the pond.

"Have you been here this whole time?" I asked, shivering from the cold. Though it was similar temperature to New England, the breeze made the day feel uncharacteristically cool for Rome.

Giada shook her head. "No, I walked over to the church. I was inside most of the time."

She seemed calm, and I assumed the fact that she was still speaking to me meant that she wasn't dumping me. But even if she planned to forgive me, I still owed her more of an apology.

I crouched on the ground in front of her, reaching for her hand. Her gaze drifted to meet my own. I brought her fingers to my lips, kissing them softly.

"I'm so sorry, Giada. I was an asshole when you didn't believe me. I swear to you, I never for a minute thought it was true, that I was…" I stopped, unable to even speak the words aloud. "I love you. I want to make you happy, and I'll do whatever it takes to earn your forgiveness."

Giada took her time answering. "Will you marry me?"

I chuckled, not just because we were already engaged, but also at the irony of *her* asking *me* when I was the one kneeling at her feet. "Si, amore, if you'll still have me," I said without hesitation.

"How about tomorrow?"

I frowned, unsure what she meant.

"Would you marry me tomorrow?" she clarified.

"Uh…" I still didn't understand what she was getting at. Our wedding was months away.

"I don't want to wait, Luca. I want to be your wife, and nothing will change that."

Hearing those words brought the first genuine smile to my face in days. "I want that too, Giada."

"I spoke with Father Ben, and he said if we wanted to have a small ceremony here, he could still perform a similar ceremony in New York. Technically we'd already be married, but we could tweak the wording of the ceremony so that our parents wouldn't have to know we'd already made things official."

I rose to the bench and sat beside her. "I don't understand. You're saying you want to elope? Here?"

After a beat, she nodded.

I shook my head. "Giada, I know you. A Catholic wedding means something to you. And you want your family there to watch."

"That's what I'm saying. We can still have an official catholic wedding. Father Ben can fax over our certificate of completion for the pre-cana classes and any other info they need, and we can be married at the church here." She paused. "I need you to go work out the details because I'm not sure they understood what I was saying, but…"

"What about your family?"

"We'll still get married this autumn in New York. No one will know we're already married except us and the priest."

I wasn't sure what to say. I'd spent the last three days terrified of losing the woman I loved, and now she was offering to permanently link herself to me. It was all too good to be true.

"I think you're rushing into this," I said finally.

Her face fell. "I thought you'd love this idea."

"I do, but I'm not sure you're thinking clearly. You're exhausted, jet-lagged, and I just dropped something huge on you. You should be mad at me, questioning if you even want to date me, let alone marry me. I'm not going to let you give up your dream wedding because of some emotional breakdown or whatever this is. You don't believe in divorce, Giada. Once you do this, you're stuck with me."

She swatted my shoulder. "We can argue about this later. Right now, I need you to go talk to the priest. I want to make sure he got the fax from Father Ben and see if he can squeeze in a quick ceremony tomorrow."

"Tomorrow,' I repeated.

Giada stood and started down the sidewalk. "We can work

out the details at dinner." Suddenly, she froze. "Do you have the rings?"

It took me a moment to realize she was asking about our wedding rings, which we'd selected weeks before. "They're in New York," I said.

A frown crossed Giada's face but disappeared before she spoke again. "That's okay. We'll pick out some others tomorrow. I figure you could wear yours on a necklace so no one is suspicious..." she kept chatting as we reached the car, but none of it made any sense to me.

She couldn't possibly be serious.

CHAPTER 5

Luca

I awoke the next morning wondering if it had all been a dream. But the moment I opened my eyes, Giada pounced on me, peppering my face and neck with kisses.

"Today is your last day as a single man," she said, grinning widely.

I nudged her back so I could see the clock. It was only 8:15, but I supposed with the time change, Giada felt wide awake.

"Are you still sure about all of this?" I asked.

"I've never been more sure about anything," she said. "Wait, you're not having second thoughts, are you?"

The fact that she could even question whether I'd hesitate marrying her was so ridiculous that I had to bite back a smile. I flipped us over so she was on her back and I was on top, appreciating the view.

"Giada, I have no doubts. I have wanted to make this official for years now." I paused. "I just don't want you to regret not having your family there."

"It honestly feels more romantic this way, just the two of us. And they'll still get to see us marry later."

I nodded and kissed her firmly before rolling off of her. "Come on, I'll take you to breakfast before we go ring shopping." Despite Giada's insistence that we marry right away, the church didn't have availability until the following day. Fortunately, that gave us time for all the last-minute things we needed to do.

I watched as Giada climbed out of bed and stretched. Her dark brown hair fell nearly to her breasts, which were currently covered in a silky black tank top thin enough to still reveal her nipples. Her black panties matched, right down to the lace trim.

I wasn't sure how I'd gotten so lucky to convince such a sexy woman to become my wife, but I was determined not to screw it up.

Giada made her way into the bathroom, styling her hair and putting on makeup before getting dressed. Since I'd joined her in the shower the previous night, it would only take me ten minutes to go from the bed to door, so I dawdled, watching her instead.

I was still seated at the foot of the bed, smiling at her, when she returned to get dressed. She slipped her top off over her head as she started to say something.

She was too tempting. I roped my arms around her waist and captured her nipple in my mouth. Giada shrieked but held me close to her, tossing her own head back and sighing happily.

Fifteen minutes later, we were working our way out of bed for the second time that morning, both of us feeling much more satisfied this time.

"He asked if you were pregnant. The priest did," I blurted out. "Yesterday, I mean."

She shrugged. "Well, I guess that's one common reason to rush a wedding. You told him no, right?"

"Yes!" I replied, mildly offended that she thought I'd lie to a priest. "I suspect the priests back home assumed we had a different reason for the quickie service."

She narrowed her gaze. "What's that?"

"Well, a wife can't be forced to testify against her husband in court," I reminded her. "So if I were in some sort of trouble—which I'm not—that could come in handy."

"Hmm. I never realized that was actually a real thing. You know I'd never testify against you anyway, right?"

"I'd never ask you to go to jail for me." I glanced at the clock then nudged her. "We should get moving."

"You messed up my hair," she said, looking in the mirror.

"You messed up my sheets," I retorted.

She glanced at the bed and made a face. "That was all you. No cleaning lady today?"

I shook my head. She began quickly stripping the bed. "Stop, I can do that," I said. "You need to put clothes on, or we'll just end up making another mess."

Giada giggled but let me toss the sheets into the laundry. When I returned, she'd pulled on jeans and a thin sweater.

"It's supposed to hit the mid-sixties today," I said, dressing in suit pants and a button-down shirt for my meeting later that day. "Much warmer than yesterday."

"Good," she said. She plopped on the bed to put on her jewelry while I fastened my watch. "Hey, I did want to ask you something."

I turned to her expectantly.

"I want this to be a secret today. Just you and me and the priests, okay?"

I nodded. "Yes. I thought that was the plan."

"Can you truly do that? Keep it from Alessio? And your father?"

I hesitated. I'd had no problem agreeing to keep it a secret in general, but I'd never really considered that I wouldn't be telling Alessio. "Of course, I won't tell my papà," I said. He couldn't be trusted not to blab to the Contis. But Alessio...I told him everything. "Alessio wouldn't tell a soul. And there might be some benefit to having him know."

"Like what?" she asked. "I know it's asking a lot, but it's more meaningful to me if it's truly a secret from everyone."

I felt my head bobbing before I consciously realized I'd agreed. But there was nothing else to say. I'd do anything for Giada. "Of course. I won't tell him," I promised.

"Can I ask another favor? I know you said you could take the next few days off. Could we maybe go to Florence for a couple days? Or Venice?"

That was an easy request to satisfy. I'd already told Alessio that he was on his own for the rest of the week. I'd figured Giada would want to head south to avoid the cold, but perhaps she was just as eager to avoid my parents as I was. Either way, I was confident I could find a romantic bed and breakfast up north, too.

~

Giada

*M*y wedding day was nothing like I'd imagined. I always assumed I'd marry at the church back home, the sanctuary bursting at the seams with all of my family and friends. I'd envisioned the huge bridal party, the loud, busy day filled with so many people and to-dos that I barely saw my spouse.

What I hadn't expected was to wake up with my fiancé's arm draped over my waist and to not feel the slightest twinge of regret that we weren't having the big, over-the-top celebration. We would have that, eventually. But today, I realized, was everything I'd never realized I truly desired.

I wanted an intimate, meaningful ceremony with my love. I wanted a collection of genuine memories from the moments we transitioned from individuals to husband and wife, not an album filled with photos of forced poses.

The priest's opening was at three p.m. that day, just before the late afternoon mass. I'd encouraged Luca to meet up with Alessio that morning, to finish up whatever work he needed to do before we jaunted off to northern Italy. We ate breakfast in bed, together, and then he left, promising to return by two p.m. so we could drive to the church together. While he was gone, I put the finishing touches on my vows, then stepped out to buy a chain for Luca to wear around his neck. I wanted to make sure it was the perfect length to hold his ring close to his heart.

~

Luca

Giada insisted on getting dressed for our ceremony separately, so we met at the church. Since Giada spent so much time in churches, no one questioned it when I asked Alessio to give her a ride to the church and said I'd meet her there for a meeting. I arrived first but only had a few minutes to panic before Alessio texted that she was on her way inside.

Giada shrugged out of her coat at the door to the church, offering me the first full glimpse of her wearing the taupe dress I'd bought for her. The silky material accented her curves without truly revealing anything. She'd curled her hair and clipped the sides to the back of her head, leaving a few ringlets cascading around her face. She looked angelic, classy, and stunning.

I opened my mouth to praise her beauty, but the words didn't come. The sight of my fiancée was literally breathtaking.

Giada giggled shyly. "You like the dress?" She twirled around so I could see the back.

An older woman popped her head into the room and smiled,

then said we could join her if we were ready. I gripped Giada's hand tightly as we walked to the altar where the priest awaited. He greeted us, then asked us to kneel while he said several prayers. When we stood, he spoke about marriage and its role in a Catholic household. He paused to allow me to translate every few lines, then asked us to pray again.

Finally, it was time for our vows. I went first.

"Giada, I love you more than I love myself. I'm a better man with you in my life, and all the good in me is thanks to you." I swallowed nervously. "I will uphold all the vows of our marriage and do my best to trust you, honor you, and please you every day. I promise to protect you, whatever the cost," I said. "And I will spend the rest of my life working to become a man worthy of your love."

Giada sucked in a deep breath, then began her vows. "Sei l'unico per me, Luca Tomas Marino. Non posso vivere senza di te. Ti voglio sempre al mio fianco."

My heart swelled with each word she'd memorized in my native tongue. *You're the only one for me, Luca Marino. I can't live without you. I want you by my side always.*

She continued in English. "My world begins and ends with you, Luca. I hope you can someday see yourself through my eyes and understand what a gift you are in my life. I pledge my loyalty to you, no matter the circumstances. I promise to respect you and to serve you. I am yours, body and soul."

I was transfixed as Giada spoke, and I stared deep into her my eyes as she did mine. While I hadn't expected her to speak any part of her vows in Italian, the words she spoke in English were more surprising. Her vow felt chillingly similar to a different oath, the kind taken by men joining the family under my command. I was certain that connection was intentional on Giada's part, and my awareness that she'd never break a promise made on holy grounds rendered her words even more meaningful than I could ever imagine.

The priest nodded politely before asking us to each repeat after him as he read the official vows. I again translated, and continued to do so as we exchanged rings. Finally, I was allowed to kiss my bride.

I asked the older woman if she'd take our picture at the altar, figuring someday Giada might appreciate one token of the day at least, and then we were done.

We planned to stick around for the afternoon mass, but we had a good half hour to talk before that started. As we walked into the vestibule off the side of the church, I squeezed my wife's hand.

"You look gorgeous," I whispered. "I don't think I've ever seen you look so beautiful, and that's saying a lot since you're always stunning."

"Thank you. You look handsome and downright delicious, husband of mine," she replied.

At her words, the breath whooshed out of me. We had really done it. We were married.

We sat on a padded bench in a cozy room at the end of the hall, simply gazing into each other's eyes. Suddenly, Giada leapt up. "Oh, I almost forgot."

I watched as she reached into her cleavage and pulled out a long silver chain.

"Give me your ring," she said.

I covered it protectively with my other hand. "I'm not ready to take it off. I kind of like having it on. It reminds me who I belong to."

"That's sweet, but I'm not sure how we'd explain a wedding ring on your ring finger. This chain should hold it right by your heart. And you can stick it down your shirt, so no one knows." She lowered the chain over my head so I could see the length.

I tucked the chain beneath my collar. "I'll add the ring later." Then, just to taunt her, I snapped a picture of our hands nestled together.

"What if someone gets a hold of your phone?"

"If they're able to unlock my phone and access my photos, we have bigger issues than our wedding rings," I teased.

She leaned forward and kissed me slowly. "I love you, Husband."

"Si, I see that. I mean, you learned Italian for me."

Giada giggled, having made it perfectly clear on countless occasions that she had no intention of ever actually learning my native language.

"The rest of your vows though, where did you get the idea? I mean, what you said… it reminded me of an oath of loyalty that um…"

"You told me once that you'd trust Alessio with your life. I want that degree of trust. And I've never been able to make you understand how much I love you, so I figured it wouldn't hurt if I threw in some familiar words."

"But…" I paused, unsure of what I wanted to say.

"I meant it all, every word of it. If you need a blood oath to believe me, I'll do that, too. There's only you, Luca. I'll do anything for you."

"I love you," I whispered, kissing her again. "You are my everything."

We were still kissing when the noise outside our little room alerted us that mass was about to start.

～

Giada

I couldn't take my eyes off my husband the entire drive to Florence. I supposed he didn't look any different than before, and he was wearing one of his nicer suits that I'd seen him in many times, but now he was mine. For eternity.

Luca had booked a suite at a small bed and breakfast on the outskirts of Florence, and he'd arranged for us to have dinner upon arrival on our private rooftop terrace overlooking the hillside. It was already dark when we arrived, but tiny flickers of lights in the distance cast a serene glow over the city beyond our private dinner. The terrace itself contained a table set for two, a cozy seating area off to one side, and a hot tub near the other corner. A heater stood in the corner, offering warmth against the cool night air. Strings of tea lights dangled above us, providing soft lighting for our first meal as a married couple.

The owners of the inn had walked us up to our room and arranged our meal on the table. Luca selected a wine from the bottles they presented, and I watched impatiently as they opened it.

Then the woman turned to me and asked a question. I glanced to Luca for translation, but instead, he simply chuckled and said "no, grazie."

Finally, we were alone.

"We could eat later," I suggested, slipping his suit jacket off his shoulders and rising to my toes to kiss him.

"I like how you think," he said. "But you'll need your energy later, so I want you fed now." He helped me remove his jacket but then wrapped it over my shoulders before pulling out a chair for me.

I sat and gazed out over the scenery. "This view is gorgeous," I said.

"Si," he agreed, except his eyes were locked on me.

I felt my skin flush. "Hey, what did that lady ask me?"

Luca's smile widened. "She offered to help you unpack."

"What was so funny about that?" I asked. Sure, it would've been a bit odd in the U.S., but it was par for the course in Italy. Italians were serious about their hospitality.

"It just amused me that she apparently didn't realize how

desperate you were to have me all to yourself. I thought you might push them off the roof if they didn't leave quickly."

I made a pouty face. "I've waited more than three hours already."

"Mmm, four if you're counting mass."

He rolled his wrist to the side, swirling the wine in his glass. "I propose a toast. To the first of a lifetime of nights spent with my beloved wife."

"Saluti," I said, clinking my glass against his. I watched his lips as he sipped, desire unfurling deep in my core and spreading throughout my torso.

With zero appetite for food, I forced myself to take a few bites of salad, focusing on the tanginess of the dressing coating the crisp lettuce. Luca broke off a piece of bread, dipped it in olive oil, then offered it to me. I opened my mouth obediently, eagerly licking his finger while accepting the bread.

"Naughty," he said.

I moved on to the pasta and veal, wondering how much I'd have to eat before he would take me inside and ravish me. Warmth spread throughout my body, thanks to the wine I'd sipped at the start of our meal which had already begun to affect me on account of my empty stomach.

Luca set down his fork and bit back a smile. "Come here," he said softly.

I was on my feet in an instant, letting his jacket fall to the concrete floor. Luca motioned for me to sit on his lap, facing the world past our terrace. He wrapped one arm around my back, then used his other hand to spear a bite of veal on his fork. He fed me that bite, then took another for himself. While I was frustrated that we were both still fully clothed, I did appreciate the contact with his warm, hard body.

I giggled as Luca struggled to feed me pasta without ruining both of our fancy outfits, but he only held me closer. Finally, when we'd cleaned off one plate between the two of us, Luca patted my behind, signaling for me to stand.

"Vita mia," he murmured. I knew that expression, *my life*. "You are stunning, Giada Francesca Marino," he said, squeezing my fingertips.

My breath caught in my throat a little, hearing the full name. In all honesty, I'd planned to hyphenate, but surely that parcel of info could wait until later. Now, I was hungry, for Luca.

His arms fully encircled me, holding me close for a long, heavy kiss. As his tongue writhed against my own, I felt the movement much, much lower. I pressed my hand against the seat of his pants, forcing his hips against me in hopes of gaining counterpressure to alleviate some of the tension blossoming deep inside.

Luca made a sound deep in the back of his throat, and I knew I'd won. He wouldn't survive prolonged foreplay any easier than I would. He released my back and began unbuttoning his own shirt buttons instead. I went to work on his belt, yanking it out of the pant loops altogether and dropping it to the ground before unfastening his pants. I carefully dragged the zipper down over the large bulge now pressing against the seam. He tossed his shirt over the back of the chair, then yanked my hands away right as I began to stroke him through his boxer briefs.

I bit back a smile, already panting, then gazed up at him. Wearing just his white sleeveless undershirt and half-undone pants, Luca was a sight to behold. I tugged my hand free and reached for his hand, pulling off the ring I'd just given him, then fastening it onto the chain around his neck. When I finished, I left my hand in place, relishing the rapid vibrations from his heartbeat.

"I love you," he whispered.

This time, there was nothing tentative about our kiss. I latched on to Luca like I was drowning, and he was my only shot at salvation. He gripped me tightly, pulling me with him towards the French doors leading into our room. We barely made it in the room before he swiveled me around, tugged down my zipper, and lowered my dress to the floor. He traced his fingers along my now bare shoulder and down my arms, his touch so light that I shivered. Luca paused, shucking his shirt, but as I was about to turn to face him, he stopped me.

When I glanced up to see why he was holding me with my back to him, I came face to face with a floor-length mirror. Luca's eyes were locked on the reflection of mine, his gaze hungry.

"See how beautiful you are?" he whispered, gently running his hands up my body.

It was impossible not to feel beautiful, with the way he was staring at me. He unfastened my strapless bra with one hand, covering my breasts with his palms the moment my bra hit the ground. I drew in a sharp breath at the welcomed contact, arching my back slightly to press my sensitive nipples further into his hands. My eyes drifted closed and suddenly, his hands disappeared.

My eyes flew open in time to see his mischievous grin. I groaned.

"I'd rather you watch. I want you to see why I enjoy pleasuring you so much." Luca's voice was low, and he spoke directly into my ear, his hot breath tickling the sensitive flesh along my neck. He flattened his palm over my belly then slid it lower, dipping inside my panties. "Mmm," he groaned. "You were ready for this, weren't you?"

I nodded. "I want you inside me," I said, begging him with my eyes.

He stroked his finger along my slick tissue then pressed it inside me.

"Not like that," I said, but I could already see my chest rising and falling faster.

Luca smiled wider, rubbing his thumb over my sensitive nub

as he moved his finger within my body. "You can have me that way too, in just a minute."

I'd barely registered his promise when his free hand roamed back to my breast, circling my nipple until a soft moan escaped my lips.

I'd never really considered watching myself, in the throes of passion like this, and it was nothing like I'd expected. Even though I felt like I was on fire, my nerve endings piqued, and my heart racing, the girl in the mirror appeared calm and cool. My face appeared relaxed despite the tension rapidly building throughout my body. If I'd seen a picture of myself out of context, I would've guessed I was drunk, yet I'd consumed less than one glass of wine.

Luca shifted his finger to the side, pressing directly against the sensitive patch deep inside me, and I shattered around his hand. My head flew back to his shoulder as spasm after exquisite spasm burst through my body like a series of fireworks. My legs went weak, but Luca held tightly to me, leaning me back against his torso.

When I regained my senses, I peered at our reflection in the mirror again, only to realize Luca had somehow removed his pants. "Still want more of me?" he asked, his eyes locked on mine in the mirror.

"Yes," I breathed. "Always. But especially now."

Luca slid my panties down my legs and helped me step out of them. I turned to face him right as he lifted me up. I locked my ankles together around his waist, and he carried me across the room, dropping me onto the bed and climbing on top. By the time I even registered my back against the soft bedding, he'd buried himself deep inside me.

"Yes," I sighed, roping my legs around him to force him even deeper.

I didn't expect to climax again so quickly after he'd rendered me a quivering wash of sensations, but I was desperate to be as close to Luca as possible. I needed our bodies to become one, just as we'd pledged earlier in the day.

"Oh Giada," he mumbled during a break in our kiss. He thrust into me harder then paused, sliding his hand under my hips to force me even closer. "You are mine," he said as our eyes met.

His simple claim of possession was all it took to rebuild the tension deep inside my belly. As he started to move again, faster now, I met him thrust for thrust. The sensation of Luca losing control and then exploding inside me pushed me over the edge. I dug my nails into his back and buried my teeth in the fleshy part of his shoulder as wave after wave of pleasure rolled through me.

~

Luca

My gorgeous wife let me feed her a few more bites of our dinner in bed, then promptly fell asleep. I watched her for a few minutes, then ducked back out to the terrace to call Alessio. I'd nearly forgotten my promise to check in.

I hadn't expected any drama, and there was none, grazie Dio. I should've known that after being dead to the world for several months with minimal effect on the business, I wasn't as essential as I purported to be. If I somehow left for good, Alessio could handle things just fine. He wasn't a leader, preferred not to make the decisions, and tended to be too impulsive when he did, but maybe with time…

A car backfired in the distance and startled me out of my ridiculous line of thinking. What did it matter anyway? I couldn't get out. My papà would never allow it, and even if he did, what then? Without the backing of the family, I'd have a target on my back for every rival family and businessman I'd ever wronged.

Besides, I didn't have enough money to support Giada

forever, especially at the level of luxury she expected. I imagined we'd have fun setting up our own bed and breakfast in Tuscany though. Giada could decorate the place and welcome the guests, I could handle the books... I supposed in that fantasy, one of us would have to learn to cook.

I shook myself out of the daydream and rejoined my angelic wife in bed.

CHAPTER 6

Giada

*L*uca and I spent the majority of the morning in bed, taking our time exploring each other, talking, and eating. We'd planned to walk into town for lunch, but somehow hadn't made it past the terrace. Luckily, the innkeepers sent up room service, which we devoured outside in the sunshine.

"I don't understand why I'm so hungry," I said. "We've barely left bed."

Luca raised an eyebrow, reminding me that while we had indeed been in bed most of the day, we had spent our morning in fairly athletic endeavors. I shrugged, and bit off a juicy chunk of pear.

"Mmm," I said, surprised by the fruit's sweetness.

Luca swiped his thumb beneath my lip to catch a drip then kissed me. "If you keep making noises like that when you eat, we'll have to return to bed right after lunch."

I shrugged. That wasn't the worst idea. "I also want you in the hot tub."

He gazed over at the hot tub then back to me. "You are insatiable."

I giggled. "I meant after dinner."

"Oh, sure." He stood and reached for my hand. "Get dressed, and we'll go into town."

We visited a vineyard and then strolled through the town together, hand in hand. I couldn't remember the last time Luca had seemed so relaxed and playful. Luca even looked more laid back than usual, wearing dark blue denim jeans, a fitted gray Henley and a black leather jacket. I assumed his demeanor was a product of our location, in his home country but a region where he had no associates and therefore no work whatsoever. Whatever the explanation, I loved it.

"Hey," Luca called, snapping me out of my thoughts. "You okay?"

I nodded, feeling heat rush to my cheeks. "I was just thinking."

"About?"

"You."

Luca grinned and stepped in front of me. He reached for my other hand and kissed me, walking us backwards as we kissed so we weren't blocking the sidewalk. I stumbled a bit and shrieked, but he just kept kissing me. When my hip brushed against a stone ledge, Luca dropped my hands, instead placing his fingers on my cheeks. I hoped the standards for PDA were more relaxed in Italy because I wasn't ready to stop kissing my husband. I wrapped my hands around his back to hold him close, then let them drop to his hips.

I froze, my hand grazing something hard and cold.

Luca quickly reached behind his back and moved my hand.

"What was that?" I asked, breaking off the kiss.

"What do you think?" He held my hand and tugged me back onto the path to continue our walk.

Stupidly, I'd assumed Luca wasn't armed. Apparently, he

wasn't as relaxed as I'd thought. "Do you really need that here?" I asked, hoping to appeal to his sense of logic.

"Hopefully not, but it's better to have it on me a thousand times that I don't need it than to need it once when it isn't with me."

I understood what he was saying, but we were in a quaint little town in northern Italy. It wasn't crime-ridden, and, besides, it was midday. Children were scampering all around.

"Amore, it's not something you need to worry about. Unless I am in bed, showering, or maybe at the gym, you should assume I'm carrying. If it's any consolation, I just have one on me now. If I were working, I'd have a backup at my ankle. Maybe my shoulder too if I was really concerned."

"You're not making me feel any better."

"Baby, come on. It's not that common here, but back home, it's really not a big deal. Just think of it as another accessory I always have on me, like a watch."

"I can't accidentally kill myself with your watch."

He rolled his eyes. "We may need a refresher on your shooting classes when we get home if you're that concerned."

I shook my head, eager to change the subject. We'd been having so much fun, and now I was stressed out. "Can we go by that furniture shop we passed on the way here? I want to see if they have anything for my clients back home."

Luca agreed without hesitation and we walked back to the car. At the shop, I spotted an amazing end table, an ornate mirror, and a gorgeous stone sculpture.

"Too bad this would be too hard to ship," I said, tapping the sculpture. Audra would love it.

Luca eyed it skeptically, clearly not appreciating its appeal. "Well, it won't fit in my car, but if they can get it to Civitavecchia, I can get it to New York or Connecticut."

"Civita…" I started to repeat, stumbling over the very Italian-sounding place.

My husband chuckled. "The port in Rome."

"Oh. But—"

"You do know that's what I do, right? Ship things? Usually between Italy and the U.S."

Honestly, I hadn't realized that. I knew he did something with exports but wasn't totally sure what. "Well, yes, but it still costs money to transport things."

He cocked his head to the side. "Amore, we use big shipping crates. As long as you're not wanting to move dozens of couches every week, I can get whatever you need back to the east coast. The only cost is whatever it takes for them to get it to the port."

I considered that for a moment. Audra had been thrilled when I'd started finding smaller items in Italy for our customers' homes and offices, but I hadn't even considered the possibility of larger items. If we could offer all sorts of custom Italian furnishings without the exorbitant prices for shipping, we could undercut all the competition.

"Don't you lose money then?"

"If you weren't my wife, I'd charge you a fee, so I suppose I'm losing that profit, but it doesn't cost me anything to add a few more items to each shipment."

"So, you're saying I can buy this stuff and just pay for them to ship it to Carav…"

"Civitavecchia. And yes."

I smiled. "Okay, I can do that." I started off towards the shop's owner.

He greeted me politely in Italian.

"Buongiorno," I said. "Parla inglese?"

The man shook his head, looking panicked.

Luca stepped up beside me, a slight smirk on his face. "Baby, can I…?"

I nodded then watched as my hunky hubby greeted the man and jabbered away in Italian. I understood nothing, except when Luca pointed to the pieces I liked. I did feel a little bad about not knowing Italian, especially now that I was married to one of their people, but I'd tried. I was comically bad at learning foreign languages.

I wandered around the shop for a few more minutes until Luca returned. "All ready to go?" he asked.

"Do you need my company credit card?"

"I paid cash. You can still get reimbursed that way, right?"

"Yes, but…" I tried to envision how he always managed to carry so much cash on him.

"It's better that way," he said. "No worries about exchange rates or fees with credit cards." He kissed the side of my head as we strolled back to the car.

~

Luca

I'd never really thought Giada would hold down a real job for any significant measure of time, so it was surprising to see her embracing this interior design gig she'd snagged. It wasn't that I'd assumed she wasn't qualified or smart enough to work, just that she'd never need the money, and therefore probably wouldn't bother.

But in a million years, I never could've imagined her job actually helping me out.

That night, after two very satisfying hours in the hot tub, I tucked Giada in bed and promised to join her after calling Alessio. After listening to his recap of the day's business, I shared my good news.

"You know how Giada has taken this new decorating job?" I began, not pausing as the question was rhetorical. "Originally, the company she liked wasn't too interested because of her lack of experience and erratic vacation schedule, but on her last trip to Italy, she found some cool local décor and stuff. She convinced the company to hire her on as an intern or something and let her shop for some of their clients."

"Okay," he said, clearly bored with my wife's work life.

"Anyway, apparently, there is a big demand for custom Italian pieces in New York, but they need a low-cost way to ship items."

"Now that's convenient," Alessio replied, finally perking up.

While some of the items we shipped were legit, my papà did still have his fair share of illicit trafficking. Nothing terrible like sex slaves or stolen organs, but the occasional shipment of leather goods or stolen watches may have made its way onto my cargo carrier. It was always a struggle to find legit items to ship to keep the authorities off our backs in any surprise inspections. Our other trick that worked, what we'd done before I left for Italy, involved claiming an entire shipment was wrong and returning it. That worked well enough, but it wasn't something we could do more than a few times a year without raising any questions from the authorities.

"Even better, I paid for the items in cash. Giada will get reimbursed from her company."

Alessio chuckled. "Does the princess know you're using her to wash your money?"

"She's always happy to help," I replied, certain he knew Giada was completely unaware of the real reason I was happy to use cash.

~

Giada

The next morning, Luca dragged me out of bed after only the most perfunctory makeout session ever, claiming he wanted to take me out for breakfast. He promised we could spend the whole afternoon in bed but reminded me I had chosen the location so that we could sightsee. Everything at the restaurant was so delicious that I didn't even protest when he suggested a hike after our meal. That, of course, worked up more of an appetite, so we returned to town and enjoyed some gelato.

"Would you ever want to move back here permanently?" I asked, stealing a bite of Luca's stracciatella.

"I never lived here. You mean Rome? Or Sicily?"

I shrugged. "Either."

"I want to be wherever you are."

I returned to my own gelato and sighed as the glorious mixture of flavors settled on my tongue. "I could live here."

"Don't you think you'd miss your friends and family back home?"

"Perhaps, but there would be plenty of gelato to soothe my sorrows."

Luca chuckled and wiped my lip with his thumb, lingering at the corner of my mouth. "There's more to Italy than gelato."

"Oh, I know. There's also sexy men, amazing designers..." my voice trailed off as I spotted the art gallery we'd planned to visit before I got sidetracked by the gelato.

"And art," Luca said, following my gaze. He stood and reached for my hand. "Ready?"

I nodded. We strolled hand in hand through the art gallery, then headed back outside to wander around the town a bit more before returning to our room. Luca's arm wrapped around my hip, preventing me from walking any faster than a snail's pace, but I didn't mind. His touch made everything better.

"Luca Marino!" I barely recognized my husband's name through the thick accent of the person who called it behind us, but Luca stiffened in an instant. He turned to face the men, then swore under his breath.

We held our ground as they approached. The men addressed Luca entirely in Italian, though it seemed a different Italian than what I was used to hearing. I could tell from Luca's demeanor that they weren't friends, but I wasn't too worried since we were in the middle of a busy square.

After a moment, Luca spoke. He, too, stuck to Italian, and didn't bother translating, but he gestured to me a couple of times.

The men replied, then one turned to me and asked a question. Of course, I didn't understand a bit of it. Luca said something then, presumably informing them that I didn't speak Italian, as they both chuckled.

"Is that true? You don't speak Italian?" the shorter man said to me, his accent unfamiliar.

"No," I replied. "I mean, yes, it's true. No, I don't speak Italian."

"We have dining reservations to get to," Luca said, tugging me along.

The men stepped in our path. "Why are you in our town?" he said to me.

I gazed at Luca.

"I already told you that," he said.

"We want to hear it from her."

I wasn't sure if I was supposed to tell them about the wedding, so I went with the safe answer. "I wanted a weekend away, just the two of us. I've never visited up here, so I thought this would be the perfect location. It's beautiful."

They seemed content with that response. They said something else, but Luca gripped my hand tighter and tugged me down the street.

I peered over my shoulder a few times, but the men didn't follow us. Luca didn't say anything until we reached the car. He looked annoyed, not scared, which I supposed was a good thing.

"What was that all about?" I asked.

He wrinkled his nose and started the ignition before reaching for my hand and peppering kisses all over my palms.

"Their family does business in this part of Italy. It's their turf, so to speak. They didn't expect to see me this far north."

"Ahh, so it's like a Westside Story thing," I said.

Confusion filled Luca's face for a moment, and then he shook his head.

"Are you not allowed to be here?" I asked.

"This is my country. I can go where I want," he snapped.

I placed a hand on his thigh, rubbing lightly then inching closer to his groin, eager to remind him I was not the enemy.

My trick worked almost instantly. A calm smile replaced his scowl, and he relaxed against his seat. "Usually, if my papà or me or someone else…higher up in the business… will be in the region where another family operates, we'll give them a heads up. But this is a purely personal trip, so it's none of their business."

I scooted my hand one inch further, then increased the pressure until Luca's body responded. He nudged my hand off his cock but smiled, shaking his head at me.

"You are insatiable. And as much as I'd love to ravish you in this car, we should head back to the inn."

CHAPTER 7

Luca

On our last night in Tuscany, Giada somehow talked me into taking her out dancing. Maybe I wasn't thinking straight after days of lovemaking and decadent meals, or maybe I only resisted the idea back in the States because of the risk of someone I knew seeing me dance. Or maybe, the promise of seeing Giada dance in her teensy purple sequin dress was too tempting to resist.

"I don't think that scrap of fabric will even cover your ass," I said, watching with awe as she began to tug it up over her hips.

"It will. It covers everything," she said, her voice full of confidence. "Well, I mean, unless I have to bend down."

"What happens then?"

Giada cringed. "I just don't bend. This is a dress for standing. Or very careful sitting."

She lifted the material up over her breasts, repositioned them, then tugged the bottom hem down a bit further before twirling to check out her own ass in the mirror. "See? Perfect." Giada was beaming.

Sure, the material did cover her assets, but only about as well as a bathing suit.

"Every man who looks at you will want to fuck you," I told her.

"But at the end of the night, only you can," she replied.

"It won't bother you, having all those men hit on you?"

She waved a hand dismissively. "You know me; I love attention."

I bit back a smile, and we headed out.

The crowd was still manageable when we arrived at the club. The dance scene in Italy tended to peak later at night—or, rather, early in the morning—anyway. Everyone who had shown up early, though, was crammed together by the bar.

"They must all be like me, desperate for a stiff drink before dancing in public," I said to Giada, motioning to the crowd.

"Let's get in line," she said with a grin.

I didn't want to drag her into the pack, so instead, I led her to a calmer section of the club, right off the side of the dance floor. I promised to get the drinks and come right back. With the horrific line, I waited over ten minutes before even getting close to the bar. And every time I turned back to check on Giada, a different man was hovering nearby her.

Usually, unease filled me whenever any man came too close to my princess, but tonight, I tolerated it. And besides, as far as I could tell, she was shooing the men away almost as soon as they came over.

I finally caught the bartender's attention and ordered our drinks, then gazed back to Giada. The man beside her at the moment had blond hair and looked to be in his early twenties. I could tell she was saying something, so the man must've been an English speaker. He moved closer, then she gestured towards me. Nothing about his posture gave me any reason to fear for her safety, so I remained at the bar, waiting on the drinks.

When the bartender returned, the man was still beside Giada.

Remembering her claims from earlier that she enjoyed male attention, I took my time getting back to her, even pausing at a table near her. She saw me and caught my eye, flashing me a clear plea to come rescue her. I smiled and winked, determined to let her handle it alone.

Finally, the blond walked away, so I rejoined my wife.

"Took you long enough," she said with a groan.

I bit back a laugh. "Who was your new friend?"

"Which one?" she asked with a grimace. "Man, you weren't kidding about this dress."

"You are the most stunning woman here. Those men have great taste."

"And no ability to take a hint and back off," she added. "I told that last guy I had a boyfriend who was getting drinks, and he said, 'oh well, I don't see him here now.' Like what kind of a lame line is that?"

"You said you enjoyed attention. I was just giving you what you wanted," I reminded her. "Besides, you can handle yourself just fine."

That seemed to placate her. "True, but now that guy thinks I was lying about having a boyfriend."

I decided to clear things up for anyone watching. I cupped her cheeks in my hands and pulled her in for a kiss. When she tried to pull back after a minute, I wrapped my arms around her back instead, holding her close for a long, intimate kiss. It was the kind of kiss that typically occurred during activities that could cause pregnancy.

When we finally separated, I smacked Giada on the ass.

"Ready to dance?" I asked her.

Still stunned, her mouth just fell open, but then she nodded.

I tugged her close again, this time whispering. "One more thing. Giada, you do not have a boyfriend. You will never again have a boyfriend. Understand?"

The second she figured out what I meant, Giada was the one

to kiss me. And this time, she was the one who kept the kiss going long after it stopped being decent for a public setting.

I danced with my wife for four songs, until thankfully, she begged me to find a secret closet or bathroom with a lock. I refused, but when we reached the Maserati, I noticed the lot was empty of people. Most patrons wouldn't dream of leaving the club so early, which meant we had a decent window for privacy.

I pressed Giada against the side of the car and kissed her, running my hands up the back of her thighs and nudging the already-short dress even higher. She stopped me at first, then gazed around us. Apparently reaching the same conclusion I had, she then reached forward, cupping me through my slacks.

"Amore, I don't think there's room for that in this car. Let me just..." I began, planning to insist on pleasuring her. But she'd already unzipped my pants. I reached around her to open the car door, positioning myself in the passenger seat before reaching for her.

She started to climb over me with her back to me, but I stopped her. I wanted to watch her the first time she came in my Maserati. I rolled the tiny dress up to her waist as she straddled my lap. Giada reached a hand between us, stroking my already hard length while I captured her lips with my own. I lifted her breasts over the top of the dress and sucked one nipple into my mouth, then the other. Giada's moan reminded me of a cat purring, eager for more attention.

I couldn't focus on her breasts for much longer, though, because she'd already positioned me at her entrance. I gripped her hips, easing her onto my cock. We groaned in unison as I slid in all the way.

"Fuck that feels good," she said, her breathy words a complete aphrodisiac.

I let her control the depth and speed, in part because I didn't have much leverage in the cramped sportscar. But letting Giada use my body to find her own pleasure was the hottest thing I could imagine. I thanked God the car had tinted windows, then I focused on the sight of my wife's beautiful round breasts bouncing up and down inches in front of my face.

Her breathing picked up, and if I'd had any doubts that she was close, her nails digging into my arms would've told me everything.

"Yes, baby," I growled.

She bit her lip and tossed her head back, then her perfect pussy tightened and released around me in wave after wave of delicious pleasure. I shifted my arms to her back, holding her tightly while I joined her and found my release.

I let her catch her breath for a moment, then pulled her dress back up over her breasts. I realized we had no tissues or cloths, so I'd just have to clean up later. Giada shifted off of me, cringing.

"Ow," she murmured.

"What's wrong?"

She opened the car door, adjusting her dress while stumbling out. I tucked myself back into my pants then climbed out of the car.

"I think I'm getting sore," she said.

I made my way around to the driver's seat, not replying until we were both securely inside the vehicle in our individual seats. I supposed what she said made sense, after days of sex, but already I suspected the discomfort wasn't enough to make her stay away from me. "I bet I could kiss it and make it better," I said.

Giada raised an eyebrow as if considering the prospect.

"Not here!" I clarified. "Later. If you want."

She giggled, and I drove back to the inn.

～

Giada

We returned to Rome the next day, but every moment with Luca still felt different than before. When we weren't alone, I still felt close to him, bonded by our shared secret. When we weren't even together, I still felt connected to him. I wasn't naïve enough to believe things would continue like that forever, so I wanted to enjoy it while I could.

On the last night of our pseudo-honeymoon, Luca took me to some fancy new restaurant, then we spent the next several hours in bed reenacting our first night as a married couple.

I was beyond content in bed beside my new husband. I was equally exhausted. And yet somehow, I still couldn't sleep. I supposed it didn't matter. I could sleep on the flight. And once we were home, I didn't anticipate leaving bed the next few days, so I could surely catch up on rest in between other, more entertaining, newlywed activities.

The gibbous moon shone through the oversized windows, casting a gentle glow on the room. In our post-lovemaking exhaustion, we hadn't remembered to pull the curtains shut, and while I knew that meant the sun would likely disturb us once it rose, I didn't dare wake Luca early by shifting. He'd fallen asleep on his back, with one arm bent behind his neck and the other arm on my hip.

From my position on my side, I had the perfect view of my husband's face. Few experiences in life were as satisfying for me as watching Luca sleep. For starters, it was a rare occasion that he actually fell asleep before me—or stayed asleep when I moved. Luca was an impossibly light sleeper, so it felt a bit like spying a unicorn whenever I actually caught him sleeping.

The other reason I enjoyed it so much was because of the stark contrast between sleeping Luca and wakeful Luca. When awake, Luca was always alert, on guard, and analyzing everything. Even if he seemed relaxed, he wasn't, and there were subtle signs that would betray his attempts to appear at ease.

But in his sleep, Luca lost all traces of tension. His facial features relaxed, making him resemble the young teen I'd had a crush on back at boarding school. He still had those same lips I'd kissed on the beach, and that same adorable nose I'd dotted with powdered sugar in the dining hall. And those eyelids... *Agh.*

Luca's eyes were stunning—mysterious, deep, and dark, but even when he shut them, something about them still mesmerized me. Maybe it was his impossibly thick, long lashes, or maybe it was just the memories of watching him nap in the courtyard in front of the science building that captivated me.

Whatever it was, I could watch Luca sleep for hours. Unfortunately, his calm appearance and even, smooth breathing also relaxed me, and I usually fell asleep within minutes of gazing at my sleeping beauty.

Tonight, I was determined to stay awake longer, to fully absorb and appreciate the man beside me. Not just the smooth curve of his ears and the masculine cut of his jaw, but the parts of Luca I couldn't see. His courage, his grit, his generosity. Even his loyalty.

No matter what may or may not have happened with some stupid dancer years before, I didn't doubt the man beside me was wholly devoted to me. He'd sacrifice everything for me, stop at no lengths to protect me. His desire for me was steadfast. Luca was even tenacious in his drive to improve.

Did I think he was perfect? No, of course not. But more than anyone else I'd encountered, Luca tried. Every day, I saw Luca fight the instincts his father had so deeply ingrained in him. His line of work forced him to teeter along the line between good and evil, but he was making progress. Making it better. Making *himself* better.

I didn't doubt Luca would ever cease striving to be a better person. Maybe he wouldn't do it for himself, but for me, he absolutely would.

I shifted my hand to his face, appreciating the contrast

between the scratchy stubble beneath my palm and the smooth flesh of his cheek against my fingers. For a breath, I thought he might've slept through the contact, that I could touch him without disrupting the sleep he deserved.

But in a flash, his hand flew from my hip, his fingers circling my wrist tightly, and I nearly giggled at my naivety in thinking I could thwart Luca's cat-like reflexes.

"Need more sleep," he mumbled without opening his eyes. "No part of me is ready for round four."

I breathed a soft laugh against his neck. "I just like watching you sleep."

He lifted my hand to his lips, kissed it softly, then flipped onto his side, shifting me along with him. His arm roped back around my waist, and his legs pressed against my own. "Get some sleep, princess," he whispered, burying his face in my hair to kiss my neck, then promptly stilling.

I tried to take his advice, to fall asleep, but I still couldn't. I replayed our wedding service in my mind, then tried to recall some of the advice Father Ben had shared during our pre-cana classes.

My mind kept drifting back to something the Father had said about how we should love our partners even more when they're struggling to love themselves. At the time the words were spoken, I'd smugly disregarded the tip, assuming I was doing that already. But was I?

To a casual onlooker, Luca oozed confidence. He didn't doubt himself or his abilities for a moment.

But I knew him better.

I understood that the cocky man everyone else saw was merely putting on a show, playing the part of the strong leader, filling his role perfectly. In reality, Luca's self-hatred bordered on crippling some days. I'd thought that by marrying him, I was showing him that I loved him despite the lie he'd told about sleeping with Carla.

Maybe what he'd needed wasn't for me to love him in spite of the perceived fault, but to believe him when he said he hadn't cheated.

The trouble there was the paternity tests. If it had just been one, I could dismiss it as faulty, or assume it had been tampered with. But two, well, that was harder to ignore. There had to be some other explanation. Luca said that the time they had done it, years before, he'd used a condom. Maybe Carla had somehow preserved his sperm and used it to impregnate herself years later.

I gazed at my husband for a moment before stealthily slipping out of bed to research that possibility. A few minutes later, I was back to square one. Apparently, sperm wasn't easy to preserve and artificially inseminating oneself wasn't a simple feat. Besides, why would Carla do that? Even assuming she was a money-hungry manipulative whore, I struggled to believe she'd go to that length to make a few bucks.

From the way Luca described her, I could believe that she wanted money, and perhaps even that she was willing to lie to get it. But when I'd seen her around Luca, she didn't strike me as some manipulative mastermind. She looked uncertain, almost frightened.

I returned to my internet search and typed in "when might a paternity test be wrong." A few seconds later, a slew of results appeared. I clicked on an article from a law office. It listed four scenarios when the DNA test results might be erroneous: if the test was tampered with, if there was a lab error, if the father was older and his sample contained mutated DNA, or if the man tested was related to the actual father.

My breath caught in my throat and I clicked to read more details about the last possibility.

Why hadn't I considered that sooner? It made perfect sense, and in a family based on lies, it wasn't a stretch to assume the dad might not have been open about other children he'd fathered. Luca knew his father wasn't faithful to his mother.

Heck, I could easily picture Camilla Marino even helping with the cover up of her husband's bastard child. Now that Salvatore was in his sixties, it was easy to imagine at least one of his illegitimate sons was old enough to have fathered Jacob. For all we knew, Luca could have dozens of half-brothers wandering the streets.

I clicked through a few more articles, searching for other specific examples of one brother mistakenly testing positive as the parent of his sibling's offspring. It was more common than I would've thought, which was disturbing. Apparently, testing both brothers was the only way to yield accurate results. Normally, I supposed that would be an easy feat, except in situations like this, where we didn't know who the brother was.

I crawled back into bed beside Luca, planning to think on it until I made sense of it all, but sleep overtook me quickly.

~

Luca

The alarm blared, yanking me from a dream where I was lounging on the beach beside Giada. I swatted my phone, silencing the monstrosity, then stretched slowly. Somehow, Giada had slept through the ruckus. I vaguely recalled her being up in the night watching me sleep, so I decided to make coffee before waking her. I would've loved another luxurious morning in bed with her, but we had a flight to catch.

Alessio was staying behind for a couple more days to visit family, but he agreed to drive Giada and me to the airport. When he showed up, she was still in the bathroom doing her hair.

I knocked on the door, opening it a few inches. "Alessio is here. We should go."

"Five minutes," she promised.

"You look beautiful now," I told her.

She grabbed my shirt and yanked me closer, kissing me on the lips before nudging me back into the hallway.

I turned to see Alessio watching, his eyebrow raised.

"Seems like things are good with you two again," he said.

I nodded, careful not to smile to broadly. "Never better."

My friend frowned. "You seem different. Did something happen?"

I shook my head. "Nope, just nice to get away with her for a few days." I turned and pretended to busy myself with something on my phone. I wasn't accustomed to lying to Alessio. It felt weird having such big news and not being able to share it with him.

Giada emerged from the bathroom then, her hair looking no different than it had earlier, as far as I could tell. "Ready," she said, latching onto my arm like we were beginning a three-legged race.

Alessio gave me a look as if her behavior were confirming his suspicions about whatever, but we left before he could say anything.

Once Giada and I were alone in the airport, she turned to me.

"I read some things when I couldn't sleep last night," she began.

"You should sleep on the plane," I said, thinking she was telling me she was tired. "I volunteer my shoulder, chest, lap, or whatever body part you choose to serve as your pillow."

"Thanks, but can I tell you about what I read?"

I nodded. She proceeded to tell me all this random research she'd done on paternity tests. At first, I was skeptical. But when she got to the part about paternity tests occasionally falsely identifying brothers of the father as the father, I listened closer. Since we had a little time before boarding began for our fight, I did my own research.

It turned out, she was right. If I had a brother, and he had a baby with Carla, that could explain my test results. But there was still a problem.

"I don't have a brother," I said to Giada.

She frowned. "You might. You don't know."

"Giada, even if we assume my papà fathered dozens of other children, they'd still just be a half-brother. Nothing in these articles says that would yield the same results."

"Nothing in the articles says it wouldn't," she countered. "And besides, for all you know, your parents had a child before you."

That was far-fetched, but I had no trouble believing my papà could've fathered other children. Except, that led to another problem. "Okay, but I can't exactly ask my papà if he has other sons. He'd want to know why I'm asking, and even if I told him the truth, there's no guarantee he'd tell me the truth." I paused. "And that is assuming he even knows about this other son."

Giada wrinkled her nose. "I hadn't considered that."

A flight attendant announced that boarding was beginning for our flight. I stood, extending a hand towards Giada. She hoisted her bag over her shoulder before entwining her fingers around mine. We reached the gate, pausing to wait in line. Giada shifted her bag to the side, so I dropped her hand, wrapping her bag over the top of the small suitcase I was rolling, leaving her with only her purse.

Just as we reached our seats, Giada turned to me.

"There is someone other than your father who would know for sure," she said.

I started to lift the luggage into the overhead compartment.

"Carla knows who she was with. And she obviously knows that person is related to you. Otherwise, why would she have tried to scam you in the first place?"

Everything Giada said made perfect sense.

Carla wasn't scamming me at random. She chose me because she knew what the paternity test would show.

Now I just had to get back on U.S. soil so I could confront her.

CHAPTER 8

Luca

Giada slept on the flight while I stewed about confronting Carla. Our plane would land mid-afternoon, New York time, but then I needed to take Giada home. I had to unpack. I had to check in at the docks and at my club. I couldn't rush straight to Carla's. And it wasn't the sort of conversation I could have over the phone, at least not if I wanted to be able to detect whether she was being honest. My confrontation would have to wait till the next day.

I'd assumed the minutes would tick by until I was able to talk with Carla, but that wasn't the case. Being back home with Giada calmed me. I'd carried her over the threshold of our apartment, then fallen asleep quickly after making love to my wife for the first time ever on U.S. soil.

That peaceful feeling lasted until I left the apartment the next day. Giada planned to run some errands then meet up with Gabby for manicures, and I had a lot of business matters to catch up on. I would've preferred to see Carla first, but I couldn't reach her until afternoon, and I hadn't wanted to risk wasting time by showing up at her place when she wasn't even home.

Her apartment wasn't too far from the club, and I was oddly relieved to see it wasn't in a terrible neighborhood. As she opened the door, I noticed a few toys on the floor and a booster seat strapped to a chair in the kitchen. I supposed that was a good sign.

I hadn't told Carla why I wanted to speak with her in person when I'd called, but presumably she was expecting me to give her money. That sure wasn't going to happen. I would've accepted the slightest chance that I was wrong about it all, except I knew I hadn't slept with her recently. There was no way that baby was mine.

"Is he here?" I asked right after she invited me in.

She shook her head, "No, a neighbor is watching him. But he's probably sleeping now, so it's not a good idea—"

"I don't want to see him," I interrupted. "I just didn't want him to overhear what I have to say to you." I paused, then looked straight in her eyes. "I don't care what your test says. He's not my son."

Carla rolled her eyes and swiveled away. "Luca, those tests don't lie. And I didn't tamper with the test, so don't even start with that."

I gripped her arm and yanked her to face me. I was skilled at detecting lies, but only when I could actually see the person. "There's a few instances where the test can be wrong. When there are brothers, for example," I began. I paused, and Carla's face blanched. Her lips parted, and she gasped.

She jerked her head away again, but it was too late. I'd already seen what I needed to see.

"Seriously? You knew all along he wasn't mine? What the hell?"

Carla backed away, but I grabbed her elbow.

"We aren't done talking yet. I want to know. How did you know we were related? Where did you meet him?"

She clenched her jaw as if trying to hold back tears. "Where did I meet who?"

I blew out an exasperated sigh. "My brother. How did you know I had a brother? Where did you find him? Why did you sleep with him? Is he in on this scam too?"

Carla narrowed her gaze. "I don't know what you're talking about."

I smacked my palm on the table. Carla jumped.

"Stop lying to me! I saw it in your eyes. You know just as well as I do that Jacob isn't my kid. I'm asking you to be honest for once. When did you meet my brother? Were you guys involved, or was it a one-time thing?"

Carla shook her head, raising her fingers to the bridge of her nose. "Christ, Luca. I didn't sleep with your brother. Jacob *is* your brother."

"What?" Nothing Carla said made sense.

"I'm sorry. I didn't want to lie to you. I didn't mean to screw up things with Giada. I just didn't know what to do."

I waved my hand dismissively, eager to hear the explanation of her earlier statement. "I didn't even know I had a brother, let alone that you knew who he was."

"You don't. Or, at least you didn't. I mean, not that I know of anyway," she said.

"I don't understand. You need to start from the beginning."

"Jacob is not your son. He's your brother. Half-brother, technically." Carla spoke so matter-of-factly that I felt like her words should've instantly made sense. But they didn't.

I sunk into the chair beside me. "How is that possible? If he's..."

Her eyes seemed to register the exact moment I pieced it together. She turned abruptly, raising her hands as though anticipating a hit.

"You slept with my papà?" I asked, flying out of my chair. I lunged at her as she inched backwards, my hand gripping her neck right when her back hit the wall.

I tightened my fist briefly, then released her throat. Tears sprung to her eyes but even just looking at her made me nauseous.

"You lied to me all along!"

"I'm sorry," she cried.

"You fucking whore!" I punched the wall beside her head before turning around and storming towards the door. I stopped myself, acutely aware that I still had more questions.

When I swiveled back to face her, I stopped dead in my tracks.

She had crouched down in the corner where I'd left her, her arms covering her chest and face. The look in her eyes was pure terror.

I bit my lip until I tasted the coppery tinge of blood. "Fuck," I spit. I was angry at myself, angry at her, angry at my fucking asshole papà. "Damn it!"

Carla trembled when I swore.

Bile rose into my throat as I realized the full implication of the situation. If she had a child with my papà, that meant that this woman…a woman I'd slept with years before…had also been with my papà. I was beyond disgusted.

"Get up!" I commanded.

She hesitantly complied.

"Jesus." I shook my head and swore in Italian. "I'm not going to hurt you. Stop looking at me like that."

"I'm so sorry," she said, still crying.

"Telling me I was the father, was this his idea, or was he in on it? Was the whole point for me to lose Giada or just to make me look like a fool?"

Carla shook her head rapidly. "No, no. Nothing like that. Salvatore has no idea Jacob even exists."

"So you came up with this all on your own? Just to scam me for money?"

She hesitated, then nodded. "I didn't mean to hurt you. I figured you had the money and if the paternity tests came back okay, I didn't think you'd even blink at paying me off." Carla paused. "The old Luca wouldn't have wanted anything to do with Jacob anyway."

I rubbed my forehead, desperate to stave off the impending migraine. The old me probably wouldn't have been so certain I hadn't slept with her the time of conception either.

"It wasn't all a scam. I mean, I needed the money, not for myself but for Jacob."

"You could get a job."

"I had a job, and I couldn't do that with Jacob. I can't support him without health insurance, and I can't get that without a job. And I can't get a job without anyone to watch Jacob." She shook her head. "I just figured if you gave me some money to help me back onto my feet, we could disappear and start a good life."

"My papà has more money than I do. Why overcomplicate things with the lie? If you know Jacob is his, why not just go to the source?"

She lowered her voice. "I know who he is, Luca. I…saw things, at the club. I'm not an idiot."

"I don't know what you think you saw, but what does that have to do with any of this?"

Carla was quiet for a moment, then gazed up again. "It wasn't even my idea. I didn't even think about telling you until…"

The abrupt way she stopped herself set off alarms in my head.

"Until what?" I asked, dread making my veins run cold.

"He looked up records or something," Carla began, shaking her head. "I mean, I don't know exactly how he got any of his information, but he knew when I'd worked for you, and he knew I had a kid. I guess when he saw a picture, he just assumed you were the father. The resemblance is—"

"Stop." I interrupted. "Who?"

She worked her lip between her teeth. I could tell Carla was afraid of identifying whoever had apparently betrayed me, but I wasn't sure why. If anything, she should be scared of what I'd do if she didn't tell me.

"I don't have all day, Carla. You've got five seconds to answer."

Carla pulled a scrap of paper from her purse and handed it to me. "He said his name was Alex but I got the impression he made that up. This is the number he gave me though."

I didn't know any Alex, but I supposed that wasn't my biggest problem at the moment. If someone was trying to get Carla to trick me into paying child support, I needed to know who and why. "And exactly what did he say to you?"

"He told me how much money I was entitled to, legally. And he said he knew you, and knew that you'd pay up to keep me quiet." She paused, her voice wavering. "He acted like you wouldn't ask questions, that after the test, you'd just fork over the money and never want to see me again. But Alex was the one who said I should go to your apartment and bring Jacob. He didn't tell me your girlfriend would be there."

"And this Alex knew about you and…Salvatore?" I couldn't even call the man my papà after learning he'd slept with her.

She shook her head. "Alex assumed Jacob was yours. And I figured if he thought the resemblance was enough, then—"

I held up a hand, shushing her. I felt sick. I didn't want to hear any more.

Carla blew out a sigh. "I'll take Jacob and we'll leave town. You'll never have to see me again. I swear we will disappear and not bother you ever again. Just please, don't tell your father."

"Why shouldn't I tell him? I don't owe you anything."

Her expression morphed into desperation. "I know, Luca, but please. You can't tell him. Think of Jacob. He's your brother."

I held up my hands. "What about him?"

"He needs his mother."

"You think my papà would hurt you?"

"Maybe me, maybe Jacob."

I wanted to tell her she was being ridiculous, that my papà would never hurt his own child or the mother of his child. Except, well, I wasn't so sure he wouldn't.

"I need to go."

Carla reached for my arm, latching to my wrist and pulling. "Please, Luca!"

I shook her free with minimal effort. "I said I need to go. I won't say anything for now, so don't leave town. I need to think." I needed to figure out who this Alex character was, and I needed to talk to Giada. She would know what I should do.

I dialed Giada as I stormed to my car, but she didn't answer. I tried to recall if she was at work or what her plans were, but my mind was swirling. I couldn't even recall what day it was, let alone where she'd said she'd be.

"I talked with Carla," I told Giada's voicemail, cringing at the hoarseness of my voice. "You were right, sort of, but..." I began, then paused. I wasn't going to tell the whole damn story to a recording. "I need you, baby. Please meet me at home."

I hung up, then dialed the number Carla gave me for Alex. I didn't expect anyone would answer, but I didn't want to hit up my tech guru for a favor if I didn't need to. After three rings, the call clicked over to voicemail. I was about to hang up, assuming it would be an automated voice, but it wasn't.

"Alex" had used his real voice to record his voicemail. Only Alex wasn't his real name.

It was Adrian fucking Patras.

The one man I couldn't punish for his betrayal.

I started the car, and headed towards home.

Giada

Spending the afternoon with Gabby had been amazing, except that I was so worried I'd ruin my own surprise about the wedding that I ended up pausing mid-sentence every time I said anything. I figured I could share details about our romantic getaway to Tuscany without blabbing the reason we'd taken the special trip. Of course, me pausing to censor everything I said piqued Gabby's interest even more than all my actual stories about my travels.

Plus, even the hint of secrecy renewed her suspicions about Luca. I tried not to take offense to her frequent suggestions that he wasn't a loyal partner. I told myself it was preferable she assume he was a two-timing jerk than a criminal mastermind. But it still bothered me that my best friend didn't love my favorite human in the world.

I hadn't heard my phone ring, but the persistent buzzing of the voice mail notification captured my attention. I ignored the manicurist's glare as I clicked to listen to my message.

"I have to go," I blurted out.

Both Gabriella and the aesthetician scowled at me.

"Is everything okay?" my friend asked.

I shook my head, then realized I should clarify so she didn't think someone had died. "It'll be fine, but Luca needs me." I turned to the woman filing my nails. "Add the bottle of polish to my bill, and I'll do it at home," I said. "And I'll pay for hers."

She raised an eyebrow but took my credit card over to the cash register.

The crease between Gabriella's brows deepened. "You don't have to treat and you don't have to rush off just because Luca says to. You're not at his beck and call, and he certainly isn't the boss of you."

I rolled my eyes. "It's not like that. He needs me." I gritted my teeth together, still unsettled by Luca's voice. I'd heard him sound stressed before, but this was different. I could tell he was truly distraught. I couldn't wait to hear what he'd learned, and I was so glad that he'd called me for comfort instead of heading out to binge drink with Alessio or something. The old Luca would've internalized whatever he was dealing with and certainly wouldn't have come to me. This was huge.

"Giada, I'm serious. I've been meaning to talk with you. I don't think this is healthy. It's like he controls you…"

I scribbled my name on the receipt with my left hand since the nails of my right hand had already been polished, then dropped my credit card into my purse along with the sealed bottle of polish.

"Gabby, I really am sorry to cut our girls day short, and I promise we will get together soon, but I don't have time to justify my relationship to you today. Luca and I are good," I said, acutely aware that was the understatement of the century. "Really good."

My friend looked completely unconvinced, but I was in a hurry. I leaned down and brushed a kiss on her cheek then dashed out, tapping a quick text to Luca telling him I got his message and would be home shortly.

He wasn't at the apartment when I arrived, and when I called his phone, he didn't answer. I toyed with painting my remaining nails, but didn't want him to think I was completely uncaring if he came home to find me with wet nails. So instead, I tidied the apartment and poured him a glass of wine.

An hour later, I called again.

Bored, and now hungry, I turned on some music and began to boil water for pasta. I chopped up a couple of tomatoes and attempted to make a sauce from a recipe online. It helped pass the time, and the sauce wasn't terrible, although I did dump a jar of store-bought sauce in with my homemade batch just for good measure.

When the food was ready, I plated up two servings but didn't wait for Luca before eating. He still wasn't returning my calls, and Gabby had already texted a pseudo apology. She said she hoped everything was okay, which only made me feel guiltier for running out on her.

I snapped a picture of my unpainted fingers and texted it to Luca, informing him that I had run out on Gabriella and the rest of my manicure to meet him. He didn't respond. I flipped through a magazine, painted my nails, and then watched three design shows on TV while my polish dried.

As the sky darkened, my annoyance morphed to concern. Unsure of what else to do, I texted Enzo and asked if he'd heard anything about Luca or knew where he was.

"I'll look into it," came his prompt reply.

A half hour later, my phone rang. My pulse raced with excitement as I reached for it, dropping back to its norm when I saw it was only Enzo.

My voice sounded dismal when I answered.

"He's at his club," Enzo explained.

"Working or just…socializing?"

"I don't know. He's with Alessio. Are you okay? Do you need something?"

I blew out a sigh. Apparently, I was wrong. People don't change. "I'm fine. Thank you, Enzo," I said, disconnecting the call, shutting off the television and rolling off the couch. I changed into my black nightgown with magenta flowers and slipped into bed.

I lay there awake for what felt like hours, but eventually, I fell asleep.

~

Luca

The apartment was bathed in darkness when I returned, a sliver of light from the moon poking through the curtains serving as my only guidepost for avoiding furniture as I maneuvered through the living room. As my eyes adjusted, I peered into the bedroom, barely able to discern a small lump in the corner of the bed. Judging from the soft, even breaths, Giada was asleep. I was relieved that she hadn't waited up, but disappointed that I couldn't talk with her now.

What I'd said earlier on her voicemail was still true. I needed her.

I'd intended to head home right after I'd called her, but Alessio had intercepted me. Dmitry Petrov had struck again. He'd tried to buy off two of the men at the docks. They weren't part of the family, but they were loyal to us. Or *had* been, rather. Dmitry's guys shot the one who refused to help him, and the other one turned out of fear. It was bad precedent.

We needed to send a message before Dmitry got too cozy. We needed to act fast.

Alessio and I called a meeting with all of our men in town, mostly to gather intel so we could formulate a plan. Dmitry didn't operate under our rules, so I knew we couldn't hope to simply reach a friendly agreement and avoid a turf war, but I also wasn't stupid enough to go after him.

After we met with our own guys, I called Marco and asked him to do the same. As a courtesy to me, he hadn't insisted on collecting his fee for the goods that would've arrived at his shipyard if not for Dmitry's interference, so he was already invested in stopping Dmitry. And the more men on our side, the better.

Alessio, Giovanni, and Thomas stayed with me at the club long after everyone else left. Adrenaline had powered me through the last several hours, but now that it was just the four of us, my exhaustion was quickly catching up to me. We weren't going to do anything about Dmitry tonight, and after the day I'd had, my brain was too fried to even finalize a plan for what to do another day.

The club was closed, but some of the dancers remained, drinking and socializing with the other workers and some of my other guys. I still remembered when Carla worked here. It hadn't been that long ago. Hell, she must have kept dancing until she was nearly six months pregnant. She'd quit without offering a reason, which hadn't raised any eyebrows. No one expected the girls to stick with this as a long-term career, though most of them were fired before they had a chance to quit.

Carla's pregnancy alone probably wouldn't have impacted her employment. Oddly enough, there was a fair number of men who had a fetish for pregnant strippers. I figured it had something to do with the sick realization that these women were even more desperate, although I'd even heard one particularly perverse guy comment about the "two for one" benefit of watching a pregnant girl strip.

Honestly, I'd never given it much thought before. The girls all made decent money, certainly more than they'd make waitressing or any other minimum wage job, and it didn't seem to be a particularly challenging or stressful job. Now I couldn't help but wonder how many of the other dancers had slept with my papà.

God. And it wasn't just my papà who betrayed me. There was also Adrian to think about. I'd thought he'd finally backed off, that he was content to just let Giada and me live our lives. Clearly, I'd been wrong. But for him to go this far, to rope me into some fake pregnancy scheme, that was too far.

Although, from what Carla had said, Adrian thought I was actually the kid's father. How was he to know my own papà was such a perv? And if Adrian truly thought I'd fathered a child with a stripper when I was supposedly committed to Giada, maybe I could accept that he was simply looking out for her best interests. More likely, he was still trying to win Giada back. Too bad for him, that ship had sailed.

I pushed against my chest, feeling for my ring through the fabric of my shirt.

"You ok?" Alessio's voice cut into my thoughts.

I washed away the sour taste in my mouth with a swig of beer before nodding. "I should get home. Giada was expecting me hours ago."

Alessio tisked. "You shouldn't keep a princess waiting."

He was right, of course. She'd called and texted while we were meeting with the crew, but I hadn't been able to respond then. Now, it was too late. Maybe she was still up, but hopefully she'd gone to bed.

It was ironic, really. I finally had the one thing I'd wanted more than anything for as long as I could remember, and I went and left her waiting. Sure, Giada claimed she'd been mine for years, but she hadn't. Not really. Marriage may just be a piece of paper to some people, but to Giada, it was meaningful. When she pledged herself to me in the eyes of God and the law, it was official and permanent. Giada wouldn't stray, and she wouldn't abandon me.

Perhaps that awareness should've made me more confident in my ability to stay out later with Alessio, but instead, it made me more desperate to be home with her.

"Everything alright with her?" Alessio asked. "You seem... distracted lately."

I stood slowly, stretching my neck to the side while rubbing the tightened muscles. "Yeah. My princess is perfect. Everything outside the kingdom has gone to shit though," I said with a chuckle. "Don't stay out too late, and don't knock up my dancers," I cautioned.

His shoulders jostled as he laughed, clearly not realizing how serious I was.

Back in the apartment, I'd watched Giada sleep for only a moment before heading to the shower, eager to wash away the day. I didn't bother with clothes after drying off, instead slipping into the bed beside Giada. I tried to move slowly so as not to wake her, but she shifted slightly and a soft purr escaped her lips.

I ducked under the covers, using my hands to gently part her legs before finding her flesh with my mouth. She startled when I made contact, and instead of awkwardly pulling her underwear down her legs, I opted to yank on the delicate fabric, easily ripping the material down the seam. I smiled for the first time all day while lapping my tongue along her tangy sweet flesh. After a moment, she shifted, granting me better access, and I rewarded her by tracing my hand up along her torso until I found her breast. Her nipple quickly hardened against my fingers, and her breathing increased.

I tugged her nightgown down below her breast so my fingers could pinch her bare flesh. I applied more pressure with my tongue, pausing only to suck on the sensitive bud, then returned to the long broad strokes along the length of her warm pussy.

Her hips lifted slightly, meeting my mouth and writhing against me, just as her hand thrust into my hair, pinning me against her. Her breathing grew more erratic, and I gripped her hip firmly with my free hand just as her pelvis began to buck against me. She moaned loudly, cried out my name, then finally stilled, gradually loosening her hold on my hair.

I lingered there for a moment, then kissed each of her thighs before sitting upright. I pulled the covers back over her, stole a sip of water from the glass on her nightstand, and settled on my side beside her.

"I missed you," I whispered.

"What did I do to deserve that? Were you feeling guilty about ditching me for a night with the guys?"

"No, something urgent came up, and I've been working since the moment I called you."

"Oh. I'm sorry. Is everything okay now?"

The legitimate concern in her tone was unsettling. I didn't want to pick a fight, but I did think it was odd that she was so eager to accept my explanation.

"Why are you so quick to believe me?"

"Because you have no reason to lie to me. And I love you. And

I'd believe anything that came out of a mouth that can do that," she said, tracing my lips with her finger.

I knew I'd never understand what I did to deserve Giada. She was so far out of my league that it wasn't even reasonable.

"I'm sorry about your manicure."

"You can buy me another," she said.

I nodded, even though she couldn't see me in the dark. "Sleep," I commanded. "We'll talk tomorrow."

"You sure? If you need…"

"I need you," I said. "Just like this." I nudged her onto her side and wrapped my arm around her, kissing her bare shoulder before relaxing against the pillow.

~

Giada

I wasn't surprised that Luca was still asleep when I awoke in the morning. I hadn't checked the clock when he returned, but I guessed it was closer to morning than midnight. I drank coffee and then left him a note that I was headed for the gym. When I returned nearly two hours later, he was still sound asleep. I sipped another cup of coffee then hopped into the shower.

When I emerged from the bathroom, feeling clean and refreshed, Luca was in the kitchen, pouring the last of the coffee into his mug. He gazed up and smiled. I couldn't help but do the same, stricken by how handsome he looked in a simple pair of grey joggers. Without a shirt to cover it, the ring I'd given him at our private wedding ceremony was clearly visible, falling right beside his heart.

"Want me to make more?" he offered, gesturing to the coffee pot.

"No thanks." I walked closer, lifted the chain around his neck, and kissed the ring. I started to retreat to sit at the bar, but he tugged me back and kissed my lips.

"We're lucky you're Italian, so no one questions you wearing jewelry," I teased.

He smiled and gazed down to his right hand, which bore his family signet ring, displaying his initials. I gripped his hand and winced, noticing that his knuckles were red and swollen.

"I suppose the other guy looks worse?" I said, unable to mask my disappointment that, apparently, he'd been fighting.

Luca appeared surprised when he saw his hand, like he didn't immediately recall what he'd done to earn the bruises. "The other guy is a wall," he finally said. "In Carla's apartment."

Clearly, that conversation hadn't gone well then.

"She thought I was going to hit her," Luca said, furrowing his eyebrows. "Apparently, I'm the type of guy that women assume will hit them."

I had no response for that, so I stood to get a bag of ice for his hand.

"You were right about two things," Luca continued.

I handed him a bag of frozen mangos and waited for him to finish.

"Jacob is not my son, and I do have a brother."

I felt my jaw drop. Yes, I'd come up with those hypotheses, but I was still shocked to hear it was true.

"Carla slept with my papà. Jacob is my brother."

"Wow," was all I could say. I had so many thoughts, so many questions, but nothing coherent came out of my mouth. Fortunately, Luca continued.

"Carla says my papà doesn't know she's in town or that Jacob is his. She doesn't want him to ever know. She's scared he'll hurt her, or the baby, or both, I guess. She says she needed money, and figured I was an easy target."

"Do you think she's telling the truth?"

"Yeah."

Luca was an excellent judge of character, so if he believed Carla, she was probably finally being honest.

"What are you going to do?"

He shook his head. "No idea. What should I do?"

"I can't decide that for you."

"I'm not supposed to keep secrets from my papà. Technically I guess this is a personal matter and not a business matter, but…"

"You don't want to tell him?"

Luca shrugged. "Carla seemed really scared of him. I don't think my papà would hurt her, and I'm nearly positive he wouldn't touch Jacob, but I don't want to be responsible if he did."

"You're never responsible for someone else's actions."

"I'd feel responsible if I told him and then something happened."

"So, you're okay with Jacob growing up without a father?"

"I don't know. I can't imagine my papà would welcome Jacob into his life with open arms."

"You could always tell your dad about him down the road if you changed your mind," I pointed out. "But what happens if he finds out that you knew sooner?"

"He'd believe me over Carla, so as long as I deny knowing, I'm fine."

It was clear that Luca already had a sense of what he wanted to do, so I asked him again.

This time, he hesitated but answered. "Would it be terrible for me to pay her off so I never have to see them again?"

I wasn't surprised that he was leaning towards that. Luca had never been stingy with his money, probably since he'd always had plenty. His go-to method of solving problems was always to throw money at them.

He stood abruptly, returning the fruit to the freezer. "Shit, I'm sorry. I guess it's not really my decision to make alone. I mean, it's your money too now that we're married."

I felt the corners of my mouth tic upwards at the mention of marriage. "You can do what you want with your money, Luca. I trust you."

He raised an eyebrow. "You shouldn't."

"Can I play devil's advocate for a moment?" I asked, pausing just long enough for him to nod. "You've always said you wanted a brother."

"Yeah, someone to share in the burden of dealing with my papà's legacy. Not a baby."

I chose my next words carefully, not wanting to get too spiritual in my explanation and risk turning him off entirely. "I'm not so sure there wasn't more to your desire for a brother than that. And all I'm saying is that while this situation isn't ideal on the surface, maybe in a way it's actually the answer to your prayers."

Luca sighed and flashed me a smile that couldn't be described as anything but patronizing but at least he didn't openly mock my faith.

"What do you think I should do then?" he asked.

"Give her a little money, but not enough to last very long. Force her to stay in touch if she wants more. Get to know your brother on your own terms."

Luca stared at me for a long time. Then his phone rang.

"Pronto" he answered briskly. He listened for a moment, then swore in Italian. He said something else in Italian, then switched back to English. "Forty minutes," he said, disconnecting and turning back to me.

"I guess that way, at least I could make sure she's spending the money on Jacob, and not on drugs or clothes," he said.

It took me a moment to realize he was talking about Carla, and not whatever his phone call was about.

He planted a chaste kiss on my forehead then went into the bedroom. I followed, lounging on the bed while he dressed in the closet.

"Was that Alessio?" I asked, curious about his phone call.

"Giovanni. I'm sorry I can't go to church with you today. I have to go back in to talk with the guys. And I'll probably be late again."

"Is everything okay?"

"Si," he answered quickly, too quickly to offer any real comfort. He finished dressing and fastened an expensive Italian watch to his wrist. Then he turned back to me.

"There's a man in town who stole something from us last week. He's bad news, and I don't think there's anything to worry about, but I'm going to ask Alessio to hang out here more. And I'd feel better if you kept Enzo with you at all times when you aren't in this apartment."

I hated having a babysitter, but I appreciated the explanation —however terse it might've been.

"I'm worried about you," I said. I stood and approached him, tugging on the collar of his shirt to confirm my suspicion that he'd worn a Kevlar vest under his button down.

Luca yanked my wrist away firmly, then kissed the palm of my hand. "Don't be. I can take care of myself, and even if I couldn't, there's dozens of other guys lined up to help me out. I don't even anticipate leaving my office today. I'm just being cautious. But I want you to do the same. Okay?"

I nodded reluctantly.

"Also, I've been meaning to tell you," he began. Then he shook his head. "Nevermind."

"You know I'm not letting it drop until you tell me whatever you were about to say."

His lips parted into a half grin. "I was just going to say that if anything ever happened to me, you need to tell Alessio that we're married."

All my breath rushed out of me. "What's going to happen to you? Luca, don't leave today. Just stay here. The guys can come meet here if they need to."

He wrapped his arms around me, pinning my own arms to my

sides. "That is exactly why I said nevermind. This has nothing to do with any current concerns. I just, well with everything going on with Jacob, I've been thinking more about taking care of people in my life. I've been meaning to tell you this since we returned from Italy."

Luca paused and glanced down at me, I suppose to ensure I wouldn't interrupt again, before he continued.

"I know he isn't your favorite, but Alessio is the person who will take the best care of you if anything happens to me. If I ever got hurt or even if I'm just out of town and you need something, you should go to him. And if anything…permanent…were to happen, which I don't anticipate, he needs to know you're my wife."

"Why? If he'd take care of me anyway…"

Luca sighed, never a fan of my interruptions. "The marriage certificate is in the safe by my desk. Alessio has the combination."

"Why don't I have the combination?"

"Because you'd never remember it and it's not the sort of thing you can jot down. And if anyone ever wanted the combination, it's safer for you to not know what it is." He kissed me to shut me up before continuing. "My guys have a strong sense of loyalty. As my wife, you will be protected and taken care of always, even if I'm not around. Your father won't be around forever, and I trust my men over your brothers, so I just need you to promise you'll tell Alessio about the marriage certificate if I'm ever…gone."

"We're getting married publicly in six months. You really think someone will kill you before then?"

"No. I really don't. But now that we've taken care of any contingencies, there is no risk." He shook his head again and released me. "I told you, I was just thinking about the future over the past few weeks, what with Jacob and all. I realized with how much I'd tried to plan for contingencies, I had neglected to do the same with you. It's just a completely unnecessary precaution, but it means I have one less worry. Okay?"

I nodded.

Luca stepped back and gazed at me for a moment. "God you're beautiful," he said, the admiration in his tone rivaled only by that in his eyes.

"I love you," I said. I went to him, and as I lifted my arms to wrap them around his neck for a kiss, my towel came untied and fell to the floor. The kiss quickly progressed from the simple, loving farewell to a full-on makeout session. His tongue teased along the edge of my lips before sweeping into my mouth and thrashing against mine. I loved when Luca kissed me that way, like he was desperate to dive inside me. I moaned into his mouth, and his hands reached around me, groping my bare hips and thighs.

Just as I started to hope for more, Luca's phone buzzed.

He swatted my ass then pushed away, staring at me hungrily before tearing his eyes away to glance at his phone. "My ride's here. Be good." He pressed a kiss against my forehead right as a pounding at the front door startled us both.

Luca frowned, but a moment later, Alessio's familiar voice called through the door. "Andiamo!"

"Let's go," Luca translated with a sigh. "Guess he's in a hurry."

I rolled my eyes and wrapped a towel around myself while Luca went to the door. I remained hidden in the bedroom, but still heard Alessio apologize for interrupting.

"Call me if you need anything, Tesoro," Luca called back to me.

"Hey, did you tell her our new numbers?" Alessio asked.

I poked my head around the corner, certain Luca had not mentioned a new phone number. Luca mumbled something then stalked closer to me, stopping short of returning to the bedroom.

"Alessio and I both got new phones. Can you put our new numbers into your phone?"

I nodded and grabbed my phone, tapping the digits as Luca recited them.

"Baby, did you get both of those?"

"Yeah." I read the numbers back to him in one twenty digit long string.

"Okay, love you," he called, shutting the door behind him a moment later. I peered out the window, watching him and Alessio climb into a black SUV idling by the curb, then made my way to the closet to get dressed.

~

Luca

I sulked the entire drive to the club. Few things angered me more in life than bad men tearing me away from a naked woman. And nothing was better than freshly showered Giada. She was warm, slippery from the lotion she massaged into her still-damp skin, and relaxed. Freshly-showered Giada loved to be touched, and she let me taste her wherever I wanted.

First-thing-in-the-morning Giada was a close runner up, but that version of my wife occasionally turned to violence if she didn't get coffee quickly enough. Maybe middle-of-the-night Giada was better.

I could've happily mused for hours, but the car jerked to a stop.

Roberto was driving, so I thanked him then climbed out, straightening my tie. Dominico and Giacamo were stationed at the entrance and opened the door for me. I headed inside to find Giovanni, Thomas, and Alessio had already arrived. About ten more men were seated throughout the area surrounding the bar, all awaiting my instruction. Gazing around, I estimated we were still waiting on three or four more captains. Even though I'd met with most of our local guys the night before, my papà's men were joining us today.

I acknowledged everyone with a tight nod, then headed back to the office. The men were all waiting to hear from me, wanting to know what my plan was to stop Dmitry's crew, but the fact was I didn't have firm plans yet. I needed to run it by my main guys.

Alessio, Thomas, and Giovanni followed me into the office.

"I spoke with your father. He said you should take the lead on the situation. Iacopo and Lodovico are here and will act as your liaisons to him," Alessio began.

I nodded curtly. For how overbearing my papà had been historically, it sure was ironic that he decided now was the time to take a laissez-faire approach and let me sort out the problem on my own. I supposed he was handling things on his side of the pond, but with Dmitry physically present in my town, I clearly had the harder job.

"So did we lose anyone in the incident?" I asked Giovanni, since he'd been the one to call me earlier. Apparently, Dmitry's guys had set fire to one of the crates at a shipyard. It wasn't Marco's shipyard, but the stuff was mine.

"No, and most of the stuff wasn't damaged either. Maybe a couple grand in damages," Giovanni answered.

"And we might be able to come out ahead if we file the insurance claim," Thomas said.

"So, I should thank our friend Mr. Petrov?" I teased.

"We need to send a clear signal, and fast. No more beating around the bush," Alessio said.

I nodded, in complete agreement. "The problem is we don't have a clear picture of who all works for him, right?"

"Right," Alessio said.

"Okay, well, I propose we cut them down at the head. Dmitry is first priority. I don't want to scare him in hiding by going after his men first, but of course, if someone goes after us directly, they become a target. Once Dmitry's out of the picture, we take out any of his guys who don't immediately leave town."

"He's never alone, and we don't have a good handle on his schedule," Alessio said, anticipating my next question about possible obstacles we could expect.

Those weren't insurmountable. "We'll start watching him twenty-four seven. I want reports at least once a day, but make sure your men all know to contact me directly with anything urgent." I paused. "Sound good?"

They all nodded, so I headed back out to the bar. I followed my papà's method in situations like this, of letting my second in command do my talking. It wasn't that I didn't trust my guys, because I did. But there was no point for me to order a hit in a large room when someone else could do it for me. It was an unnecessary risk, a potential liability. And I may not have agreed with my papà on everything, but I did have to admire how he'd avoided indictment and prosecution in both countries where he worked.

Besides, delegating left me time for one task I was eager to complete on my own.

Once Alessio emerged from the meeting, we started outside together. Right as we reached the car, Alessio's phone buzzed. I glanced at him as he read the text, his cheeks flushing almost as quickly as his eyes widened.

"Everything ok?"

He cleared his throat then tapped on the last message and angled his phone towards me.

It read, "You're destroying my panties this week." I shook my head and chuckled.

Alessio eyed me warily. "I assume she mixed up our numbers. I swear I haven't touched her panties."

I gazed down at the phone again, this time checking who the message was from. The sender was LP. I assumed that referred to La Principessa, the same one saved in *my* phone as Giada.

"Cazzo," I swore under my breath. I dialed my wife. She answered quickly, panic filling her voice.

"Hello?"

"Baby," I said, unsure of where to even go from there.

"Luca? Why are you calling me from Alessio's phone?"

I rolled my eyes towards the sky. "This is my phone, not his. Remember when I gave you the new numbers? I know you were distracted, but—"

"But if this is your phone, then his number is…oh my God."

I could practically hear the mortification in her voice.

"But you got my text though, right? I mean, he didn't see it, did he?"

"Uh no, he did in fact see your text, since you sent it to his phone and all."

"Omigod." Giada sounded a little like she was about to hyperventilate. It was cute, and hopefully she'd actually learned her lesson about not paying attention when I gave her important information. "Please tell me he didn't get the photo at least."

"There was a photo?" I practically shouted, flashing Alessio an accusatory glare.

He winced and held up his phone again. I scrolled above the text where there was, indeed, a photo. Luckily, the picture was of her skimpy (and now torn) lace panties, and not her actually wearing them. I slammed the phone back into his hand to focus on my conversation.

"So have you learned a lesson?" I asked Giada.

"Me? What lesson would I learn? You're the one who rips underpants. Maybe you should learn a lesson in patience."

"*What lesson?*" I repeated, aghast. "Seriously? Maybe double check the number before sexting someone."

"Oh please, that was hardly a sext. If you want to see dirty texts—"

"Giada!" I interrupted. "Switch the numbers please. Okay?"

"Okay," she reluctantly agreed.

I hung up and turned to Alessio. "Those had better be deleted."

"On it," he said, making no attempt to hide his laughter.

~

Adrian

𝒯edious regulations for estate taxes consumed my thoughts as I walked home. I detested the class, hated all tax-related courses, really. I didn't understand why law students were forced to study such matters when people like accountants would willingly deal with numbers and the minutia all day.

The moment I lifted my key towards the lock of my apartment door, my thoughts flipped as if controlled by a switch. Now, my focus was dinner. Well first, I'd go for a run with Scruffy, then I'd make dinner. I'd picked up fresh shrimp the day before, and I had a handful of recipes I was eager to try.

The key hit an obstacle in the lock, jolting me out of my thoughts. I dropped a glance to the key, confirming it was the right one, then reached for the handle. The door opened with ease, and I cringed at the realization I'd forgotten to lock my apartment in the morning. I supposed that was what happened when I thought too hard about tax law. I'd be more careful going forward, although, I wasn't too concerned about robberies. Scruffy was much too friendly to be a guard dog, but he was big and had an intimidating bark.

He greeted me the moment I pushed open the door, tongue dangling and tail wagging. I kicked the door shut behind me dropped my backpack on the floor in the entry. As I reached for Scruffy's leash so I could take him out to pee, movement across the room caught my eye.

My muscles stiffened, and my body tingled with adrenaline as

I gazed to my couch. My eyes honed in on the tuft of black hair before scanning down to take in the man calmly seated on my couch.

"Luca," I murmured, heart pounding.

"Hope you don't mind I let myself in. I thought we could have a little chat." He rose to his feet, straightening his jacket and stepping closer with no hint of urgency.

"How did you get in?" I asked.

His lips quirked into a grin, and he reached into his pocket. He held up a small metal key. "I had a copy made ages ago. Thought it was about time I tried it out."

I made a mental note never to give any future girlfriends a key to my place. Especially if said girlfriend had mob connections.

"You can have it back, but you should probably change your locks anyway," Luca said, dropping the key on the table.

"What do you want?" I asked. I tried to take comfort in the fact that he seemed to be alone, although I didn't doubt Luca was capable of carrying out his own dirty work if properly motivated.

"Nothing. *I* have everything I want, Alex. But I think you could use a reminder."

My throat ran dry. There was only one person I'd given that name to, and I truly hadn't expected her to sell me out. And even if she had, how had Luca figured it out?

"Your voicemail was a dead giveaway," Luca said, as if reading my mind. "Have a seat." He motioned to my couch as if I were a guest in my own home.

"I need to let the dog out."

"He can wait. I won't be long."

"If anything happens to me, she'll know it was you."

Luca rolled his eyes. "Your confidence is a tad misplaced. You are so far off Giada's radar right now that I'm not sure she'd even notice if something happened to you."

His words hit me like a gut punch. I still didn't sit.

Luca blew out a sigh, clearly exasperated by my stubbornness.

"Look, I came here to offer a gentle reminder to back off. If you were anyone else, we wouldn't be having this conversation right now. Or at least, you wouldn't have all your fingers and toes left after this conversation," he began.

Nausea churned in my stomach at Luca's smug grin.

"I'm telling myself you keep intervening because of some misguided theory that you're helping her out," he continued. "And I can respect that. If you truly were helping Giada, I'd support your endeavors."

Luca stepped closer. "But the thing is, you're not helping anyone. Your latest misguided antics have caused my fiancée undue stress. And she doesn't need that right now. She's busy enough with the wedding plans."

"She deserves to know what kind of man you are before the wedding," I said, suddenly bold.

Luca dipped his head in a nod. "Adrian, Giada knows me better than I know myself. That woman knows me in every possible sense of the word. And the thing is, our lives are so entwined by now that it wouldn't even matter if she changed her mind. Her father and I are working together now. He loves me like a son. I'm headed to their house for a family dinner tonight, actually."

"Does he know about your son?" I asked.

Luca shrugged. "I don't have a son, and if I did, Marco wouldn't mind. But to answer your larger question, Marco knows everything. I wouldn't keep secrets from him, nor could I. And all you've accomplished by trying to out me for some ancient one-night stand is upset the woman I love."

"I know he's your son."

Luca took another step forward, his body so close to mine that I felt his breath on my face. "You know nothing, Patras."

I pushed past him, stepping further into my apartment.

"She's happy now, Adrian. You pretend you're the good guy in this scenario, so maybe you should act like it. Giada is picking out dresses and floral arrangements with her aunts. We've got appointments to sample cakes. She's got a job she loves and a man that fulfills every single one of her needs. Her life right now is complete perfection." He paused. "Anything you say or do will only fuck that up."

"She deserved to know," I repeated.

Luca rolled his eyes at my brazenness. "What she deserves is to be happy. And I take that seriously. I feel like my job as her husband-to-be is to do whatever needs to be done to ensure she is happy." He paused. "Now you are your own man, and I can't control what you do, but if you keep popping into our lives, you need to understand that won't make her happy. And if Giada isn't happy, I'm not happy."

I stared into his cold, dark eyes, but said nothing.

"Do you understand, Patras?"

My middle finger shot up.

"Very mature," he sighed. "I've got to go. Shall I tell my fiancée you said hello?" he asked.

"No," I croaked.

Luca smiled tightly, then showed himself out the door. I waited by the window until I saw him climb into a car and drive off before exhaling the breath I'd been holding.

Scruffy nudged my thigh with his nose, whimpering softly. I wiped my damp palms on my jeans and reached for the leash. "You're a terrible guard dog," I told him, patting his head despite that fact.

CHAPTER 9

Giada

I reluctantly invited Gabriella to church that afternoon, followed by dinner. I told her it was Luca's treat since he felt bad about making me leave early the previous day. With Enzo driving us, we didn't have much chance to talk in the car, but I wasn't surprised when Gabby brought it up at dinner.

"Was everything okay when you got home last night?"

I didn't understand what she meant.

"The way you rushed out to see him, I figured there was some emergency."

"Oh, yeah. It was, sort of, but then he got called back into some work stuff, so he didn't even end up getting home until late."

"And he's working today?"

I nodded.

Gabriella's expression tightened, so I braced myself for the impending lecture. Instead, all I got was another question. "Giada, are you positive Luca isn't cheating on you?"

"Yes."

"I know you love him, and your family loves him, and blah blah blah. But you have to admit. All the signs of infidelity are there. Like one hundred percent of them."

I wondered if my friend would still brazenly toss about such accusations if she knew what Luca did for a living, or who he really was.

"I appreciate you looking out for me, but I am positive he isn't cheating on me. He's going through some stuff lately, and it's really taken a toll on him. In the past though, when he had to deal with stuff like that, Luca would've shut me out and drank more. Now he's confiding in me. I don't want to betray his trust by blabbing about it, and I also want to make sure I'm there when he needs me. I really just need you to believe me when I say he's the man for me."

Gabriella eyed me warily for a beat, then shrugged. "Okay. But if you ever decide otherwise, let me know, and I'll help you trash his apartment."

I giggled at the ridiculous notion and focused on my food until she changed the subject and started telling me about her potential dates to my wedding.

"Do I get to bring a date to the rehearsal dinner?" she asked after listing a handful of prospects.

"Sure, if you want," I said. "You're the Maid of Honor. You can do whatever you want."

Gabby smirked. "Okay, so how about I bring one guy to the rehearsal dinner and then a different one to the wedding?"

I bit back a laugh. "You'd get them mixed up, and if by some miracle, you managed to keep them straight, you know my mom wouldn't."

"Nor would Matteo," she agreed.

"Only because he still likes you."

Gabby rolled her eyes. My brother had been crushing on her ever since the first time I brought her home during college. They'd actually make a great couple, aside from the fact that I didn't want to hear my best friend talking about my brother in a romantic sort of way. Gabby was an over-sharer about her boyfriends, and I'd probably barf if she offered me any of the details about Matteo that she usually included in her post-date phone calls. Besides, I didn't want her getting caught up in his business, either.

"Let's table the final decision about your dates," I suggested. "By the time the wedding actually rolls around, you may have a whole different list of contenders."

That idea seemed to satisfy my friend.

~

Luca

I'd told Carla to meet me at my office at the club that night if she wanted money. I hadn't specified for her to come alone but wasn't surprised that she didn't bring Jacob with her. Alessio was just heading out when Jordan, one of the newer recruits, brought Carla back to me.

"Hang on," I said to Alessio, trusting him more than Jordan. "Can you check her for wires and then hold on to her purse while we talk?"

"I'm not leaving my purse with him," Carla said with a scowl.

"Give it to one of the dancers then. I don't care," I said.

I could've checked her for wires myself, but the thought of seeing even a fleeting glimpse of the intimate body parts of my brother's mother disgusted me. Carla headed into my office with Alessio.

"Hey! What are you doing?" she snapped when he reached for her shirt.

"He's checking to see if you are wearing a wire or have any other way of recording. If you don't want to talk with me, he can see you out now. If you do, hold still and let him check."

Alessio mumbled something in Italian about how I would've enjoyed this job back in the day, but I ignored him. Carla appeared to consider my offer then held her arms out to allow Alessio to search her. I focused on my phone while he quickly confirmed she had no method of recording our discussion.

"I'll be right outside," he said, reaching for her purse.

She scowled but let him have it.

"Have a seat," I said, once we were alone.

"No thanks."

I sighed and leaned against my desk. "After you lied to me and attempted to swindle me, I don't have the highest regard for your character. If I'm going to give you money, I want to ensure you're spending it on Jacob."

"He's my son. Of course, I'll spend it on him. I only want what's best for him."

"You can't blame me if I need some oversight. You've given me no reason to trust you, and, after all, Jacob is my brother, so I have a vested interest in his wellbeing." I paused. "Here are my terms. I will give you cash payments every few months. I want to be able to spend time with Jacob on occasion, though."

"I'm not leaving you alone with him."

"That's fine. You can stay with him. And you can tell him I'm a family friend."

"You won't tell your father?"

"No. I won't say anything about it to him, unless I have a reason to. If he sees you or Jacob with me, I could tell him I'm the boy's father. He'll believe I wanted to keep it secret so Giada wouldn't know. If you ever choose to tell him he is the father, I will, of course, deny ever having any inkling of that being the case."

Carla rolled her eyes dramatically. "Why would I ever tell him?"

I shrugged. "I don't know, but that is why Alessio searched you. So that you have no proof of what I do or don't know."

She made a face, so I explained further.

"You blackmailed me once before, so I'm being cautious." I reached into my desk drawer and pulled out a stack of bills. I slid it across the desk to her. "It's only two grand, but that seems more than fair considering he's not my financial responsibility," I said as she cautiously reached for the money. "I'll contact you when I'm ready to give you more. I don't want to see you in the meantime."

I paused. "Oh, and if your little friend Alex ever contacts you again, you will not say anything to him. That isn't his real name, and he's just using you as collateral."

"Did you tell him about Salvatore?"

"No, and I'm not going to. He can go on thinking I'm the father for all I care."

Carla nodded. Without her purse, she was forced to awkwardly clutch the money in her hand.

"Oh, also, don't put that in the bank," I said. "Use it for small cash purchases."

Her lips parted to complain, but fortunately, she restrained herself.

"Anything else?" I asked.

Carla hesitated before shaking her head. "Thank you," she mumbled after another lengthy pause.

I dipped my head in acknowledgement of her gratitude before brushing past her to open the door.

"That was fast," Alessio said with a wink, handing me her purse. I passed it along to Carla.

"Not that type of a visit," I replied, even though I figured he knew that. "Can you walk her out?"

"Yep, but then I want to talk with you."

I dipped my head in what I hope resembled a calm nod, then panicked for a solid five minutes until Alessio returned. If he had figured out what was going on with Carla, surely my papà could have, too, and that was a problem.

Alessio dropped into a chair in my office when he returned, casually leaning back and spreading his knees. I inhaled slowly, hoping he'd put me out of my misery by speaking soon. Thankfully, he did.

"You know Anton Volkov?"

I frowned. "The Russian guy that owns the club near Giovanni's place?"

"Yeah, that's the one. Anyway, remember a while back, when I hooked up with a roommate of one of his dancers?"

I squinted, as if that would help show me the relevance of his question. I did recall Alessio mentioning a woman named Irene, but only because he'd also said she had "titties to die for"—while we were in a church, which almost caused my sweet Giada to suffer a heart attack. Of course, Irene's roommate was the one Alessio had been with, but still none of that seemed relevant now.

Alessio must have read the frustration on my face, as he continued.

"Look, point is, we've kept in touch, and I learned last night that we share a common enemy with Anton."

My pulse slowed as I realized what Alessio was saying had nothing to do with Carla and everything to do with a possible solution to the Dmitry issue. "Dmitry Petrov?"

Alessio grinned and nodded. "Yeah, apparently Anton's crew is bratva and Dmitry's isn't, or something like that. Anton hates him, and my source says Anton has been tracking Dmitry's movement." He leaned forward. "I took the initiative and got in touch with Anton, asking if we could meet up and swap intel."

"And?"

"Good news and bad. Anton's happy to pass along everything he knows, but he's not the most trusting man. We need to go in person to his club to meet with him."

"Done," I said. That wasn't a big ask at all.

Alessio wrinkled his nose. "He wants to keep it social. Asked you to bring Giada."

"How does he know about Giada?"

My friend quirked a brow but kept his smirk to a minimum. "Everyone's heard of the princess. But maybe he doesn't know what she looks like. You could bring someone else and either pass that girl off as Giada or just let Anton think you're the two-timing jerk everyone assumes you are anyway."

I didn't love either option, but I'd make it work. "How soon can he meet?"

"He's free this week," Alessio said.

I nodded, relieved we at least had one lead in the Dmitry Petrov mess.

CHAPTER 10

Luca

"You sure you don't want to bring someone else?" Alessio asked, his eyes leaving no question as to his opinion on the matter. "I could get Lila or Katie ready in a half hour."

I'd already considered this option. Several times. And each time I'd come to the same conclusion—it wouldn't work. Anton wanted to keep things social and he'd invited Giada by name. He was expecting her, and while it wasn't unheard of in our community for someone like myself to bring a different date to such outings, doing so would signal that I didn't believe him when he said tonight would be purely social.

Obviously, I didn't believe him. I was certain it was all about business, if not draped in the guise of casual drinks with our ladies. But he didn't need to know that.

Giada emerged from the bedroom while I was still looking at Alessio. His eyes widened and his jaw dropped noticeably. I turned to follow his gaze.

Giada wore a skin tight black dress. It barely covered her ass, and if there hadn't been straps on the shoulders, I would've questioned its ability to contain her breasts. She looked absolutely stunning, but everyone else would think so, too.

"You sure about that?" Alessio said, turning to me after finally peeling his eyes off Giada.

I blew out a sigh, adjusted my pants and tried to focus on the evening's mission.

"You like?" Giada asked, twirling.

I still couldn't even formulate words. She looked hot. Too hot, really.

"Luca?"

I shook my head. "Jesus. I don't know if I should fuck you or throw a blanket over you."

Alessio chuckled softly. Giada wrinkled her nose and pouted.

"Your, um, hair looks nice," I finally said.

She rolled her eyes. "You're not looking at my hair."

I tore my gaze away. Alessio shrugged and held up his hands as if to say "what can you do?"

"You said it was high end-club attire," Giada said.

Damn. I had said that.

"Well, the upside is that Anton's men will all be distracted," Alessio said.

He didn't have to say the downside, that there was absolutely no place to conceal a small handgun under Giada's dress. That much was obvious.

There was no way Anton would let me waltz into his club armed—and if our roles were reversed, I'd do the exact same. But I had been banking on him not performing a full pat-down on Giada.

"What?" she asked, her hip thrust to the side.

"We were hoping you'd be able to…carry something for me," I said.

Her eyebrow rose.

Alessio gestured to the handgun.

"That ain't happening," she said.

"No shit," he agreed.

"You said we were perfectly safe tonight," Giada reminded me, her tone firm.

"You are," I reassured her, shaking my head dismissively at Alessio. I'd come up with a solution.

"If I switched to a bigger purse…" Giada began.

"No!" Alessio and I replied in unison.

"O-kay," she said, drawing out the word. She turned towards the kitchen and opened the refrigerator door, retrieving a bottled water. She held it up as an offering. I shook my head. Giada shrugged, closed the fridge, and uncapped her water, sipping it while perusing the pantry.

"Didn't you just eat?" I asked.

She flipped her middle finger at me without turning then grabbed a granola bar. As I watched her slip the snack into the miniature sequined purse she clutched, an idea came to me.

"I need a small baggie and duct tape," I said to Alessio. I held my fingers about three inches apart to show him the size I meant.

He glanced at Giada then back to me. "Duct tape?"

I winced, knowing what he was thinking. "I can't risk it not sticking."

"I have medical tape. It'll hold." Alessio was out the door before I could reply.

"Why do I suspect I'm not going to like what you have in mind?" Giada asked me, still sipping her water.

I walked around her, dropping a kiss on the side of her neck as I reached into the drawer beside her. I grabbed three nine-millimeter bullets right as Alessio returned.

"That was fast," Giada said, still clearly uncertain.

I dropped the bullets into the baggie, pressed it closed, then motioned for her to sit.

"I'll be over here if you need me," Alessio said with a chuckle, handing me the tape.

"What are you doing, Luca?" Giada asked.

I crouched in front of her and slid her dress up her thighs. I only needed to shift it about an inch since it was so short. My hand may have drifted a tad further though, discovering that there was another item she wasn't wearing. I glanced down for visual confirmation.

"Seriously?" I said, completely distracted by devious sexual thoughts. Again.

"I didn't want panty lines."

I squeezed my eyes shut for a moment, regaining focus, then pressed the baggie against the upper portion of her left thigh. I positioned it slightly to the front so that it wouldn't rub against her other leg but also wouldn't be visible when she sat. I secured the bag with tape, then smoothed her dress back down.

"Good?" I asked

She frowned, shifting side to side. "That is not the word I would use, but I guess it's okay. I don't understand how you plan to get this off without ripping off my skin. Or how you plan to use these bullets."

I confirmed each of my guns was loaded then slid them back into their holsters right as Alessio spoke.

"We gotta go."

"Why I even have ammo strapped to my thigh when you're carrying two loaded guns," Giada continued, her tone growing more agitated.

"Three," I said with a smile, guiding her out of the apartment and towards the SUV. "And it is just a precaution. No one needs any ammo or guns tonight. I'm only armed because I'm playing a part. It's all just for show. They need to see that I am the man they think I am."

She frowned. Alessio slid behind the driver's wheel while Giada and I climbed into the back. Alessio pulled away from the curb the moment we shut the door.

"Do they need to see my ammo?" she asked.

"No!" Alessio and I replied in unison.

"Do not show anyone that no matter what and don't tell anyone it's there," I said.

"Then what role am I supposed to play?"

I sighed. We'd gone over this before, when I'd agreed to this outing. Now, I was starting to regret it.

"You should just be yourself, only dumber. They will expect you to be obedient and oblivious to my work."

"Obedient," she repeated with a snicker. "Not my strong suit."

I pressed a kiss into her forehead. "You'll manage for one night."

∼

Giada

We rolled to a stop in front of an unmarked building. I noticed two women smoking cigarettes a little further down the block and a couple making out against the painted brick wall a few yards away. Nothing else even indicated there might be a club inside.

Luca climbed out of the SUV and offered his hand to me. I accepted it and awkwardly slid across the seat, careful to keep my dress down. Now that we'd arrived, I was nervous. I tried to pretend we were on a normal date, but having a baggie of bullets strapped to my body made that fantasy difficult to buy.

"In bocca al lupo," Alessio said.

"Crepi," Luca replied.

I raised an eyebrow.

Luca frowned. "Good luck," he translated. He pressed his hand firmly into the small of my back and guided me up to the building. "It's an expression, it means into the mouth of the wolf."

I paused, suddenly nervous.

"Hey," Luca said softly, gripping my hips in his hands. "Relax.

We're fine, and you look beautiful." He tilted his head down and kissed me squarely on the mouth. I'd expected a brief peck, but he lingered, tracing his tongue along my lips.

When he finally broke away, he paused. "You had lipstick on, didn't you?"

I giggled and wiped the pad of my thumb along his lips, erasing all traces of me. Then Luca nodded to Alessio.

The feeling of Luca's hand against my lower back comforted me as Alessio drove away.

"Great, there goes our ride home," I joked. "Are you sure we're even in the right place?"

Luca guided me towards the solid gray, unlabeled door. I turned to him, wondering why he hadn't answered me. I noticed his eyes focused on a small camera above the door.

"Yep," he replied, right as the door swung open.

A heavily muscled man stood at the door. "Name?"

"Luca Marino."

The man pressed his finger to his ear as though waiting for a response through his earbud. After a moment, he nodded. "Right this way. Mr. Volkov will be with you in a moment."

He motioned for us to step into the long corridor. Now, I could hear the pulsating beat of a lively dance floor, but I still didn't see anything that looked too promising. The walls were bare and the ground was poured concrete. The hallway was dimly lit.

I glanced at Luca again. He looked cool as a cucumber. Bored, even. Just before we reached the end of the hallway, the door swung open and a burly man stepped through. He smiled warmly, but the smile didn't quite reach his eyes.

"Mr. Marino, it's a pleasure to finally meet you in person." The man said, reaching forward to shake Luca's hand.

"Please, call me Luca."

The man nodded and patted his chest. "Anton." Then he turned to me.

"Anton, this is Giada Conti," Luca said.

"Giada," the man purred, reaching for my hand. I offered it but instead of shaking it like he had Luca's, he raised it to his lips and kissed it. "Enchanté." Then he paused and turned back to Luca. "Sorry, that's French, isn't it? How do you say that in Italian?"

Luca's smile looked natural and relaxed. "Piacere."

"Piacere," Anton said to me.

I smiled, unsure of the correct response.

Anton stepped beside Luca and placed a hand on his bicep, leaning in to whisper. "She is stunning," he said, plenty loud for me to hear.

"Yes she is," Luca agreed as we followed him into the club. "Won't Laura be joining us?"

"Of course, of course. She's in here somewhere. I'll track her down in a moment. We actually need to stop off with security for a moment. I'm sure you understand."

We'd passed through the doorway into what appeared to be a normal club, albeit one with a totally hidden entrance. The main club was dimly lit, but bustling with activity.

Anton guided us into a small room off to the side. A large picture window overlooked the rest of the club. I turned and came face to face with a beast of a man with two guns holstered to his chest. Instinctively I took a large step backwards, slamming into Luca's chest. He slipped his hand around my waist and kissed the back of my head.

"Relax," he whispered before releasing me and stepping to my side.

"We don't allow concealed carry within the club," Anton explained.

I peered over at Luca to see his eyebrow raise.

"Clearly," he said, pointedly staring at the heavily armed men in front of us. Luca's gaze shifted then and I looked past the security booth, where I realized men within the club were armed as well.

Anton chuckled. "Well, I make exceptions. But not for new friends. You can leave anything with my friends here. I assure you Alex and Sergey will take excellent care."

Luca smiled at the two men, then crouched down to his ankle. He pulled out a handgun and placed it on the table beside us. Then he reached into the front of his suit jacket and retrieved another. I assumed he'd stop there, but he went on and tugged a third gun from his waist band.

He didn't set down the third one. He held it by the barrel and turned to Anton.

"This one's registered, so I don't make a habit of letting it out of my sight ever," he said. "In my world, there are too many looking to frame someone for something."

Anton nodded but didn't speak.

Luca then twisted something and removed the bullets, placing them on the table. "Compromise?" he said.

Anton confirmed the weapon was in fact unloaded, then nodded. "For a friend, of course." Then he motioned to the security.

The guards stood and the taller one performed a thorough pat-down of Luca. He paused on his pocket, and pulled out Luca's wallet. A moment later, he located Luca's cell phone. When he'd apparently checked everywhere on Luca, he handed him back his wallet and phone.

Luca wedged the unloaded gun back into his lower back and I realized all eyes were on me.

"I suppose we don't need to check Ms. Conti," Anton said. "Although that would be fun."

"Open your purse," the shorter guard said, apparently opting to ignore the creepy comment.

I did as I was told, grateful I didn't have tampons or anything embarrassing stashed in the tiny clutch.

After a moment, Anton motioned for us to follow him. He gave us a brief tour, then led us up a winding staircase to the VIP area. Plush armchairs and cordoned-off booths filled the dimly-lit space overlooking the main dance floor.

We were seated, ordered drinks, and then a woman named Laura joined us. She looked about my age, which was surprising since I'd put Anton closer to forty. She was pretty, but didn't talk much, and when she laughed, it was over the top. Our drinks arrived and I eagerly reached for mine, desperate for something to calm my nerves. But then I froze. What if the cocktails were drugged?

I gazed at Luca, who simply patted my hand and then reached for his own glass.

"Saluti," he said with a grin.

Anton smiled back, said something I assumed was Russian, then translated "To our meeting, to a new friendship."

Luca clinked his glass against Anton's, then Laura's, then mine, and finally, he sipped his drink. He skated his fingers across the back of my hand, his touch so light it tickled. I understood he meant to calm me, though, so I sipped. My drink was delicious, and tasted exactly as I'd expect.

I tried to follow along with the conversation, but it was boring, so I found myself gazing out over the club. After a moment, I realized everyone was looking at me.

"What led you into that line of work, Giada? Design?"

I panicked momentarily, not sure if I'd missed something else he'd said. Finally, I answered with a brief version of the truth. "I just really like pretty things."

Anton chuckled, raising his glass to his broad lips. "I think the same could be said for your boyfriend here."

"Fiancé," I corrected, blushing at my own rashness.

"Of course. My apologies," Anton said with a slight nod to Luca.

"Join me in the restroom?" Laura said suddenly, knocking into the table as she stood abruptly.

Thanks to the water I'd chugged before we left the apartment, and my nervous bladder in general, I did sort of need to use the bathroom, but I'd fully planned to hold it until we got home. I wasn't about to leave Luca.

He glanced over at me, nodding encouragingly.

"I don't need to…" I began, but Luca cut me off with a clear of his throat.

"It's fine, you ladies go touch up your makeup or whatever. Leave us men to chat for a bit," Luca said.

Condescension dripped from his tone, but I reminded myself he was merely putting on a show. Terrified, I stood slowly and followed Laura across the room and down a winding staircase.

For a moment, I wondered if she was leading me somewhere other than a bathroom, but finally we walked through a small doorway at the end of the hall. The large, clean, space housed one toilet in the open and an oversized sink. Just seeing the toilet made my urge to pee that much stronger, but I wasn't about to use the toilet in front of Laura. Even if it were a true emergency, I still couldn't go, because of the stupid secret goods strapped to my thigh.

Laura dropped her purse on the counter and pulled out a baggie of her own. I was torn between my curiosity about what she was doing and my discomfort at watching her. She tapped some powder out and quickly snorted it, tapping her nostril with her finger while sniffing repeatedly once the powder was gone. She blinked a few times, then rinsed her hands in the sink before turning to me.

"You want some?"

"Oh no, I don't do…" I stopped myself, not even certain what drug she was offering.

Laura laughed and dried her hands. "Your boyfriend doesn't let you sample his goods?" she teased.

I started to insist he wasn't a drug dealer like her boyfriend, except… "Fiancé," I said instead.

"Right," she said, giggling. "You mind?" she gestured to the toilet.

I shook my head and turned around.

"So what's the deal with you guys anyway? Anton said your dad is a pretty big deal and that Luca's is too."

"Yeah," I said, cringing over the sound of her using the toilet.

"So was it like an arranged courtship or something? Do they still do that sort of thing in Italy?" She flushed and rejoined me by the sink, washing her hands again.

I hated when people looked at Luca and assumed he was with me because he had to be. I knew it was stupid and shallow, that the opinions of others meant nothing in the grand scheme of things, but it drove me bonkers.

I wanted the universe to know that Luca's world began and ended with me, the he'd do anything for me, that he would literally die for me.

"We met through our fathers," I said through gritted teeth. "We've known each other for years though."

"Seems like he keeps you on a pretty tight leash," she said, shaking her hands before drying them.

I opened my mouth then closed it several times before deciding not to respond at all. "So, um, how long have you and Anton been involved?"

She smirked at my use of words. "We've been… together… off and on for maybe a year now."

"Do you think you'll get married?" I asked her, touching up my lipstick.

"That's not really on my radar now. Anton is a complicated man and I don't think marriage really fits with his business model. Or any sort of perceived monogamy, really." She paused and chuckled. "He treats the women he likes very well though. You sure you don't want any?" She tapped the baggie again.

"I'm sure."

She crammed the bag into her purse and swung open the door, then paused. "I don't know if they're done talking yet. Do you want to go dance or something?"

"Um, Luca doesn't really like when I dance without him," I replied, cringing at how lame it sounded.

Laura rolled her eyes and then laughed like I was some pathetic puppy. "You know, a little coke really would loosen you up."

She was probably right, but I had no intention of ever finding out, and not just because Luca would hate it. "I guess we can dance for a bit. Can I get another drink first?"

Her smile widened as she led the way to the bar. Laura whispered something to the bartender and a moment later he returned with two drinks. She let me choose first, so I grabbed one and sniffed it tentatively.

"It's Russian," she said. "Strong but sweet. I think you'll like it."

I downed a small sip, concurring with her assessment. We made our way out to the dance floor, and luckily no one came near us. I supposed probably people knew who she was and that they shouldn't touch her. Mostly, I nursed my drink, but so as not to look completely out of place, I also swayed to the music.

After an eternity, my skin tingled with that odd feeling of being watched. I gazed around, then spotted Luca. He stood on the opposite side of the floor, holding a drink in his hand and staring at me. His eyes were dark and serious, but he wasn't angry. I could tell by the way his lips ticked slightly upwards in the corner. I motioned for Luca to come to me, and he did, stepping behind me and clasping his hands around my waist.

"You look really hot," he whispered, his breath tickling the side of my neck. He kissed just behind my ear as I curled into him, welcoming the comfort after being so nervous.

"Are you done talking shop?" I asked.

"Yeah, we can go now."

"I think you owe me a dance."

He lingered behind me for a moment before swiveling me to face him. "Alessio will be here in a moment. But since you're all dressed up, I could take you to one of our clubs."

"Our?"

Luca grinned. "What's mine is yours now, right?"

I laughed, swaying against him to the beat of the music for another minute before he tugged me off the dance floor. I waved politely at Laura and then followed him out. We stopped back at the security checkpoint and picked up his other weapons, then climbed into the back of the SUV with Alessio.

I exhaled with relief.

~

Luca

"Success?" Alessio asked as we drove off.

"Yeah, I think so. Thanks for setting this up," I said. I'd give Alessio the details later, but for now, we were good to celebrate. Anton had shared a few pertinent tidbits about Dmitry with me, but the most valuable piece of information he'd offered had been the address of Dmitry's mistress.

"Anytime," Alessio replied.

"Let's go to Rize," I said, tugging Giada's legs up across my lap. "Giada wants to dance."

I slipped my hand up her skirt, eliciting a squeal from her. I noticed Alessio staring in the rearview mirror, but figured he'd look away after a moment. Once I located the baggie against her thigh, I slowly picked at the tape, loosening it gradually.

Alessio cleared his throat. "Dude," he said.

I laughed, chucking the newly freed bag of ammo into the front seat so my friend would know what I was doing with my hand up Giada's skirt. Still, Alessio kept looking in the rear view. After a moment, he switched to Italian.

He told me that the car behind us had been following us since we left Anton's. I turned around to see if I recognized the driver, but I didn't. The passenger, though, looked a lot like one of Anton's security guys.

"Great," I mumbled, wondering what their plan was.

"Still to the club?"

"Yes. Who's in charge tonight?"

"Thomas."

I called Thomas, explained the situation and asked him to have a few guys outside for protection when we arrived. I didn't think Anton's crew meant us any harm, but I wasn't taking any chances.

"What's wrong?" Giada asked, tensing beside me.

"Nothing, amore. It's fine."

As Alessio pulled to a stop in front of the club, I watched the mystery car pulled in a few spots behind us. Thomas stepped towards the SUV and I turned to Giada.

"Go inside with Thomas. I'll be right behind you in a moment."

She looked uncertain, but for once in her life, Giada did as I asked the first time.

Alessio and I took our time getting out, waiting until the two other guys approached to move to the entrance. I turned to the one I recognized.

"Hey, you're uh Anton's guy, right? Not sure if we formally met. I'm Luca. This is Alessio."

"Sergey and Alex."

"Good to meet you. Did you need something, or just here to check out the place?"

Sergey mumbled something about wanting to verify where we were headed, so I motioned for him to come on in. "Enjoy yourselves. Drinks are on me tonight," I said.

"Weapons can go in your car," Alessio added, staring pointedly.

They seemed to comply, so I went on through the club and back to my office where Giada was waiting. She was seated on my desk, her legs crossed above the knees. The position forced her dress up ridiculously high.

I bit back a smile, certain she hadn't intended to look quite so delicious.

"Oh no. Don't you get that look in your eye. You promised me a dance, not a quick fuck in your office."

"I could take my time," I bluffed, stepping closer.

She slid off the desk. "Is everything okay?"

I nodded. "Yeah, some of Anton's men followed us. Not sure why, but seems harmless."

"They're here?"

"Yes." I draped my suit jacket over the back of my chair. "One dance," I said, certain she'd never relax if I didn't give in.

Few things interested me less than dancing in my own club, but for Giada, I'd do it. Luckily, the main floor was packed, so no one would really be able to watch us. I let Giada lead me through the crowd to the center of the action, then tugged her close to me. She roped her hands around my neck and began to sway to the music. I gripped her hips, dropping my forehead down to rest on the top of her head.

As Giada danced, her dress slithered even higher up her thighs, indecently so, although I realized no one would ever complain. My hands were desperate to drift below the hem, to stroke her warmth, to confirm she was as wet as I suspected.

Giada tilted her head back to me, her eyes narrowed but her lips quirked up in a half smile, and I couldn't help but smile back. Then she broke free of my grasp, swiveling until her ass pressed against my fly. She stretched her arms above her head, still swaying as she ground against me. I groaned, not that she could hear it over the thumping bass.

After one more song, my devious wife finally had her fill of dancing. She leaned her head back against me, peering up at my face. I hunched over to plant an upside down kiss on her, then paused with my lips by her ear.

"I bet you're so wet right now," I breathed against her ear.

She squirmed against me and grinned mischievously. "You could find out," was all she said.

That was enough for me to haul her off the dance floor and back to my office. I dodged eye contact with all of my men, certain they had no doubts what I was about to do with the gorgeous half-naked woman scurrying behind me. I locked my office door then turned, just in time to see Giada shove a stack of notebooks off my desk. They hit the floor with a thunk, but before I could even complain about her trashing my desk, she had draped herself across it, ass up.

A lump rose in my throat and I nearly forgot how to breathe. I stepped closer, skittering my fingers up the length of her thigh then right along her tender slit, swirling them in her ample juices. I groaned, glad I'd been right, then used my other hand to unzip my pants. I stroked her for a moment longer, then coated my length in her moisture.

I planted a kiss on her bare shoulder before whispering in her ear. 'Hold on, baby."

Giada gripped the edge of the desk above her head, and I thrust fully into her. Her moans spurred me onward, so I pumped against her harder and faster until I felt her internal walls tighten around me. One of her hands flew to her mouth, and I nearly came at the sight of her biting her own fist to muffle her satisfied moans.

I pulled out of her, gently lifting her enough to turn her over. I was close myself, but I wanted to see her beautiful face when I came. Giada grinned up at me, drunk with pleasure, her hands reaching for me.

I slid back into her and it felt like coming home. Her eyes fluttered shut, but I kept my gaze locked on her.

Giada was always beautiful, but this was the way I liked her best—smiling softly, hair messed, makeup faded and lipstick long gone. Her dress had slipped lower on her breasts, revealing their full swell and all of her softness.

I ran a hand along her midline and her eyes opened. Giada grasped for me, tugging my shirt until my face neared hers. I cradled her head in my palms, lifting her towards me and kissing her hard. I was tempted to pull out, to come all over her, marking her as mine and permanently removing the tiny dress from her rotation. But I resisted the urge, instead filling her with my seed then dropping my head to her neck.

"I love you," she whispered.

All I could do was sigh.

Giada

I was exhausted the evening after we went to Anton's club, but Luca stayed out late again the next night. By the time he came home, I'd already enjoyed three hours of sleep. Luca's thumping woke me, but he made it up to me twice...first with his tongue, then with the rest of his body. And then he snuck into the kitchen and returned with a tub of chocolate chip gelato. I was half asleep as he spooned the first bite into my mouth, but the creamy sweetness perked me up.

"Where'd you find this?" I asked.

"Some specialty grocery near L'Occhio," he replied. "The carton claims it's better than the fresh Italian kind. It's not."

Maybe I was just extra sleepy, but the gelato tasted pretty good to me. "I'm not sure you've given it a fair chance," I said. I straddled his lap, then scooped the bite off the spoon, leaning in to kiss him with the gelato still on my tongue.

"Mmm," he groaned. "You're right. That is better." The spoon fell to the floor as he flipped me onto my back, kissing me till I forgot all about the dessert. We made love again, and then, exhausted, I fell asleep.

After the restless night, my body craved sleep more than anything else. But the next morning, as the hand on my hip slid down to my thigh then up again, my body slowly tugged my brain out of the fog of sleep.

I shifted, pressing my face against the pillow, but noticing a twinge of pain lower. "I'm still sore from last night," I told him. "So you can do whatever you want with your tongue, but I'm gonna need a few more hours before I can handle any more attention from your big—"

"Giada!" A man's voice cut me off. The voice was definitely not Luca's.

Not-Luca cleared his throat awkwardly, and I groaned into the pillow, realizing my mistake. Suffocation was decidedly less mortifying than ever facing Alessio again.

"Right, so, Luca had to leave early, and he wanted me to wake you up. The plans changed, and you're meeting the florist an hour earlier now. I'm supposed to drive you, and he'll meet us there." Alessio paused, clearing his throat again. "I'll, um, give you a few minutes."

I felt the bed shift as he stood, but I listened for the door to shut before I turned over to face the world. I grabbed my phone, ready to send a snippy text to my darling husband for ditching me, but Luca had already texted. And his messages weren't snippy at all. His were…*oh*.

My pulse rocketed, and my face flushed. Suddenly, I didn't care what was sore anymore. Luca could stick whatever he wanted wherever and I would love it.

Except Luca wasn't here.

I groaned again, this time from a different type of frustration. I set about my morning routine, happy to see that Alessio had at least left a cup of coffee on my nightstand before rudely waking me.

By the time I'd gotten dressed and fixed my hair and makeup, I'd all but forgotten about the conversation with Alessio. I made my way to the kitchen to refill my coffee. I cringed when I saw Alessio hadn't left and was seated at the island, but since he seemed focused on his phone, I just ignored him.

He'd been hanging around the apartment a lot since we returned from Italy, and for the most part, I didn't mind. There was something relaxing about the knowledge that I'd never have to worry about my safety, or really anything else, even when Luca wasn't home. But on occasion, it would've been nice to be truly home alone. Privacy was totally underrated.

I dumped some Greek yogurt into a bowl and then added berries and homemade granola—literally the only thing I'd learned to cook since college —and sipped my coffee. It felt wrong to stand a few feet away from Alessio and not even acknowledge his presence, so I opted for dumb small talk.

"Any idea what prompted the new time for the meeting?" I asked.

"Uh, I think Luca just realized he had more to do today and needed to get an earlier start."

Alessio's eyes were locked on his phone screen, but his fingers weren't moving, so either he was a slow reader, or he was just staring at nothing simply to avoid me.

"Have you checked the weather? Will I be okay in this today?" I continued, smoothing my hands over my short-sleeved blouse and onto the tops of my jeans.

"High of sixty something," he said, still not peering away from his phone.

I sighed, willing the strength to face the awkwardness head on. "You can't even look at me," I mumbled. Then I turned and topped off my coffee with a little more from the pot. When I swiveled back to the counter, Alessio was staring straight at me, a wolfish grin on his face.

Suddenly, I regretted taking the confrontational route. "I had hoped you hadn't heard me."

"No such luck, Princess."

"I thought you were Luca."

"Yeah, I got that." He pressed his lips together to stop his grin, but it spread nonetheless.

"You could've just knocked to wake me up."

"I tried. You were basically comatose. And Luca said to make sure you were in a good mood."

"So, you thought an upper thigh massage was the way to go?" I flung my hands in the air. This misunderstanding was not entirely on me.

He shrugged. "I couldn't tell what I was touching. Your room is dark. And I'm not exactly in the habit of waking up other people that aren't in my bed."

"You wake Luca all the time."

"I could whisper his name from a different room, and he'd wake. It's different."

He wasn't wrong.

"Okay, so we're in agreement that you'll just forget what I said, and I'll not tell Luca you basically grabbed my ass?"

Alessio leaned back in his chair, crossing his arms as he cocked his head to the side. "I don't know. I'd rather lord it over your head for a while," he paused. "And I have questions. When you said 'big,' I mean, is it really that big? That would explain the ego, and why the ladies all seem to like him, but…"

I chucked a bagel at his head and stormed back to the bedroom to get my jewelry.

"We're leaving in 15 minutes, Princess," he called after me. "If you need to sit on an ice pack or something, just bring a towel. I don't want to mess up my car's interior."

I slammed the bedroom door, but had to laugh. I could see why he and Luca got along so well.

∾

Adrian

With final exams fast approaching, I'd focused fully on school and lining up a summer internship. The prosecutor's office had offered me a paid gig, but I wasn't sure I could handle another round with them, not without it bringing back memories of my summer with Giada. So now I was toying with a summer internship at a law firm. The money would be better, and surely it would keep my mind off of Giada.

It was time for me to move on. Past time, really.

I'd been obsessed with showing Giada what kind of a man Luca really was, and it turned out it didn't matter. When I'd first discovered his secret love child, I'd been certain that the awareness he'd cheated would be the final nail in the coffin of his relationship with Giada. But the last time I spoke with Carla, she assured me Giada had seen the child, and according to Angelo, Giada and Luca were still happily engaged.

I'd assumed Giada would realize it was Luca's kid, but maybe she hadn't. I'd assumed she'd never forgive him for cheating, but maybe she had. And I'd assumed that Giada would never get over the fact that this kid's mere existence was proof to the entire world that Luca didn't love her as much as he claimed. But I guessed I was wrong.

Whatever had happened, I was done plotting. Luca knew what I'd done, and Carla had blocked my number anyway. I had no fresh ideas, and I was starting to realize that good guys really did finish last.

Hence, the focus on school.

Spring had finally arrived in full force, so I had taken my notes to an outdoor café. I wasn't in my usual neighborhood, so I didn't anticipate running into anyone who might distract me from my work. But between the gentle breeze and the birds chirping, I had zero interest in reviewing my notes. It was the perfect day for a long run with Scruffy or a barbecue with friends. Yet here I was, hunched over a laptop trying to memorize commercial law theories.

Just when I was thinking studying couldn't possibly get more miserable, I heard a familiar laugh. Hoping it was an audible illusion, I peered up, but of course, there she was, just across the narrow alleyway.

She tossed her head back, laughing again as her wavy hair cascaded down her back. Her fingers clasped loosely around Luca's as they walked. As they passed a tree, I got a better view of him, and could see he was grinning widely, too.

For some reason, seeing Luca deliriously happy nauseated me more than the sight of him making Giada happy. Actually, since I'd rarely seen him smile, any measure of happiness from Luca was unnerving. As I watched them, Luca suddenly stepped in front of her, wrapped both arms around her so tightly that her toes lifted off the ground, and kissed her.

The moment was so intimate that I had to look away. I could see how, to a complete outsider, they probably looked adorable, but honestly...stopping in the middle of a busy sidewalk? That was just rude. Selfish, even.

Typical for them.

I glanced back just in time to see Luca swat Giada's butt as he set her down. I winced, but I couldn't stop myself from watching. They probably would've seen me too if they'd bothered to look, but they were both oblivious to anyone else. They took a few more steps, and then it looked like Luca threw something at Giada. Popcorn maybe? Or some candy? I could tell she was trying to catch it in her mouth, but she missed widely.

Luca tossed a handful of the same item into his own mouth and Giada swiveled suddenly, grabbed him by his necklace, and yanked him to her. I half expected him to look angry at this, but of course, he only grinned more, like he didn't have a fucking care in the world. Giada kissed him, then pulled back abruptly and stole the small bag in his hand.

She scampered a few feet ahead of him, but he quickly caught her, lifting her into the air and setting her down again while dropping quick kisses all over her arms. I watched the bag drop from Giada's hands as she turned to Luca, wrapping her arms around him, and kissing him as though he'd just given her a million bucks.

I groaned. I must've racked up some really horrific karma to have to endure this nauseating scene.

"Can I get you a refill?" the overly perky waitress asked, her coffee pot blocking my vision.

"Sure," I grumbled, annoyed that she'd interrupted my spying. I thanked her once she'd poured, but as soon as she walked away, I realized they were gone.

Fuck. I really needed to get laid.

~

Luca

*A*fter the perfect spring afternoon, Giada and I returned to the apartment. As we kicked off our shoes and tumbled onto the couch together, I was acutely aware of how relaxed I felt. Nothing, aside from the slight body of my perfect wife, was weighing me down. I couldn't remember the last time I'd felt this light, this carefree.

Maybe it was the idyllic weather. Maybe it was the fact that I'd actually done it—I'd taken an entire day off work, not even thinking about any of my pending business matters.

Really though, there was nothing to think about. I'd worked out a solution for the Jacob problem that actually seemed to make all of us happy. And I'd decided to just ignore Adrian's involvement in the whole debacle. Business was thriving, wedding plans were coming along, and Giada hadn't shown any sign of becoming the bridezilla type guys had warned me about.

Life was good.

The Dmitry issue was still there, but in the back of my mind. I hadn't forgotten about him. I wasn't in denial that we'd have to do something, and soon, but it wasn't in the forefront of my brain. My guys were following him, and once they found an opportunity to take him out, we'd act.

In the meantime, I wasn't going to stress it. I'd faced much bigger problems and worked them out, so this would be the same. In a matter of months, it would all be a distant memory, I knew.

"Why are you still dressed?" Giada asked, interrupting my thoughts as she tugged on my jeans.

"Ladies first," I replied.

She rose to her knees above me and lifted her shirt up over her head. My mouth practically watered as she reached around to unfasten her bra. Giada had the most perfect breasts I'd ever seen, and that moment when they first tumbled free always drove me crazy.

Giada hesitated, her sly grin suggesting she knew I was about to pounce, and she was right. The instant her bra fell to the floor, I sat up, capturing her nipple between my lips. She tilted her head back, giggling, but after a moment, her playful laughter gave way to soft moans, like it always did.

After a minute, I released her breasts and shifted so I was sitting on the edge of the couch and nudged her legs around my waist. Her arms drifted to my neck as I lurched forward, standing with her in my arms. Her gaze caught mine, and she smiled, her peacefulness mirroring my own. I walked slowly, wanting to remember this moment of pure happiness before our baser desires overwhelmed us.

When I reached the bedroom, I gently placed her on her back, kissing her lips before dragging her remaining articles of clothing to the ground. I pressed my mouth into her abdomen and felt her fingers rifle my hair before she yanked my necklace to get my attention. As I lifted my eyes to stare at her, she pulled my shirt up.

Her fingers trailed down to the faded scar on my chest, the last remnant of the bullets I'd taken for her. Her expression changed and it was obvious she was remembering, and worrying. I wondered how often she thought about me dying. The possibility was fresh on her mind, maybe it always would be. With my line of work, she said, there was always a risk of dying.

Even with all my usual worries, death wasn't one of them. Not my own, anyway. I wasn't oblivious to the risks, but I didn't see the point in worrying. If I was killed, it would be over. There'd be nothing left to worry about. I wasn't going to waste precious brain space stressing about the when or how of it all.

I did, however, worry about others dying. Usually, Giada was my concern, and logically so. Not only did my actions place her at great risk, but I was certain without a doubt that if anything ever happened to her, I couldn't go on. I also entertained fleeting concerns about Alessio and my other guys dying. They pledged to protect me, but I knew the guilt I'd feel if anything ever happened to them would be crushing.

Occasionally, I also worried about my papà's death. It was inevitable, and it carried with it the finality of being the leader. The last Marino standing. The official boss of the family. As much as strife burdened my relationship with my papà, I wanted to delay that future as long as possible.

"I lost you again," Giada murmured.

Her voice drew my eyes back to hers, and I couldn't help but perk up at the sparkling brown eyes and thick black lashes before me. I was about to apologize for my distraction when she sat up, finished where she'd left off with my pants, then wrapped her soft lips around my cock.

Instantly, all of my worries left as quickly as they'd set in. All I could focus on now was the warmth of her mouth, the gentle pressure from her tongue, and the tickle of her hair cascading across my thighs as she moved her head back and forth.

I groaned. As perfect as the sensations inside her mouth were, I'd enjoy being buried deep inside her body even more.

I nudged her backwards, returning my lips to her breasts as she relaxed against the bed, her arm draped above her head. After I'd lavished enough attention on each of them, measuring my success by the speed of her breathing and the drunken look in her eyes, I positioned myself over her. She parted her thighs and positioned me at her entrance, both of us moaning as our bodies became one, reuniting as if we'd been separated for more than the afternoon.

Married life was good, I decided.

When we were both satiated, Giada sprawled across my chest, her eyes closed. I let her relax for a moment, then reminded her of our evening plans.

"Hey, I promised you dinner," I said.

"And a movie," she added, yawning.

I couldn't remember the last time we'd had just a normal date. Maybe never. Or at least not since high school. I owed her for sure.

"I just need a little nap before dinner," she said.

I laughed. It was already dinnertime. If Giada fell asleep, there was no chance of her waking and getting dressed for a restaurant. We'd do takeout and maybe a movie on the couch. I was fine with that, but that was nothing new. We did that all the time.

I was debating my options when my phone buzzed. It was the alert tone I'd reserved only for Alessio, and since I'd instructed him not to contact me unless it was urgent, I didn't hesitate to crawl out from under Giada.

She groaned, but quickly replaced me with a pillow.

"Take your nap," I said. "I'll shower."

I grabbed my phone and went to the bathroom. His text had been simple, reading "what's up?" But I knew what that meant.

The more casual the text, the more serious the situation because the more expertly we needed to cover our asses

I dialed his number. "Hey," I said as he answered.

"Giovanni called. Dmitry just went into his lady friend's apartment. He drove himself."

I clenched my jaw and reminded myself to breathe. This was big. Since my guys had begun shadowing Dmitry, they'd never seen him alone. But with Anton's intel about the mistress, we'd lucked out. Each time, Anton went to her apartment, he'd disappear inside for about an hour, then emerge looking calmer. It didn't take a trained spy to guess what he was doing in there.

The woman's apartment building faced an alley. A poorly lit, generally empty alley. It was the sort of place normal folks avoided at night, the sort of place where bad things happened all the time and no one seemed to care. It was the perfect place to kill someone without any witnesses.

In the past, Dmitry had always been driven to and from these meetings. His driver always waited in the car, but we all knew this person was likely well trained and well armed.

If he was alone, though... This was it. This was the golden opportunity we'd been waiting for, and it was much sooner than I'd anticipated.

"I can meet up with Giovanni and take care of it," Alessio continued. "I'll call you when it's done."

"No," I said. As much as I wanted to delegate this, I couldn't. It was too big. "Where are you?"

"I can get to you in ten minutes."

"I'll be ready."

I clicked off my phone, already feeling jittery from the adrenaline coursing through my veins. I grabbed my clothes off the bedroom floor, redressing in the same outfit as earlier, but adding in my Kevlar and my gun holsters. Giada seemed asleep, but I brushed a kiss across her forehead just in case she was still awake. She didn't stir.

I locked the apartment, switched my phone to silent to avoid any potential distractions, then jumped into Alessio's car as he pulled up. He barely slowed to a stop before we were on the road again. We didn't want to arrive too early, as the risk of being spotted outside the apartment increased the longer we were there, but if we missed him altogether...

"Giovanni is across the alley, sitting on a stoop, head down, playing on his phone. If Dmitry comes out early, he'll handle it," Alessio said, reading my mind.

I blew out a sigh. "I need to be the one to do this."

Alessio cast a sideways glance at me. He wouldn't openly question my judgment, but he was clearly thinking it.

"It has to be me," I repeated. "I'm not putting a target on your head."

Alessio was quiet for a moment. Then he grabbed a burner phone from the center console. That way, we could call Giovanni when we were close, and he could tell us when to drive up. "Use the gun from the glove box," he said. I reached in and quickly found the weapon, wrapped in a clean handkerchief. I confirmed that it was loaded, then focused on my breathing.

"There should be plates in there too," Alessio said, startling me.

I reached back in, but waited until he stopped to hand him the requested item. It resembled a legit license plate, but of course wasn't. It was likely an unnecessary precaution, but caution had served us well so far. There was no reason not to cover our tracks. He was back in the car in under a minute, and I knew without having looked that if anyone had seen him, it wouldn't have mattered. Alessio, with his dark baseball cap, dark letterman-style jacket, and black jeans, would've kept his head down. He was utterly unmemorable and unrecognizable.

I dialed Giovanni from the burner phone, waiting for him to tell us the moment he saw Dmitry leave the apartment.

We were close to the apartment, probably less than two

minutes away, and with every passing moment, my pulse increased. The plan was simple, but not foolproof. Giovanni could be wrong—Dmitry might have a guy someplace in the area that he just hadn't seen. Or we could be late, arriving after he already reached his car. And, there was always the possibility of witnesses.

The gun Alessio had given me was pre-fitted with a silencer, but the gunshot would still be audible to anyone within a few blocks. The only way to muffle the noise further would be to press the gun against Dmitry while pulling the trigger, but that obviously carried other risks not present if I shot from the car.

I considered my aim and knew what I had to do.

"Drop me at the corner," I said. Assuming Giovanni had gotten the time right, Dmitry had been in the apartment for exactly an hour. He should be leaving any minute now.

"No," Alessio quickly replied.

I shot him the look that was supposed to remind him who was in charge. Instead, he simply shook his head.

"I don't want to miss," I said.

Alessio furrowed his brows together. Then he swore under his breath and yanked the hat off his head. He reached over and stuck the hat over my head. He slowed the car, and I spotted Giovanni as we rolled past. Had I not known Giovanni was there, I wouldn't have noticed him at all. I doubted anyone else had, either.

I wedged the burner phone into my pants pocket right as Alessio slowed behind the building. He nodded encouragingly, but the worry in his eyes was still apparent. I climbed out, shoving the gun into the front of my pants.

Keeping my head down, I walked around the back of the building. The temperature had dropped markedly since I'd been out with Giada earlier, but the fresh air felt good, invigorating, even. I knew the sweat on my palms wasn't from the heat of Alessio's car, though.

Nightfall had erased all lights on the street, yet there were still people milling about. I slowed my pace, hoping to appear inconspicuous to anyone who passed me. I held the phone to my ear, but aside from my heavy breathing, there was only silence for the next two minutes.

Finally, Giovanni spoke. "He's walking," was all he said.

I clicked off the phone, shoved it in my pocket, and picked up the pace. I was in front of the adjacent building, so I should be able to catch Dmitry and walk up right behind him before he reached his car, rather than walking straight at him. Even in the narrow sliver of daylight remaining, Dmitry was sure to recognize me if he saw me coming.

Fortunately, he was focused on his phone. I wondered if he was texting his wife, telling her he'd be home soon. Or maybe he was thanking his mistress. More likely, he was communicating with his guys, the same way I did throughout the day. Dmitry Petrov and I were more alike than I wanted to admit, but we differed in two very important ways.

He was about to die. And he deserved it.

I didn't often see the world as black and white. People were rarely all good or all bad to me. But Dmitry Petrov was the exception to that rule. He was a bad man. Dmitry Petrov was void of any good, and well past the point of redemption. Even if he hadn't jacked my shipment, Dmitry should've been on my hit list. He hurt women and children, and he gave a bad name to all of us who operated outside the law.

I did one last visual sweep of the alley before turning onto it. I pulled out the gun, clutching it tightly in my hand, and sped up as much as I could without my footsteps making noise. I gripped the handkerchief from the car in my other hand and just before Dmitry reached his Mercedes, I lifted my arm and aimed.

I said a quick prayer as the gunshot rang out, piercing the relative silence of the alley. I knew the noise could attract residents of the apartments on both sides of the alley to their windows, so I was now on a definite timeline.

The bullet had stopped Dmitry in his tracks, and his phone had fallen to the cracked pavement, but he still stood upright. Two more wide strides brought me to him, so I grabbed his shoulder with the handkerchief, pressed the gun firmly against his back, aligned with his heart, and pulled the trigger two more times.

He went limp against me, so I backed up, waiting till he slumped lifelessly against the street beside his car before taking off. Head down, I jogged to the end of the alley, turning the corner before hopping into Alessio's waiting car.

Neither of us said anything. I watched in the rearview mirror, but saw no one appear from the woodwork.

Alessio had placed a large plastic zip-top bag on the center console, so I dropped the gun and the handkerchief inside.

"Burner?" he said.

I added the phone, then zipped the bag shut.

"I'll wipe your prints and get rid of it all in separate locations," he said. It was an unnecessary statement, since there wasn't a doubt in my mind that he would take every possible precaution to lose all the evidence.

"Anyone see you?" Alessio asked. His tone was clipped, signaling he shared the anxiety I'd felt.

"Probably. At least two dozen windows lined that alley."

"It's New York. People don't run to the window over loud noises. Could've been a car backfiring."

In a neighborhood like that, people knew the difference between a car backfiring and a gunshot, but I didn't argue. Alessio was trying to make me feel better.

"I would've done it," he added.

"I know."

Alessio turned to me and grinned. "Your aim is better than you think. Those last two shots were out of spite."

They weren't, but I appreciated the vote of confidence. He drove for a few more minutes before hopping out to switch the plates back. The fake ones would go into the bag of items to be disposed of.

Alessio dropped me in front of my club, L'Occhio. "Give me an hour or two to deal with this," he said, gesturing to the bag of evidence. "Then, I'll meet you. In the meantime, you should celebrate, Boss."

I left his hat on the seat of the car and climbed out. I went in the back entrance of my club and made my way straight to my office, where I changed clothes. Then I walked back out, certain to pause in front of the security cameras. At least I'd have partial proof of my whereabouts that night if it came to that.

I went to the bar and Nick, our best bartender, poured me a double shot of whiskey.

"You look like you could use it," he said as I thanked him.

I downed the drink in record time, then jumped as a hand clapped against my back. It was Thomas. His wide grin told me he'd already heard of my achievement.

"Nicely done, Marino. Alessio says you put us all to shame."

I motioned for Nick to refill my glass, but already felt my lips tugging upwards.

"Should I call a meeting for tonight?"

"No. I haven't decided yet if we are taking credit for this. Just let it ride, and the news can spread naturally. I'll gather the captains tomorrow night probably."

Thomas hesitated, then nodded. I knew he was pondering the dilemma. On the one hand, every other criminal in the area was familiar with Dmitry, or at least his name. To take credit for his death would give us immense power.

However, it could also make us a target. Even without Dmitry, his crew might prove a worthy opponent. Besides, the authorities still might investigate the murder of a scumbag like Dmitry, especially if they thought they could pin it on someone in my family.

CHAPTER 12

Giada

When I awoke the next morning, I was alone. I pouted for a moment, then checked my cell phone to see if Luca had texted. Nada. Groaning, I dragged myself out of bed to make coffee. Having gone to bed before eight, I actually felt well rested, but if I was going to survive a day at work and track down Luca, caffeine would help.

I barely made it to the kitchen before noticing Luca's shoes and jacket on the floor. Next to his jacket was a black handgun. I concluded that he was home, and that he had returned home drunk. I peered into the guest room and confirmed my suspicions, since my husband was sprawled across the bed on his stomach.

I rolled my eyes and then proceeded to make my coffee. I ate breakfast, showered, and dressed for work before returning to the guest room. Perching cautiously on the edge of the bed, I poked him.

Luca groaned, so I jabbed harder. He winced and tugged a pillow over his head.

The last time I'd seen him that hung over was after Carla showed up with Jacob. Before that, well, I couldn't even recall another instance. Luca had a drink most days, sometimes even two drinks, but he rarely got sloshed. He was too much of a control freak for that. Usually.

"I'm leaving for work, but I thought you should know there's a gun on the floor by our kitchen."

He groaned louder.

"So much for the dinner and movie."

Luca didn't answer, so I left. I returned with a cup of coffee, set it on the nightstand, then took off for work.

We had a team meeting at ten where my boss Diana showed us all pictures of a new client's home. The property had a classic Mediterranean feel, and the owners loved unique, authentic items. My mouth watered at the thought of all the gorgeous pieces I could find them in Italy.

I texted Gabby after the meeting to see if she wanted to meet up for lunch. I knew she'd be sympathetic to my complaints about Luca, but she apparently had plans already. It was just as well because when I left my desk around noon, I saw Luca saunter up to the receptionist's desk.

He didn't see me, so I hung back, watching him as he grinned at Cami, the receptionist, and gestured to a bouquet of flowers in his hands. He was such a natural flirt. Also, he looked like he'd recovered from the hangover. I made my way over to reception.

"Hey Giada, good timing," Cami said. "You have some flowers." She pointed to Luca.

I smiled. "Wow. They sure have hot delivery guys doing their work these days," I said.

The confused look on the receptionist's face told me she didn't realize I actually knew Luca.

"I'm sorry, Cami, this is Luca Marino, my..." I froze as the word 'husband' nearly flowed off my lips.

"Fiancé," Luca supplied, offering Cami his hand.

"Nice to meet you," she mumbled, now blushing.

"I owe you a meal," Luca said to me. "Can you get away?"

I considered playing hard to get, to punish him for abandoning me the night before, but that would be immature and besides, I wanted to see him. "Wait here. I'll run these to my desk and grab my purse."

I returned a minute later, and we stepped outside. It was colder than the previous day, but when Luca wrapped his arm around me, I felt plenty warm.

"Does Italian sound good?" he asked as we walked.

"Italian always sounds good," I replied. "So where did you run off to last night?"

"I went to the club to help Alessio with something."

"You were working?"

He hesitated. "There was some drinking involved after."

"Some?"

Luca shrugged. "A lot. I thought I'd just be gone an hour or so, but after the first few drinks, I sort of lost track of time."

"Uh huh," I said. I actually believed him, but I wasn't entirely sure how he let himself get into the position where he was drinking that much on a Tuesday night.

"I think I'd just been under so much stress lately, I needed to get it out of my system."

"I thought we were going to spend the night together. Have a real date or something."

"Tonight?" He gazed at me, his expression hopeful. Suddenly, he grimaced. "Shit, actually I can't tonight. Tomorrow night?"

"I told Gabby I'd go to that poetry reading with her."

Luca frowned. "Friday. You're not working, right? We can do lunch and catch a matinee."

I nodded. That sounded good.

"I want to go to church with you this week too. Saturday? Or Sunday? Or both, I guess."

"Both?" I repeated with a giggle. "Sounds like someone has a guilt complex. You didn't kill someone, did you?"

Luca blanched and looked around us furtively. "Jesus, Giada. Why would you even say that?"

I scowled at his harsh tone. "I was teasing. You don't usually offer to attend mass twice in one weekend."

"I was trying to be nice. I feel bad for leaving you alone all night."

I squeezed his hand.

We turned the corner and reached our destination, a seedy-looking corner shop selling the best New York style pizza slices in the borough. We ordered, then Luca carried our tray of food to a booth in the corner.

"You know, you can't just buy me cheap pizza and expect me to forgive you for blowing me off. That's not how this marriage is going to work."

He grinned at the word "marriage." I loved that the mere sound of our relationship status brought a smile to his face. That was enough for me to forgive him, but I wasn't about to admit that.

"I also got you flowers," he said.

I quirked an eyebrow, indicating that wasn't adequate either. Luca shrugged sheepishly, then reached into the inside pocket of his jacket and pulled out a small, flat jewelry box.

"Not what I meant," I said, even though I supposed we both heard the lie. I opened the box, biting back a smile as I saw the delicate rose gold bracelet with an oval-shaped cobalt blue gem in the middle. The bracelet was simple yet beautiful. I suspected Luca had paid close to two hundred dollars or more, but it wasn't a flashy or over-the-top piece like he used to choose for me.

I held my wrist out so he could fasten the bracelet for me. He did so, then kissed the palm of my hand.

"I love it," I said. "Thank you."

Luca and I were on different schedules the next few days,

passing like ships in the night. I'd barely seen him since our lunch, so on Thursday, he stretched out on the bed to watch me get ready for my night with Gabby.

"I spoke with your father today," he said, as I debated between two pairs of boots.

"Why did he call you?" I asked, figuring since he was my dad, he should call me.

"Work stuff. He actually wanted to congratulate me."

I froze. "How did he find out?"

Luca frowned, then shook his head. "Not about us. Work stuff." He paused. "You know that Russian guy I mentioned a while back? The one that, um, stole some stuff from us?"

"Yeah."

"I think we got his whole group to leave town."

"So that's why you've been so busy this week?"

Luca simply nodded, then continued watching as I put on my jewelry. "What about your new bracelet? Aren't you wearing that?"

I had been planning to, but it was still fun to tease him. "You just want me to wear it so Gabby will notice and think you spoil me."

He grinned.

"But then she'll want to know why you gave me a bracelet."

"You could tell her the truth. That I'm just that thoughtful and perfect."

I leaned in to kiss him, but the doorbell interrupted us.

"She's early," he groaned.

"Be nice."

Since I was expecting Gabriella, I opened the door without checking the peephole. Instead of my friend though, it was Alessio. Apparently, I didn't hide my surprise well.

"She didn't look before she opened the door," Alessio said over my head.

"Tattle tale," I snarled. Luca was adamant I never open the

door without being completely certain who was standing there and why. It was one of his less charming neurosis.

"Bad girl," Luca whispered teasingly, swatting me on the butt. Then he turned to his friend, who clutched a fancy-looking bottle of Scotch in his hand. "What's that?"

"Another thank you gift arrived for you. Didn't want to leave this one at the club unattended."

Luca reached for the bottle and held it admiringly. "Holy shit. That's beautiful. I don't know if we should drink it or just sit around and admire it." He tore his gaze away from the bottle to look at his friend again. "Who's it from?"

"Giancarlo DeLuca," Alessio answered.

The name meant nothing to me, aside from the obvious Italian heritage to it. "Why would you sit and look at a bottle of scotch?"

"Because it's a one-of-a-kind aged Scotch."

I wrinkled my nose. "Aged as in expired?"

"Aged as in really expensive. This bottle is probably worth fifteen hundred," Luca said, heading to the kitchen. He retrieved two glasses and placed a couple ice cubes in each.

"Seventeen hundred," Alessio corrected. "I checked."

Luca poured a small amount in each glass. He handed one to Alessio, and they clinked glasses.

"Salute," they said in unison.

I watched, bemused, as the guys swirled the rich amber colored liquid around in their glasses, sniffed it, then finally each took a delicate sip. They groaned at the same time. I couldn't help but roll my eyes.

"Oh, come on baby, you have to try this," Luca said, tugging my hand.

Reluctantly, I sampled a tiny taste. The liquid rolled easily down my throat, having an almost syrupy texture and a slight maple flavor. It wasn't bad, but it wasn't great either. And once it hit my stomach, I felt the slightest bit queasy. I shrugged. "Not my thing," I said.

The doorbell rang, and I raced over, relieved to be saved by the bell.

"Look first!" Alessio and Luca both shouted.

"Yes, Daddy," I mocked, confirming it was Gabby before answering.

She smiled as I opened the door, then peered over my shoulder at the guys.

"They're making me drink old whisky," I explained.

"Scotch," Alessio clarified.

I reached for my purse then turned to Luca.

"Be good," he said, the side of his mouth angling upward mischievously.

"I feel like you're more likely to get in trouble than I am," I said.

"Come home early, and we could get in trouble together," he whispered into my ear before kissing my neck.

I squealed at the ticklish sensation, then rejoined my friend.

"He seemed…happy," she said as we walked out to the street.

"Yeah. Something went right at work for once, I guess."

"At the strip club?" Her tone made it clear how she felt about Luca's business holdings, as if I hadn't already known her feelings on the matter.

"No, the shipping business," I replied. "Are you excited for your trip?" I asked, eager to change the subject. She was headed to the west coast in about a week for a work trip, but planned to extend her trip a few extra days so she could explore.

"So excited," she said. "I have a list of about fifteen places I want to eat, which might be tough to squeeze in with such a short trip."

I giggled. "You could do like a progressive dinner each night."

She nodded, clearly considering that possibility. "Hey, I meant to ask. I'm making my spa appointment for next week, so I can get everything done before my trip. You in?"

"Sure. What day?"

"Maybe Wednesday late afternoon?"

"Yeah, that'll work."

"You want the usual?"

I nodded again. Our usual involved a facial, mani, pedi, and eyebrows.

"I'm getting a bikini wax too. Just in case. You want that too?"

I didn't ask if she meant just in case she met someone or just in case she wore a swimsuit. "Umm, not next week. I'll probably be on my period."

Gabby made a face. "Really? Mine was last week. I thought we were on the same schedule."

I considered her point. We had been on the same schedule for as long as I could remember. I'd read somewhere that it wasn't uncommon for good friends or roommates to have their cycles sync up like that. But I definitely hadn't had my period the prior week. Or the week before that. I tried to recall when I'd last actually had a period.

"Wow, I guess we've finally lived apart long enough to become independent women in every sense of the word," my friend mused, interrupting my thoughts.

We both laughed at the sentiment. We reached the café and snagged a table in the middle. We weren't so close that the people at the mic could see us mocking their terrible poetry, but we were still in the middle of the action. We each ordered a glass of wine and then chose a few tapas to share.

As the readings began, I listened closely to the first two, then found myself growing distracted by our earlier discussion. I definitely hadn't gotten my period in Italy. In fact, I was pretty certain I'd had it the week before the trip. Since switching birth control a year or so ago, my periods had been delightfully light, but still noticeable. Surely, I would remember if I'd gotten mine since

Italy. I wished I were one of those super organized girls who actually tracked her cycle on the calendar, but that wasn't me. I usually relied on my sudden crankiness to tell me when it was coming.

I reached for my wine and took a sip, my stomach souring the moment I swallowed. I noticed Gabby's glass was almost empty, and she hadn't mentioned it seeming rancid. I sniffed the wine and winced, scooting the glass away. I caught the attention of our waitress and ordered mint tea instead.

Gabby eyed me warily.

"That stupid scotch messed with my stomach," I said. "You can have my wine."

My friend accepted it willingly and returned her focus to the action ahead of us. She divided her focus pretty evenly between the readers and the audience. Gabriella was in between boyfriends at the moment, so I knew the real reason we were here was for her to scope out decent potential suitors. She loved the artsy types, so this was the perfect venue for her to find her next Mr. Right.

I hated that I couldn't tell her about Luca. I didn't imagine I'd actually feel married until the whole world knew, or at least my best friend. And the handful of months until the official wedding felt like an eternity. My jaw tightened as I accepted the tea from the waitress, and I recalled what the priest had asked Luca in Italy when we said we wanted to get married right away. Of course, he'd assumed I was pregnant, and now, my period was late.

What if God was punishing me for eloping by making my birth control fail?

I couldn't possibly be pregnant yet. I wasn't ready. Luca wasn't ready. And everyone would assume that was why we got married early.

My heart began to race. I wasn't pregnant. I couldn't be pregnant. Even thinking it was ridiculous.

Except, well, I was late.

Probably.

And Luca and I had engaged in plenty of behavior that traditionally resulted in pregnancy. I mean, seriously. We'd done it multiple times a day in Italy and once nearly every day since. But none of that should matter since I was on birth control. That was the whole reason I'd switched from the pill to the shot, so I didn't have to worry about getting busy and forgetting a dose. I only had to get the shot a few times a year, and I'd just gotten my last one…

I pulled out my phone to check the calendar. Of course, I hadn't marked the appointment anywhere, but surely looking at the dates would jog my memory. I'd definitely gotten the last one before a trip to Italy. Except…which trip?

Gabby cleared her throat loudly, eying me pointedly.

I flushed and sheepishly wedged my phone back into my purse. But I couldn't stop the what-ifs from running through my brain.

It wasn't late when Gabby and I returned home, so I hoped to talk with Luca right away. Maybe he'd remember when I'd last gone to the doctor and, if not, at least I'd have someone else to reassure me that I was panicking over nothing. But much to my chagrin, Alessio was still at the apartment, and they'd been joined by Thomas and Giovanni.

I greeted everyone before retreating back to the bedroom. I needed to do some research in private. I thought I'd been warm enough, but Luca quickly followed me back, so clearly, I hadn't hidden my concerns well enough.

"What's wrong?" he asked.

I shook my head dismissively.

"Did something happen tonight with Gabby?"

"No, she's good. We had fun."

He frowned. "I can get rid of the guys now if you want. I just thought they'd worked so hard lately, and we haven't had much of a chance to relax and celebrate…"

It was obvious from his tone that he didn't want to send his friends away yet, even though it seemed like they'd done plenty of celebrating already this week. "I'm just tired. I'm going to read for a bit."

He hesitated for a moment, then left.

~

Luca

Giada was already up when I awoke the next morning, and while I expected her to be annoyed that I'd let Alessio crash in our guest room, she didn't seem to be. To the contrary, she was over the top with her affections and praise, telling me how handsome I looked and how excited she was about our lunch.

"Excited?" I repeated, hoping for more specifics.

She shrugged. "There's something I want to talk with you about," was all she said.

"Uh oh. Am I in trouble?"

"No," she said, straightening my tie. "Just…something about our future."

That struck me as odd, but since Alessio and I needed to make our rounds at a few businesses that morning before I took Giada to lunch, I didn't have long to dwell on it. Besides, whatever she wanted to tell me or discuss was probably something related to wedding planning. I confirmed where she wanted to eat, then made reservations, and promised to pick her up at a quarter after noon.

Business went smoothly that morning, but we were running behind, so Alessio drove Giada and me to the restaurant. When she'd seen we wouldn't be alone on the drive, Giada was visibly disappointed, but I couldn't pinpoint why. If she wanted to talk, we could do it at the restaurant or later.

"Are you okay?" I asked Giada, once we were seated.

She nodded unconvincingly and then stared at the menu as though trying to memorize it.

"You seem...distracted," I said. Actually, the more I watched her, it seemed like she was nervous.

Giada shrugged, not glancing up until the waitress arrived to take our drink orders.

"So, what did you want to talk about?" I asked.

Her lips parted, but then she stopped herself from speaking. The sight of her pretty red mouth momentarily distracted me from my eagerness to hear what she had to say. I stood, leaning over the table and pressing my hand against the back of her head, holding her still as I pressed my lips to hers. I lingered in the kiss for a moment, but didn't press my tongue past the seam between her lips.

As I returned to my seat, her skin flushed, making her even more enticing than before.

"What was that for?" she asked.

"Do I need a reason to kiss you?" I countered, pressing my hand to my chest. Giada bit back a smile, telling me she knew exactly what lay beneath my fingers.

"Let's order, then we can talk," she said. I motioned for the waitress, then nodded for my wife to order first.

As the waitress disappeared with our menus, I turned back to my wife. Her eyes were on the table as she absentmindedly fiddled with her napkin, so I stole the chance to check her out. Her dark hair covered her shoulders, partially obscuring the view offered by her v-neck shirt, and she wore minimal makeup. I was just about to comment on how heavy her earrings looked when she spoke.

"I can feel you staring at me," she said, slowly raising her eyes to meet mine.

"I can't help it. You're beautiful."

"And starving," she said.

"We could get an appetizer," I said, right as my phone buzzed.

I glanced down in no particular hurry, then froze when I saw the all-caps message from Alessio. "COPS," was all it said.

"Cazzo," I said, swearing in my native tongue. In an instant, I felt intolerably warm, like the room was not only on fire but also closing in on me. Time slowed down as I turned to the window, unable to see anyone yet.

I told myself it was nothing, that they were just here to eat, but I knew in my heart that wasn't true. Alessio wouldn't have texted me if it was just a couple of officers or if they looked like they were about to enjoy a casual meal.

No, I felt it in my bones. This was it.

My time was up.

"Giada, take this and listen closely," I said, my tone low but serious. I switched off my phone, dropping it into her purse along with the gun from my side holster under my jacket. Then, I tugged a roll of cash out of my pocket and wedged that into her purse, too.

Giada looked panicked.

I gripped her hand tightly. "I love you so much, Giada. I need you to take your purse and go to the bathroom now. Hide there for a minute, then sneak out the back and call Alessio. Don't turn back. Don't say a word to anyone other than Alessio or your father. Or Enzo, Thomas, or Giovanni. Do you understand? Go!"

I nudged her, but she didn't move.

"Luca what is going on?" she asked.

I glanced to the door again and saw two men in suits, flanked by several uniformed officers, approach the manager, then glance our way. "Give Alessio my phone and yours when you see him. Go now!"

I didn't miss the recognition in Giada's eyes as she saw the police approaching us. She leaned in and kissed me. "I love you too," she whispered. Then she slowly backed away from the table.

"Stop!" an officer shouted.

Giada froze in place. I slowly raised my hands and leaned back from the table. I felt the eyes of every patron in that restaurant glued to me as three of the officers stepped closer, tugged me to my feet, and cuffed my hands behind my back, but I kept my gaze on Giada. She was crying, but as I mouthed, "I love you," she nodded, and I knew she'd get through this.

"Luca Marino, you are under arrest for the murder of Dmitry Petrov."

Giada's eyes widened further, but after years of practice, I was confident my face showed no emotion.

"There's a handgun on my left ankle," I said as the officer began his pat-down.

I felt naked the second they'd removed it, but the moment I glanced up, I saw that Giada had disappeared.

Good girl, I thought. I prayed they hadn't nabbed Alessio also and that she'd only have to wait a couple of minutes before he came to get her.

They began walking me to the car while reciting my Miranda rights, but I'd already stopped listening. I hadn't been arrested in the States before, but that didn't matter. I knew the drill. Until my lawyer showed up, I was done talking.

At the station, they conducted a more thorough search and then offered to let me make a phone call. I declined with a simple shake of my head. A phone call wouldn't solve anything, and it wasn't necessary. I may not have been the most trusting person, but I had faith in my men. They knew what to do, and they would get it done.

They seated me in an interview room and unfastened the cuffs before launching into their interrogation. I had no concerns that I'd actually answer any of their questions aloud. Moreover, to ensure I also didn't inadvertently reveal any information with my body language or facial expressions, I didn't even listen to their questions.

Perhaps the most valuable thing my papà had ever done for me was lecture me so extensively that I mastered the art of mentally escaping my surroundings. I was still facing the officer, but I was completely tuned out.

In my mind, I was trying to weigh the pros and cons of various honeymoon locales. Giada loved the beach, and I would never turn down a chance to see her in a bikini, but it was hard to top the beaches of Sicily. And if we were going to go there, it would feel just like everyday life. Maybe a trip to France would be better. Do some sightseeing, make love in a room overlooking the Seine or maybe even with a view of the Eiffel Tower. Actually, maybe a cruise would be nice.

I snapped back to reality as a second officer joined.

"He's not saying anything," the first one said. "I'm not sure he can even hear me." He waved a hand in front of my face. I cocked an eyebrow.

"He has dual citizenship. Maybe he only speaks Italian."

"Do you need a translator?" the man practically shouted as though his volume had been the problem.

"No," I replied before returning to my daydream.

CHAPTER 13

Giada

The five hours after my lunch date with Luca passed in a blur. At Luca's instruction, I'd ducked out the back entrance of the restaurant, shocked when the three officers stationed by that door simply let me pass. I'd started walking as fast as I could down the street, using every ounce of self-control not to turn and watch what was happening with Luca.

Stupidly, I'd assumed that getting myself away quickly as he'd requested was the best thing for my husband, but in retrospect, I should've stuck around. What if I'd given up my last chance to see him for a while? What if I could've helped somehow?

I wasn't sure how long I'd walked when I stumbled across a bustling coffee shop. I stepped inside and locked myself in the single-stall bathroom. I debated calling my father or maybe Enzo, but I figured I should follow Luca's instructions and dial Alessio.

"Si?" his voice was clipped, frantic, but I was certain it was him.

"Alessio? I thought I should call you," I began, wincing when I remembered Luca's rule of never using names on phone calls.

"Princess, thank God. Where are you?" The relief in his voice was palpable. "I need to get you someplace safe now."

I gave him the name of the coffee shop but couldn't even remember the cross streets. He said to stay in the bathroom until he texted that he'd arrived, so I did. While I waited, I called Enzo.

"They arrested Luca," I said the moment he answered.

"What? Who?"

"I don't know, police." I started hyperventilating while I thought about it. What if it hadn't actually been the police? What if it was some bad guys masquerading as the police?"

"Did they get anyone else?" Enzo asked. "Are you alone now?"

"I...I don't think so. He told me to hurry out, so I went to a coffee shop. Alessio said he'll come get me."

"Okay good. That's good, Giada. Just stay put until Alessio gets there, and then do what he says. Don't talk to anyone else at all."

"I don't want to be with Alessio. I'm scared, Enzo!"

"I know, sweetheart. But he'll keep you safe. I'll talk with your father, and then I'll try to get to you later tonight."

I didn't stop crying until I ducked into Alessio's car. He looked panicked too, which wasn't reassuring. But I was distracted by all the clutter in his car. For how much Alessio hung around Luca, the neatness sure hadn't rubbed off on him. Luca kept his cars meticulous, but Alessio's had a handful of fast food wrappers in the front seat, a notepad, and some random receipts.

"I thought you were a vegetarian," I said.

"I am. That's not all mine, and besides, every place has meat-less options."

I stared out the window, dazed. "Where are we going?"

"A hotel."

"What? Why?"

"We need to keep you out of sight."

"Am I in danger or something?"

He glanced at me at a stoplight. "No. Luca has a contingency plan for everything. We follow the plan. That means I am taking you to a hotel on the outskirts of town. You will stay there, out of sight, until Luca tells me otherwise."

"I need to get some things from the apartment," I said. "Or my parents' house if we can't go to the apartment."

Alessio ignored me and drove to the hotel. He told me to go to the lobby restroom while he checked in. When I emerged, he met me at the stairs and we went up to the room. He'd gotten two adjoining rooms, which I supposed was reassuring, except that there was no way I'd actually stay overnight at this establishment.

"I need to make some calls," he said, unlocking the adjoining door. "I'm going to leave this open so you can get me if you need anything, but do not open that door for any reason, okay?" He gestured to the main door which exited to the hotel hallway.

I nodded. I needed to call Enzo again anyway.

"Did Luca give you his phone?"

I started to say no, but as I reached into my bag, I realized he had. I handed it to Alessio.

"Give me yours too."

"I need to call Enzo," I said, clutching mine to my chest.

Alessio hesitated. "Luca said I needed to take your phone immediately. That is the plan. I can call your father for you from my phone."

I hesitantly handed him my phone. "Call Lorenzo, not my father. Please," I said.

"Okay." Alessio turned on the television and tossed me the remote. As if I'd touch that germy plastic thing. "You probably shouldn't eavesdrop," he explained. "Lock this door as soon as I leave."

I followed him to the hall door and locked it as instructed. I then prepared to be alone, but a moment later, Alessio came through the adjoining door, propping it open, then starting a phone call. His first call was entirely in Italian, so I wasn't sure why he was concerned I'd eavesdrop, although I could gather the general tenor of it.

Alessio made several more calls in quick succession, then when there was a lull in his conversations, I piped up. "Did you call Enzo yet?"

Alessio made a face but dialed something on the phone, then switched it to speaker phone and handed it to me.

"Enzo? It's me, Giada," I said when he answered. "You're on speaker phone with Alessio too," I said, not wanting him to say anything that could get him in trouble later.

"Your mother packed you a bag. I can bring it to you. Where are you?"

Alessio hesitated but told him where we were.

"I'm an hour away," Enzo said.

I groaned.

"Alessio, Mr. Conti would appreciate you keeping him apprised of any developments, and of course he is happy to offer any assistance he can."

"Sure," Alessio mumbled, not sounding extremely grateful for the offer.

When they disconnected, I had dozens of questions for Alessio, but he gave me virtually no useful information.

Instead, he shook his head. "Luca told me you ask too many questions, but I had no idea." He started back into the other room. "Don't worry about this. I am handling it."

"If you don't tell me what is going on, I'm leaving," I said, startled by how resolute I sounded.

Alessio paused and turned back to me. "Your fiancé has been arrested for murder. He doesn't want anyone questioning you about anything because he doesn't think you can keep quiet, so instead of putting all my efforts into helping him and connecting with his legal team, I'm here, babysitting you. I really don't know anything else yet. I'm waiting for a call from the lawyer and then we can…" his voice trailed off as his phone buzzed. "Ahh speak of the devil," he said.

"Ciao," he answered the phone, all but slamming the door in my face.

I tried to eavesdrop on the call, but Alessio spoke very little. What he did say was largely monosyllabic words. The call went on for nearly twenty minutes. When they hung up, Alessio immediately made a series of other calls. Finally, he returned to my room.

"Well?" I demanded. "Was that the lawyer?"

"Yes. And he's already spoken with the police."

"Is Luca okay? I mean are they treating him…"

"He's fine, Giada. This isn't some Siberian work camp," the man sighed as though my concern was unwarranted.

"Anyway, once Thomas works out the alibi, the lawyer will go meet with him and make sure everyone is on the same page with the story."

"He has an alibi?" For a moment, I felt hopeful.

Alessio turned to me, confused.

Suddenly, there was a knock at the door. Alessio popped up and peered through the peephole before unlocking.

"Enzo!" I said, relief flooding me.

"Hey, princess. Your mom sent me with some things for you."

He tossed a duffel bag onto the second bed. I jumped up to hug him. We were still embracing when Alessio's phone rang. I turned at the noise and stiffened at the stern look of disapproval on his face.

"I've got to take this," he said with a shake of his head, ducking back into the hall.

I told Enzo about the arrest and caught him up on every minute of my life since then before pausing to breathe and launching into my questions.

"Alessio says Luca's okay."

"I'm sure he is. He knows not to say anything to anyone until his lawyer is there."

"What if they torture him?"

"They don't do that here." He reached over and placed his hand on my back, rubbing up then down. "He's fine, Giada. I promise. Luca is tough, and he's been through much worse things than a night in jail."

"You think he'll be there all night?"

Enzo frowned and his voice became uncharacteristically high-pitched. "Giada, you need to prepare yourself. He might be there until trial."

"What?" I flew to my feet. I had nowhere to go but suddenly felt useless just sitting there. "What about bail?"

Enzo made a face. "He successfully disappeared for six months once before, and he's got unlimited funds, dual citizenship, and no legitimate ties to the community. They'd be crazy to let Luca out on bail."

"But…" I started to protest, when suddenly, the room was spinning. I heard a voice that vaguely resembled mine mumble something about being sick, and then everything went dark.

When I came to, I was in bed on my back. Both Alessio and Enzo were hunched over me. I swatted them away, rolling to my side.

"What are you doing?" I asked.

"You fainted. Are you feeling okay?" Enzo pressed a hand against my head.

I shoved his hand away and tried to sit up. He pushed me back down.

"No, I'm not okay," I snapped. "Luca is in jail, and you're all acting like it's no big deal."

"We should be working our asses off trying to make sure we get him out, and instead we're babysitting you," Alessio retorted. Then he switched to Italian to continue his rant.

"Go," Enzo said to him, with more authority in his voice than I'd heard in the past.

Alessio made a face, but left.

Enzo propped pillows up behind my back and slowly helped raise me to a seated position. "Drink," he said, holding a glass of water by my face.

I accepted the water and sipped timidly.

"Have you eaten?"

I thought back. I had coffee at breakfast, but hadn't eaten because Luca and I were meeting for an early lunch. Of course, then he'd been arrested before our food came, so… I shook my head slowly.

He rifled through a binder on the cheap particleboard desk across the room, then held up a pizza menu. "What do you want?"

I shrugged. He perused it for a few minutes, then called and ordered enough food for an army and gave Alessio's room number for delivery.

"Why am I here?" I asked.

"Because the police will want to question you, and we don't want you talking to the police."

"I can't do that from home?"

"No, because if you're at home and you won't answer their questions, they know you're avoiding them. If they just can't find you, they can't say you're not cooperating."

"How is running away and hiding in a seedy hotel cooperating?"

"They don't know you're running away."

"Can't I just plead the fifth if they question me?"

"No, because you're not accused of anything."

I treaded carefully on my next question. "But if we were married, then they couldn't force me to testify against him, right?"

"Right, but…" Enzo shrugged. "Don't stress it, Giada. The lawyer will meet with Luca in the morning and make sure everyone is on the same page with his alibi. Then he will answer all of their questions."

"What if they question someone else? Is Thomas in hiding?"

Enzo's lips ticked up in a smile. "They might try to question someone else, but you'd be the first priority. The rest of us won't give them anything useful and they know that."

"I wouldn't give them anything useful!"

"Giada, I know you mean well, but you don't have much practice being evasive. You're an honest person, and you have a tendency to overshare."

"I do not."

Enzo blew out a sigh. "It's not an insult. You're sweet and innocent. You are not a career criminal, so you don't know how to handle the police like some of the others in Luca's life might."

I rolled my eyes. "Do you guys go through training or something? Is that part of the initiation?"

"Yes, there is training. And there are some basic rules."

"Like?"

His eyebrow raised. "Like don't discuss the rules with outsiders."

"I'm hardly an outsider. Besides, I need distracting."

"No texts, no paper trail, no voice mails, limit phone calls, use burner phones when needed. Never volunteer information, never talk in public."

"None of that is a big mystery. Tell me something I don't know."

Enzo considered that request for a moment. "We value the traditional roles. Respect for women, taking care of them, that sort of thing."

"Chivalry?"

He nodded.

"Again, not news to me. I've had an entire life of men treating me like a child because I wasn't born with a penis. What's the number one rule?"

"Loyalty." He paused. "I know Alessio isn't your favorite, but the reason Luca trusts him so much is because he will do anything Luca tells him to do. If it came to it, he would die for Luca."

"Really?"

"Yes."

"Would you die for Luca?"

There was a long pause. "I don't work for him."

"You would die for my father?"

He hesitated but then nodded once.

"Why?"

"Because that is how this works."

I shook my head. That was ridiculous. Obviously, I loved my father and didn't want anything to happen to him, but Enzo was so much younger. He had a lot more life left to live. Before I could dwell on that too much, Enzo stood.

"I'll be back with the food. Don't open the door or answer the phone for anyone. I'm right next door."

I nodded. As soon as I was alone, I slowly stood and made my way to the bathroom, dragging my bag in with me. I grimaced at my streaked eye makeup, but twisted my hair up into a loose knot on top of my head. I splashed some cold water on my face then left the faucet on so the water could warm up before washing off my makeup. My eyes were still puffy, but otherwise I looked normal.

A wave of nausea washed over me and I stilled. Once the feeling passed, I turned to the side and lifted my shirt. My stomach was still flat, practically concave at the moment actually thanks to my unintended fast. I puffed out my stomach muscles, trying to envision what I'd look like in six months if...

God, I couldn't even finish the thought. It had been a terrifying enough notion before, when Luca and I were together and the rest of our future was certain. I'd planned to tell him my suspicions today after lunch, but even by the time we'd ordered, I'd already panicked so much that I probably would've postponed another day. There was no point in telling him if I wasn't sure, but...

I searched for my phone, to check my calendar again, in hopes that maybe I'd just miscalculated the dates, but of course I didn't have the device. Alessio had confiscated it.

There was a single knock at the door followed by the sound of a lock clicking.

"I have pizza, Giada," Enzo called.

"Okay," I replied, my wavering voice betraying my mood.

I rummaged through the bag until I found a pair of yoga pants, then pulled on a camisole. I tried to focus on dressing myself, but my mind kept drifting to the what ifs. What if Luca had to stay in jail until trial? I couldn't live that long without him normally, let alone if I was pregnant. Would I even be able to see him, to talk to him? I couldn't keep the information from him forever. But telling him seemed cruel. If he was in jail, it would kill him to know I was going through it alone.

I closed the lid on the toilet and sat, too exhausted to even care that I was in a disgusting hotel bathroom. Would this be my life until Luca was free? I couldn't live this way. I wasn't sure I could survive like this overnight, let alone until trial. And, oh God, what if he was convicted? Surely that wasn't a real possibility, was it?

I was too tired to fight the tears any longer. I let it all out, crying until I didn't even remember where I was.

When I finally opened my eyes, Enzo was crouched on the ground in front of me.

"Don't cry, princess. We'll take care of you."

"And Luca?"

"Him too," he promised. He helped me to my feet, then nudged me out of the bathroom. "You need to eat something."

"I'm not hungry." The fragrances from the excess of foods they'd ordered assaulted my senses as soon as I stepped out of the bathroom. I fought back the nausea and focused on just making it to the bed.

"One breadstick," Enzo said, handing it to me.

"Not hungry," I repeated.

"Not negotiating."

Alessio rolled his eyes. Judging from his plate, this ordeal had zero effect on his appetite.

I nibbled the breadstick tentatively. My mouth was so dry that I struggled to swallow, but once the food hit my stomach, I felt better than I would've expected.

"You said he has an alibi," I began. "So there's no chance they could convict him, right?"

Enzo and Alessio exchanged a glance.

"What?"

"Nothing," Enzo quickly said. "That's right."

Alessio snorted.

I turned to him. "What?" I repeated.

"Well, I mean, it wouldn't be the most airtight alibi," he said.

"Why not? Who is his alibi?"

"We don't know for sure yet."

"You follow him around like a puppy dog. How do you not know who was with him at the time of the murder?"

"I do know. It was me. I was with him," Alessio said.

Enzo shot him a dirty look.

"So you're his alibi?"

"I could be, but I don't have the most credibility."

"Why not? Do you have a record?"

"They know I work for him."

"So? When you swear an oath before testifying that means you're telling the truth and so they'll just have to believe whatever you say," I insisted, knowing it was every bit as ridiculous as it sounded.

"Even if I said *I* was the one who did it, they wouldn't believe me," he said.

"Alessio!" Enzo gritted his teeth and glared.

"Why would you…" I squeezed my eyes shut again as my surroundings grew wobbly again.

I pieced together what he meant, Enzo's sharp reaction having tipped me off. "You're saying Luca actually did it. And since you are his real alibi, anything you say to help him would be a lie."

"Giada, it doesn't matter what he says. They know how we operate, and they'll believe nothing Alessio says, whether he's under oath or not," Enzo said.

"It does matter though." I couldn't even fathom a world where the fact that my husband actually murdered someone was an irrelevant point in the discussion. My stomach rolled, and I covered my mouth. "I'm going to be sick."

Enzo dashed over to my bed with a stack of napkins and began rubbing my back again. "You're not going to be sick. You haven't eaten anything. Just take some deep breaths and it'll pass."

Luca wasn't a murderer. He had promised me he wouldn't do that ever again. "He promised," I mumbled.

"He didn't have a choice, and this guy was a monster. He was an arms dealer and sex trafficker. He sold kids for sex, Giada."

I rubbed my forehead, too exhausted and overwhelmed to launch into an ethics discussion with Enzo. Despite my silence, he continued rambling on about the many misdeeds of my husband's latest victim.

"I just want to sleep," I said, after several minutes. "And the smell of that food is making me nauseous."

Alessio stood and began packing up the food. I heard the click of the door as he left, presumably to deposit it in his room.

Enzo held out the rest of my breadstick. "Finish, Giada. I know you're not hungry, but think about how it would make Luca feel to know you weren't taking care of yourself when he couldn't be here to take care of you."

Enzo was right, but I also felt like Luca maybe could've thought of that before murdering someone. I nibbled the breadstick slowly.

"Here," Alessio said, holding out his hand. I startled, not having realized he'd even returned. "This will relax you."

I grimaced at the small yellow pill in his hand.

I glanced at Enzo, but his expression suggested he thought it was a good idea. I had to admit there was something tempting about just taking a pill and sleeping till morning, especially since nothing was going to be resolved tonight. I reached for it, then stopped.

I couldn't take some mystery drug. Not if there was a chance I was pregnant.

"No thanks."

"Giada…" Enzo began.

I shot him a look that shut him up.

"Have a drink at least," he suggested, walking over to his suitcase.

I shook my head. "I'm just going to sleep." I crawled under the covers.

I watched as the two men exchanged another glance, then seemingly acquiesced to my plan. Enzo reached into his bag and began pulling out various items on the second bed in the room.

"You can't stay here," Alessio said.

"I want him to," I said. I hated being alone in hotel rooms, and without my cell phone, I'd feel even more vulnerable. Besides, the moment the lights were off, I knew I'd start sobbing. With no one there to disturb, I couldn't imagine anything would stop me from crying.

"We can't just leave her alone," Enzo agreed.

Alessio scowled. "When Luca gets out, the last thing he's gonna want to hear is that I let *you* spend the night with his girl. You are literally his least favorite person."

"Not Adrian?"

I rubbed my stomach and tried to ignore the dumb argument, but Enzo did have a point. If Luca were going to hate someone, it should be the man I actually slept with, not the guy I just kissed.

"Why would he hate Adrian? No one could blame Adrian for falling for Giada. But you—you touched her knowing exactly who Luca was and that Giada was his."

Enzo rolled his eyes and started a retort, but I interrupted.

"Nothing happened, it wasn't his fault, and oh my God that was ages ago. Can we drop it already?"

The guys both appeared to consider my plea.

"I'm not leaving her alone," Enzo repeated.

"What if I need something? I don't even have my cell phone." I reminded them.

Alessio scribbled his room number on the notepad by the old fashioned phone beside the bed. "Call next door if you need anything. Or knock on the wall. Under no circumstances are you to answer the phone or door or leave the room."

I supposed I could handle that.

Enzo was still frowning. "I'll stay till she's asleep."

"It's fine, Enzo. Go next door," I said, remembering that Alessio was the one who had caught Enzo and I together that one fateful night years ago.

God, I'd been so young then. I'd just learned Luca was cheating on me and that Adrian was dating someone else. I hadn't known Alessio was spying on me when I'd launched myself onto Enzo's lap for a memorable makeout session. He'd stopped it before we went too far, but still earned himself a brutal beating when Luca was back in town.

That had been the first time I'd realized the horrible things Luca was capable of. Now, I had convinced myself he knew better, that he wasn't that person anymore.

Except it seemed the evidence pointed to the contrary.

~

Adrian

I'd seen the short news clip when I was finishing my final set of box jumps at the gym. I hadn't given it a second thought. Some guy—not a good one, from the way the anchor described him—was shot dead in the streets. His name was Dmitry Petrov. The crime had happened at night, but in a residential neighborhood, where potentially hundreds of witnesses could've helped solve the murder. Police asked residents or other potential witnesses to come forward with information, and the anchors speculated it might have been a mob hit since the victim's wallet wasn't stolen. As they'd described the victim as a major player in another crime organization from out of town, the theory seemed more than plausible.

I wasn't totally jaded by life in the greater area of the Big Apple quite yet, but there was nothing unique about that particular shooting. I had no reason to care, or even to remember the details. I grabbed my water bottle and left the gym, already debating whether I should blend up some bananas to add to my usual post-workout peanut butter protein smoothie. I probably would've never given the crime a second though, except for Matteo's call.

I'd resolved never to answer a call from anyone in the Conti family, but somehow, Matteo seemed a justifiable exception. Besides, I was still in an easy-going mood, the exercise endorphins still coursing through my veins.

"Hello?" I answered.

"Adrian, hi. It's Matteo," he began. He sounded breathless, less certain of himself than usual, but before I could ask if he was alright, he continued. "I don't know if you've seen the news, but Luca was arrested."

I stopped dead in my tracks. "Luca Marino?" My lips parted into a wide smile, and I covered my mouth to keep from chuckling aloud with glee.

"Yeah," Matteo said.

"What did he do this time?" I asked, regaining my cool and continuing the walk towards my apartment.

"Nothing, obviously," he snapped. "But they're trying to pin a murder on him."

My smirk weakened at that bit of information. Just because I hated the guy didn't mean I wanted him to go down for murder. Well, actually I did, but I didn't need Matteo to realize I felt that way.

"Anyway, I just thought you should be aware. If the cops or anyone asks you about it, just say you don't know anything."

"I *don't* know anything," I replied pointedly.

"Right, yeah."

The conversation seemed to have concluded, but Matteo didn't hang up. I wondered if he was waiting for me to ask more questions, to at least pretend I cared.

"I assume everyone is cooperating with the police," I said.

"Uh, yeah. I guess. I mean, I haven't spoken with them, but..." his voice trailed off.

"Has your sister?" I couldn't even bring myself to say her name.

Matteo paused. "No. They, um, I guess the cops came to the house asking if anyone had seen her, but no one had. Looks like maybe she's out of town."

Something about his statement seemed fishy. "You don't know where your sister is?"

"Well, no, but—"

Suddenly it all made sense why he was calling me. "Jesus, Matteo, she could be in danger. I haven't seen her since..." I paused, recalling how damn happy she and Luca looked when I'd spotted them a few days before. "Well, I don't know where she is. Have you checked with Luca's guys?"

Matteo blew out a breath. "Adrian, calm down. I'm sure she's fine."

"Her boyfriend just got arrested for murder, and now she's missing. That doesn't seem fine."

"I didn't say she's missing, just that we don't know where she is. I'm sure the police want to question her and of course we'll notify them the second we figure out where she went, but at the moment no one knows."

I gritted my teeth together as it all clicked. Giada wasn't missing; she was hiding. They knew she couldn't hold together a coherent lie for the police so they'd whisked her away to someplace the police couldn't find her. Presumably, all of Luca's guys would be similarly impossible to locate until after they'd figured out whatever unified story they wanted to present.

"I see. Well, I haven't seen her, so afraid I can't help," I said. I was about to hang up when it occurred to me that I had another question. "Who are they saying he killed?"

Somehow, I knew the answer before Matteo even spoke.

"Dmitry Petrov," he said.

Well, wasn't karma a bitch?

CHAPTER 14

Giada

Every detail about the moment felt so unreal that I knew I was dreaming. But I didn't care. Perched on Luca's lap, his arms wrapped tightly around my waist, basking in the sun on his boat off the coast of the Mediterranean, I was in heaven. The sun shone brightly, heat warmed my bare arms, and a gentle breeze kept my hair from sticking to my neck. Luca peppered my shoulders with kisses and I squirmed against him, ticklish, but eager for more.

Right as I turned to face him, a rogue wave smashed into the boat. We both flew overboard, separated by several yards. I sucked in a breath of air then swam towards Luca, pleased to see I nearly bridged the entire distance between us. But then another wave smacked into me, dragging me even further from Luca than before. Every time I'd make any measurable progress swimming to Luca, another wave would hit and force us further apart than before.

Soon, my arms were shaking, my lungs burned, and I was choking on mouthfuls of salty water. I started to feel discouraged, certain the powerful waves would knock me under the sea long before I reached my Luca.

"Shh, Giada, it's okay. You're dreaming."

The words jolted me from sleep, but I didn't move. I needed a moment to acclimate myself to reality. Well, or maybe I didn't. Without even opening my eyes, I recalled that Luca was gone and I was all alone.

I didn't need to be awake to feel his absence like a hollow in my soul.

Enzo's hand rubbed soft circles on my bicep, and I appreciated the gesture, even if my thoughts when awake weren't any less terrifying than my nightmare had been. I wiped my eyes and steadied my breath. I turned towards him, then gasped.

Lorenzo wasn't the one sitting beside me, soothing me from my dreams. It was Alessio. He must have noticed my shock, because he explained.

"You were talking in your sleep," he began. "Loudly."

"I'm sorry," I said, suddenly feeling very naked despite my pajamas. I tugged the sheets higher, tucking the hem under my armpits.

"You don't have to apologize. I don't need a lot of sleep." He paused and glanced around the dreary room. "Do you want me to make you coffee or do you want to try to get more rest?"

I knew I'd never fall back asleep after that dream, but I also recalled that caffeine was bad during pregnancy. Without my phone, I couldn't confirm anything, but it wasn't worth the risk. This baby would have enough trauma to overcome, and if Luca came back to me soon, I sure didn't want to have to tell him I may have damaged our baby with my coffee habit.

"Is there decaf?" I asked, quickly adding, "In case I want to nap later," so Alessio wouldn't be suspicious.

He flashed me a peculiar look, but busied himself making coffee.

I located my hoodie on the floor next to the bed and tugged it over my head.

"Are you really just going to sit here and babysit me all day?" I asked him.

Alessio's gaze dropped down to his watch. "No, I have some business I need to take care of, so Thomas will be coming in an hour or so."

"You guys don't have to babysit me. If it's better for Luca that I stay hidden, I'm not going to go anywhere."

"That's good to hear, but we still aren't leaving you alone." He handed me a sugar packet, plastic tub of creamer, and a stirrer, then set my decaf coffee on the nightstand beside me. "Luca told us to take care of you, so we are."

I doctored up the coffee as best I could with the limited hotel resources before gazing up at Alessio. "Did Luca tell you why we went to Tuscany?" I asked, watching his expression carefully.

"Some romantic getaway?" His face was relaxed, just like his tone.

"Yeah, but did he tell you what happened before?"

Alessio frowned. "I mean, he mentioned you guys argued about something. I think he said you accused him of doing something, and he hadn't done it so he was mad that you didn't believe him."

I cocked my head to the side, surprised Luca not only hadn't told Alessio about our marriage but also hadn't told him exactly why we'd fought. *Interesting.* I decided to change the subject before he got too suspicious.

"Your girlfriend won't mind you staying in a hotel room with me?" I asked.

Alessio choked on his coffee. "Girlfriend? No. Not me."

"I could've sworn Luca said you were seeing someone."

Alessio regained his composure. "Giada, you are all the woman I can handle right now."

I rolled my eyes, then pushed off the bed. I needed to brush my teeth and shower. I started across the room, then stopped. I actually did not need to do any of those things.

I didn't even need to get dressed. I had nowhere to go. I was literally trapped in a hotel room while my husband rotted alone in jail. I clapped a hand over my mouth right as a fresh wave of sobs erupted.

Alessio's arms wrapped around me before I even registered him having moved. "Hey, come on now. Luca is fine. You don't need to worry about him. He's got a great attorney, and he'll be home before you know it."

I wanted to be comforted by that, but there were so many unknowns. "What if you're wrong? What if he stays there until trial? What if he's convicted of something?"

Alessio didn't release me from the embrace, nor did he answer my rhetorical questions. Instead, he just held me tight against his chest, not saying a word as I soaked his shirt with my tears. He didn't loosen his grip on me until I calmed down. As my tears dried up, I could hear the steady thrumming of his heartbeat. At first, the repetition soothed me. But then, that simple sign of life reminded me of the other thing I was facing.

"I can't do this alone," I sputtered, pushing back from him.

This time, Alessio gripped my forearms, angling his head around until he caught my gaze. "You are not alone Giada. Whatever happens, I promise, you will never be alone."

I bit back my tears, forcing a nod. Then I excused myself to the bathroom, where I could cry undisturbed in the shower.

～

Luca

"They want your alibi," my lawyer said the moment we were alone.

"Yes, I gathered as much. We'll get to that. How's Giada?" My attorney was my only connection to the outside world at the moment, so he'd been tasked with relaying messages back and forth between Alessio and me, as well.

"Well, apparently, the authorities haven't been able to track her down to ask her any questions," he began.

I smiled for the first time all day.

"Alessio says she's fine though."

"They need to make sure she's eating. She tends to skip meals when she's worried," I said. "And she shouldn't be left alone, even if she says she wants to be. Giada's used to a big overbearing family, and if it gets too quiet, she'll just worry more."

"She's fine, Mr. Marino. She's in good hands."

"Can I write her a note? Alessio could read it to her."

My lawyer frowned. "We don't have that much time, and I can't have any loose pages—"

His voice trailed off as I swiveled around the notepad so it was facing me. I wrote quickly.

"Amore, so sorry I messed up our lunch plans. I meant what I said to you in Rome before Mass, every single word of it. I can't wait till I'm back home and show you my gratitude for our amazing vacation together. Ti amo, Luca. P.S. You would hate the food here—they haven't served gelato once. It's better than boarding school, though."

I handed the legal pad back to my lawyer. "If someone could text Alessio a photo of the note, I'm sure Giada would like to see it in my handwriting," I said.

The man stifled an eyeroll and then turned to a fresh sheet of paper."The best alibis are the ones who aren't connected to you. Even if your associates, employees, girlfriend, or family was with you at the time and can testify to your innocence, the prosecution will just poke holes in it. Now if there was a stranger who saw you—"

"What about someone who hates me?" I asked, the brilliant idea coming to me all at once. Thanks to some minor reconnaissance I had my guys do lately, I knew exactly where my alibi had been the night in question. And I knew exactly who could convince him to deliver the court performance of his life.

My lawyer looked intrigued. "I suppose it would hinge on whether that stranger was a law-abiding citizen who couldn't easily be impeached on the stand."

I felt my lips curl into a smile as I spoke the name that was to spare me. Then, I added, "Alessio can work out the details and you'll get back to me."

The man jotted down some notes. "They won't let me return to talk with you again today."

"That's fine. I won't speak with them tonight or tomorrow until you return." I passed along a few other messages for him to take to Alessio, then I said goodnight to my loyal advocate.

With any luck, Alessio could pull enough strings overnight to smooth out any details or potential issues with my alibi, and I'd be a free man by dinner the next night.

~

Adrian

When the knock came, I figured it was a classmate or a salesperson. Possibly even one of Marco's guys coming with an update. Never did I expect to see Giada. Especially not alone. I barely recognized her, either. She wore baggy sweats and an oversized sweatshirt with the hood pulled up over her face.

I opened the door, but instead of speaking, I simply stared. She looked exactly as I remembered her, and not a day older. She wasn't wearing much makeup, but her perfect skin had a natural sheen to it making her look like one of those models from a glowing magazine ad. I hated that I still found her attractive, particularly now, when it was apparent she'd done nothing to try to improve her appearance.

I turned away to break the trance. "Come in," I mumbled, shuffling towards the kitchen. I started for the fridge, then decided something stronger than beer was merited for this discussion. I set two glasses on the counter and reached for the whiskey.

"Drink?" I offered, gesturing to the bar to show her I also had vodka or rum, since she'd never loved whiskey.

A peculiar expression crossed her face, then she shook her head before turning and settling onto my couch. I tilted a swig of the whiskey into my mouth, letting the flavors wash over my tongue and sting the back of my throat before swallowing. Then I refilled my glass and sunk onto the armchair across from her. The further from her, the better, I figured. Although now that I was seated, I realized it may have been wiser to sit beside her simply so I didn't have to stare directly at her.

Just as the silence was about to become untenable, she spoke.

"I'm here about Luca."

"I figured as much."

Her eyes lightened. Her gaze filled with hope.

"I'm not involved in his case. I really don't have any advice for you," I said. "You had to know this was inevitable. It was only a matter of time before…"

"He has an alibi," she said. "Once they interview his alibi, the case will be dismissed."

I sincerely doubted that. As hard as their associates worked to keep their names squeaky clean, there was enough suspicion surrounding each of those guys to raise character questions if any of them testified.

"You should prepare yourself for a conviction, Giada. I'm not saying it's a guarantee, but you have to know the prosecution will question the credibility and character of his alibi. They know how his kind works. They know his guys have to back him up or risk death."

"His alibi isn't one of his guys. His alibi is an upstanding citizen, totally uninvolved with his family or mine." She paused, chewing on her bottom lip. "His alibi has no reason to lie for him."

I frowned, actually letting myself think, for a moment, that she was telling me that Luca was actually innocent, that someone really saw him at the time of the crime. "Who is it?"

She hesitated, swallowing nervously. "You."

I stared at her for a minute, trying to decipher if she was joking. Unfortunately, she appeared dead serious.

"That was an unfortunate choice on his part. I'm not lying for your boyfriend. Or, uh, fiancé is it now?" I chugged the rest of my drink and stood to get a refill. "And if I go missing, or worse, after he names me as his alibi, that'll be the final nail in his coffin."

"No one is going to hurt you regardless of what you do, Adrian. You know I would never let—"

"Actually, Giada, if there's one thing I've learned over the years, it's that I don't really know you at all. The Giada I thought I knew would've never tolerated this. That Giada was kind, honest, and faithful." I shook my head, too annoyed now to even attempt to mask my disgust. "You're just like the rest of them now."

She stared at the window and inhaled slowly. I could tell she was trying her damnedest not to cry, and that only reinforced my point. The old Giada would've been a weepy mess by now. The woman in my living room now was as coldhearted as her lover. Boy had I dodged a bullet.

"I didn't know he was going to name you as his alibi. It wasn't like, my idea or anything. But you have to admit it's brilliant. It really could work, and it's not like you have to do much."

"Except lie," I interrupted again. "I literally just took an oath to uphold the dignity of the court, and you're asking me to perjure myself. And for what? So a monster can get away with murder?" The fact that she didn't see what a big deal that was told me a lot about her character as of late.

I paused, then asked her the key question. "Did he do it?" What I really wanted to know wasn't whether or not Luca was guilty. That was irrelevant. He'd killed before, and he'd kill again. So whether this blood was on his hands didn't matter to me.

What I needed to know now was whether Giada would even answer my question.

She did. Her head dipped in an almost imperceptible nod. "He's not a bad person, Adrian."

"No, he is. He's the stereotypical definition of a bad guy. The world is better off with him behind bars." My mind flitted back to the article about the murder. It wasn't some heat-of-the-moment shooting during a fight. It wasn't self-defense. It was a full on ambush-style mafia hit. The guy was just walking along a street then shot at point blank. The only thing that could've made it more cliché would be if they'd thrown his body in the Hudson River. Or possibly buried him under the concrete of some new development they were planning.

When the case went to trial, the prosecution would use words like "premeditated." They'd describe the commission of the crime as "in cold blood." They'd be right. Legally speaking, it was the worst of the worst. The first-degree murder type of shit. Our justice system maybe wasn't perfect, but it wasn't that far off. Good guys didn't go down for first-degree murder.

"I need him, Adrian." Giada's desperate words interrupted my thoughts. Her expression softened now, her hard shell finally cracking and revealing beneath it hints of the vulnerable, uncertain woman I'd once known.

"Giada, if I were to help him get off this time, I'd be partially responsible for all the horrible shit he did after. I don't need that on my conscience."

Her mask slid back into place. "You don't know much about how these guys operate if you think that. Luca can do just as much damage behind bars, if not more. At least when he's home, with me, he has a reason to try to be better. He has something good in his life to work towards."

I opened my mouth to reply, to point out that she wasn't doing a great job of convincing me he was a good person by admitting he could orchestrate even more crime from prison. But I stopped myself. It didn't matter. I wasn't going to lie for him regardless. Or for her.

Giada drew in a sharp breath, her exhale uneven. "He's trying, Adrian. He's not a perfect man. He'll never be as good as you, Saint Adrian, but he's already changed. And soon, he'll be out of this life altogether. He's got to get everything in line, and then we can go and leave this life far behind." Giada paused again. "I could have everything I want, Adrian."

I licked my lips, suppressing an eye roll. I couldn't tell if she was playing me or if she truly believed he would change. If that was the case, she was more foolish than I thought. Maybe the old, naïve Giada hadn't really disappeared.

"It wouldn't work anyway. I don't know where I was that night, and if there's a single hole in my story, he's a goner."

Giada hesitated, leaning forward to let her hair cascade over her eyes. "You were here, in your apartment. You were alone."

"How do you know that?"

"Because my cousin Antonio was watching you."

I frowned, unable to place this cousin in my memory. "Why would he be watching me?"

"My father was suspicious. He saw you with a former associate of his and wanted to know why."

I shook my head. "I don't know anything about any of your dad's former or current associates. I want nothing to do with your world."

"I know. And he knows that now, too. But the fact remains

that Tony saw you come home alone at five-fifteen that day, and you didn't leave until the next morning. The security cameras outside your apartment weren't working that night so no one has any way of disproving anything you say about anyone who may have been at your apartment that night."

"How do you know the cameras weren't working?" I asked, feeling foolish the moment the words left my mouth. Obviously, they had been working just fine. But someone had subsequently broken them or deleted the footage. Of course. These guys left no stone untouched. That was why it was so hard to ever nail one of them down.

I thought about my former boss at the prosecutor's office, Jeremy. He was a good guy, a hard worker. Winning a case like this would lock his career. He deserved that.

"Why would Luca have visited me?"

"To talk with you. To tell you that we were getting married and that you needed to stay out of my life for good so I wouldn't keep running back to you."

I didn't respond right away. This was all too ridiculous. Every time I thought I'd gotten away, somehow Giada and her famiglia would worm their way back into my world and fuck everything up all over again.

"You'd tell them you got home around five-fifteen and that you'd done some work and then watched the six o'clock news followed by two episodes of Walking Dead on Netflix. You'd just turned it off when he arrived. You assumed he wouldn't stay long so you preheated the oven right after he arrived, and then you baked a frozen pizza. He still hadn't left when it was done, so you turned the oven off and let it stay in to keep warm. But he stayed so long it burned. He finally left sometime after eight-thirty and you called to order Chinese food after he left since your dinner was ruined."

"I did order Chinese food that night," I recalled. "Around eight forty-five."

She nodded, and I realized she already knew that. Of course.

I reached for my drink but it was already empty. "Fuck," I said, angrily nudging my glass across the coffee table before standing to pace. I stomped back and forth for a moment before ending up at my corner window, looking out at the street. It was relatively calm this time of night but there were a few stragglers, all calmly going about their simple, honest lives, void of any of the type of bullshit I was currently facing.

"You don't understand how much you're asking, Giada," I finally said.

"I do," she said, her voice startling me by its proximity.

I turned to face her and saw that now, her eyes were red and glossed over with tears. I gazed at my feet, unable to hate her when she looked so sad.

"I'm so sorry he put you in this position, Adrian. If there were any other way, I wouldn't even be here. I know you're a good person, and I know how much integrity matters to you. I will do whatever it takes to pay you back for this. I meant it when I said he's changing. He's trying to find a better way. You don't know what it's like for him. He's never known another way of living, and now he's got all these people that depend on him. And this guy was after his friends, his family…my family."

I shook my head and tried to walk around her, but she didn't budge.

"You still hate me for everything I've put you through, and I understand. I'll never forgive myself either." She tilted her head to catch my eyes. "But I'll die without him, Adrian. I mean it. I don't know how to get through it all without him."

"Giada, stop. This is ridiculous. You can just move away. Start fresh. No one will ever hurt you. Go start a fashion company in Milan. Join an interior design firm in L.A. Hell, just move to New York with Gabriella. You have options. You're not stuck with Luca. Just because he goes down for something doesn't mean you have to. This is your chance to walk away."

"We're already married," she blurted out.

That stopped me dead in my tracks.

"We eloped. Weeks before all of this."

I couldn't fathom why she'd ever do such a thing, and then it hit me. "So you can't be forced to testify," I said.

She shook her head. "Luca didn't know he was going to get arrested. Are you kidding? In his mind, he's invincible in his mind. No, we eloped because we were worried everyone else was getting too much input on our wedding day. We wanted something special, just for us. It was my idea."

"Fuck," I said again, this time under my breath, although at less than a foot away, Giada surely heard me. Still, this didn't change anything. "You can still leave him. It's not that hard to divorce someone in prison."

"You know I don't believe in divorce."

I snorted. Of all the things for her to be a stickler about. "So murder is okay, but divorce…"

She squeezed her eyes shut for a moment, raising her hand to her lips as though trying not to vomit. She paused for a beat, then resumed her cool demeanor.

"Do you even know anything about the guy they say he killed? He was an arms dealer. He literally supplied guns to criminals. He was arrested two years ago on suspicion of sex trafficking. They found four teenage girls in a house he owned and all of them showed signs of sexual abuse and trauma. They were all runaways and all hooked on drugs when they found them. None of them would testify against him, but every single one of them had a clean record before they'd gone missing." Giada paused.

"That's the kind of guy that's no longer here, Adrian. That's the kind of monster they want to ruin Luca's life over. That's the guy who could ruin my life."

"It doesn't have to ruin your life Giada," I began, but suddenly she swayed, as though about to pass out. I reached out to steady her and she fell limply against my chest. I held her tightly for a moment before walking both of us to the couch.

"Hey, you alright?" I asked, lowering her to the cushion and sitting beside her.

She nodded, but she clearly wasn't.

"Have you eaten anything today?"

"Yes. I'm fine. I've just been getting lightheaded lately."

As she spoke, my eyes lingered on her untouched drink. Giada had never before turned down alcohol in a stressful situation. She pressed her hands against her abdomen, a flicker of worry crossing her face.

Suddenly it all made sense. Bile rose in the back of my throat.

"You're pregnant," I said, all the breath rushing out of me so fast I worried I might pass out. I caught my head between my hands and held it for a moment until the world stopped spinning. Then I turned to look at her.

She averted her gaze, but her answer was obvious.

"Shit, Giada. Why wouldn't you..." I sighed. There was no point in blaming her now.

"We were traveling a lot, and I got behind on my shot," she said apologetically. "I'm not even sure I am. I haven't taken a test yet. I just, I keep getting these dizzy spells, and well, I'm late."

"How late?"

"A week," she said, "Maybe two."

I squeezed my eyes shut, wishing this were all a nightmare.

"You can't say anything to anyone. It would kill Luca if he knew and he couldn't be there for me. Especially if he knew I told you before him."

"Why won't you just take a test, Giada?"

She stared at me for a long time before answering. "Because then it's real, and I don't think I can handle anything else right now."

"You're stronger than you think."

"I'm not. Not without Luca. I can't do it without him."

I reached for her glass and began chugging its contents. "Whether or not I say he was with me that night, there's a good chance you're going to have to do it without him. You understand that, don't you? If he doesn't go down for this, it'll be something else. Or worse. He might just get himself killed."

I barely had time to set down the glass before Giada burst into tears. It wasn't a soft, timid cry, but rather a full heaving sob. *Shit.* I wrapped my arm around her and tried to focus on my current messy predicament and not on the fruity scent of her hair. She pressed her face against my shoulder and cried like she hadn't had a chance to process any of her feelings for days. When she finally caught her breath and pulled herself together, I stood to get tissues for her.

I sat beside her again, handing her the tissues. "I need time to think."

She dabbed at her eyes, her efforts having no effect on the redness of her pupils. "He gave them your name tonight. The police will come to question you in the morning."

I shrugged, having figured as much. I could dodge them for the day, but I would have to make up my mind fast.

"I misplaced my cellphone, so don't call it if you want to reach me. Call my church back home at any hour and leave a message for Father Ryan. He'll make sure I get the message. Okay?"

As I nodded my understanding, she lurched forward and hugged me so firmly that I stumbled backwards a step. She clung tightly to me, and I desperately tried to ignore the tantalizing fragrance of her hair or the all too familiar way her body fit against mine. In another world, things could've been so different.

"Take care of yourself, Giada," I said, pressing my lips against her head.

CHAPTER 15

Luca

My second day in jail had passed quickly. I was formally charged with the crime, I announced my plea of not guilty, and the attorneys had argued about bail. As expected, the prosecution insisted I was a flight risk, thanks to my dual citizenship, international connections, and wealth. When they referenced my many ties to known organized crime families, my lawyer objected and accused them of ethnic profiling. Since I hadn't expected to actually be released on bail, I felt no disappointment when the judge sided with the prosecution.

My lawyer had moved to dismiss the charges against me, claiming my alibi was airtight. The prosecution—as predicted—complained that I had produced no alibi, and my attorney responded that I had been too scared to talk. My lawyer then launched into his rant about how I was being harassed and targeted by the police. He argued that the police were using this crime against a known felon as an excuse to arrest me because of an unrelated grudge. The judge seemed particularly interested in hearing what a horrific person my alleged victim had been.

We left with the judge giving the prosecution forty-eight hours. In that time, they must either come up with some shred of hard evidence connecting me to this crime or dismiss the charges against me. Without a gun, fingerprints, or any material evidence, my lawyer seemed confident I'd be home soon. Still, the alibi would guarantee my freedom.

As the bailiff escorted me out of the courtroom, my lawyer promised to meet with me in a moment.

"Are you ready to give your alibi?" he asked me.

I nodded. We hadn't received word that Adrian wasn't going to cooperate, so this would have to do. I hadn't spoken to any of my men since my arrest, and they knew better than to attempt to visit or attend my court hearings. I trusted that they were working to ensure the alibi was airtight and that any leftover manpower would go to tracking down whatever cretin had told the police that I was with Dmitry Petrov at the time of his death.

I met with my attorney for nearly an hour, and then we spoke with the police. Answering their questions proved infinitely harder than remaining silent. I had to monitor my facial expressions, my tone, and of course, my actual words. I needed to follow the script, without letting them distract or anger me. I couldn't offer a single word more than necessary.

My future depended on it.

The only time I faltered was when they asked me about Giada. It was easy to tell the police I didn't know where she was and hadn't spoken to her since my arrest, because that was all true. I didn't deny that we were involved, but when they asked me the nature of our relationship, I hesitated. Not even my lawyer knew we had married. I assumed the marriage was public record, but since we'd done it in Italy, well…maybe no one here knew about it yet. It was important to Giada that her family believe the upcoming summer ceremony was the real thing, so if at all possible, I didn't want to ruin that illusion.

"Guys, what does his girlfriend have to do with any of this?

Stop harassing him," my lawyer had interrupted. "Actually, you know what—I think she's part Italian too, so maybe you want to throw her on the suspect list also. Maybe every Italian-American should be investigated."

Luckily, his rant had distracted them, and they'd moved along to other topics.

My second night in jail was worse than my first. With everything worked out about my alibi—assuming said alibi cooperated—I had nothing to focus on, no problems to solve. I wasn't used to so much downtime. It reminded me of my time in the cabin, immediately after my "death." But thinking of those days only made me miss Giada even more. I would've killed to be back in her bed...

~

Giada

I kept my head down after speaking with Adrian, following the roundabout route Thomas had instructed me to follow to get back to the car. We hoped no one saw me go to Adrian's. Or that if they had spotted me, that they hadn't recognized it was me. Thomas assured me that even if the authorities somehow did see me, we had plenty of options. I could've been visiting as an old friend, seeking comfort. Or I could have even known Luca was with Adrian that night.

But still, I was terrified. If I hadn't convinced Adrian to lie for Luca, or, worse yet, if I had but it still didn't matter, I couldn't live with myself. It was bad enough being away from Luca, but being away and knowing it was all my fault would be worse.

My body was shaking by the time we returned to the hotel. Thomas parked the car and jogged over to my door, wrapping his arm around me as we walked to the room. I wasn't sure if he realized he was the only thing holding me upright, or if he was simply trying to shelter me from any prying eyes.

He locked the door behind us, helping me to the center of the small room. I sat on the foot of the bed, but as soon as Thomas released me, I slid down the front of the bed until I was resting on the floor, my back supported by the bed. I brought my knees to my chest and wrapped my arms around my knees, still trembling.

Panic filled Thomas's eyes. I'd told him in the car what Adrian had said, so he knew there was nothing to do but wait, and I could tell he wanted answers maybe as much as I did.

"Giada, you're shaking. Are you…cold?" He winced as though certain that wasn't the explanation.

"I'm…" I gave up trying to speak and instead just shook my head.

"I'll call Lorenzo. Would that make you feel better?"

I started to nod, a hint of comfort creeping over me at the familiar name, but then I stopped. "I want Alessio," I said. He was the only person who loved Luca as much as I did, albeit in an entirely different way.

Relief washed over Thomas. "He's already on his way."

I nodded and squeezed my eyes shut, replaying every moment of my conversation with Adrian. Overanalyzing that part of my day proved infinitely less stressful than letting my mind wander. Thinking about Luca, trying to guess how he was feeling, where he was sleeping, what he was doing…all of those questions made my pulse roar behind my ears.

My eyes flickered open at the sound of voices. Alessio had appeared in the room, and was deep in hushed conversation with Thomas. They spoke in Italian, so I wasn't sure why they bothered to whisper. A moment later, Alessio had kicked off his shoes and dropped to the floor beside me. He scooted behind me, pulling my back against his chest.

His arms wrapped tightly around me, letting me release my

firm hold on myself. Alessio's embrace left no room for me to shake, nor to take the deep gulps of air my anxious body craved. He didn't say anything until I began to still, my body slowly relaxing into him.

"You did great, Giada. Adrian is going to come through for Luca, and everything will be back to normal soon," he promised.

I opened my mouth to ask questions, but he kept talking.

"But you need to calm down. Luca's asking about you, wants me to tell him if you're eating and sleeping okay. You know I can't lie to him. But how do you think he'll feel if he hears you're like this?" he pauses, but his words cut into me like a knife, filling me with guilt. "You're strong, Giada. And you just have to be patient a little longer. Okay?"

I closed my eyes. "Okay," I whispered.

Alessio held me for several more minutes. Exhaustion mixed with my newfound calmness, and I nearly drifted off. Maybe I actually did. When I opened my eyes, Thomas was pulling tubs of cream cheese from a paper sack and the scent of fresh bagels filled the small room.

I shifted forward, surprised that my stomach didn't recoil from the smell. I was famished, but up to this point, the thought of eating had disgusted me more than the fear of continuing to suffer hunger pangs.

Alessio slowly helped me up, not releasing his hold on me until I demonstrated I could stand independently.

"Luca recommended we bring you carbs. He said you'll eat bagels when you're stressed and that this is your favorite bakery," he said. Then he made a face. "He also made some comment about how you'll need all the carbs you can get before he gets home, but I'm not really sure I'm comfortable translating everything he said."

Heat rushed to my cheeks and I bit back a smile. "You talked to him?"

Alessio shook his head. "Not directly, but his lawyer, he passes along messages. I'll tell you more while you eat."

I lifted the sweatshirt over my head, suddenly suffocated by its thickness. I gazed around the room, quickly locating my leggings, then went to the bathroom. I changed into my own pants, washed my hands, and splashed cool water over my face. My eyes weren't nearly as splotchy as I'd expect. A low growl erupted from my stomach, prompting me to return to the room.

The guys had spread multiple drinks across the small table, so I chose a ginger ale. Thomas offered me a glass with ice, which I accepted, pouring the light amber liquid over the cubes and watching the foam and bubbles rise towards the edge. I surveyed the bagel options, then dropped a blueberry one onto a paper plate. Luca always scoffed at my choice, insisting blue was not a natural color for a bagel, but I loved the subtle sweetness of the variety. I broke off a piece a stuck it in my mouth, relieved when its warm softness settled against my tongue instead of churning up nausea.

I chewed and swallowed the bite, washing it down with a long sip of soda. The bubbles stung the back of my throat, but once the liquid hit my stomach, a renewed thirst overwhelmed me. I gulped down the entire glass, then gnawed another bite of bagel. Thomas refilled my drink while Alessio spread cream cheese on a bagel for himself.

"I'm eating," I said. "Now talk."

The men exchanged a glance, then Alessio began. "Luca's lawyer is the best. He knows our family, but he's independent. He thinks they'll drop the charges if the alibi comes through."

"And if it doesn't?" I interrupt. "If Adrian won't—"

"They still have nothing. No weapon, no fingerprints."

"Then why did they arrest him? What made them think it was him if there's no evidence?" That was the question that kept running through my mind when everyone insisted there was nothing keeping Luca in jail.

Alessio hesitated. "We aren't sure. They say they have an eyewitness and a motive."

"Who?"

He shrugged. "They won't tell. The name is sealed."

"You think someone was following him? Or, like, a rat?"

"We don't know. We'll find out eventually, but that isn't the priority."

Plucking out traitors within the ranks seemed pretty important to me, but I had too many other questions to argue. "How many people knew what happened that night?"

Thomas chuckled, and Alessio shot him a look. I cocked my head to the side until Alessio answered.

"Everyone. Giada, it wasn't just our family that wanted Petrov gone. Your family was after him too. So was Anton Volkov. Literally everyone with any relevant business in the area wanted him out. If everyone in our world knew that Luca could take out another powerful leader, that ensures no one messes with us for a while. And it made them all grateful. Everyone owes us favors now."

"The scotch," I groaned. "That was a thank you gift?"

He nodded.

"So basically, you all threw Luca out there on a platter to be arrested, telling the whole world he did something illegal just so people wouldn't mess with you? Did no one think about him, about what would happen when he got arrested?" Anger bubbled up inside me, threatening to erupt.

Alessio placed a hand on my arm, keeping me in my seat. "Luca made all the decisions, Giada. No one did anything *to* him, and it was a calculated risk. One that still looks like it'll pay off."

"If everyone knows, couldn't dozens of people come forward and corroborate the witness's story?" I asked, pressing a napkin to my lips, my nausea returning. "What's to stop someone else from talking?"

"Omertà," Alessio replied.

"What is that?"

He shrugged. "It's a code amongst men."

"A code of silence," Thomas clarified.

Alessio nodded. "It's a pretty big deal in our world. No one talks to the authorities unless they have a death wish. Not even if you're ratting out an enemy."

I wasn't sure how comforting that information should be, but I filed it away to ponder further later.

"Luca wrote you a note, but I'm not showing you until you finish your bagel," Alessio said.

I glared at him over that taunt, but resumed picking at my food. "Where is Salvatore? Has he been visiting Luca?"

"He's in Palermo."

"Luca's own father didn't even come back?" I made no attempt to hide my disbelief.

"There's nothing for him to do, Giada. He'll fly back once Luca's home, and he'll help us pin down who went to the cops."

I said nothing, focusing instead of finishing the bagel as fast as possible.

"Giada, if anyone ever questions you about any of this, you say nothing, okay? No matter how innocent the question, you don't answer. Even if they just ask your name or your birthday, you tell them you want a lawyer or you stay silent. Understood?"

I nodded, then gestured to my now empty plate. Alessio pulled out his phone and clicked on an image. I snatched the phone out of his hands, smiling at the familiar scrawl of Luca's penmanship. His note was short, but it served its purpose. Luca was okay. He was still himself. And if he could get through this, so could I.

"I'm impressed you got him to go to mass in Italy," Alessio said after a moment, interrupting my seventh read-through of the note. "What did he say to you?"

I glanced away from the phone, taking in Alessio's innocent expression. He was only trying to distract me from my worries with happy thoughts, but his question served a much greater purpose. "I can't believe he didn't tell you," I said. "I asked him not to, but I never really thought he would actually keep his word."

"Didn't tell me what?" he asked, exchanging a look with Thomas.

I smiled and shook my head, reaching into the bag for a miniature chocolate chip muffin instead of answering.

~

Adrian

I was awake and ready when the police arrived on my doorstep at eight o'clock the next morning. I hadn't slept much the night before, but thanks to a cold shower and some coffee, I looked relatively normal. When the officers told me they had some questions pertaining to an active murder investigation, I said I'd be happy to help but that I needed to take care of something that morning and could meet them at the station by half past nine. They'd made a quick phone call, then left.

I was ready to leave, but I needed to do one final thing before selling my soul to the devil. It had occurred to me overnight that since I hadn't received any threats from Angelo or bribes from Marco, perhaps they didn't know Giada wanted me to be Luca's alibi. And if her own family didn't want Luca free, then who was I to tarnish my good name on his behalf?

I dialed Marco before I could second guess myself, and he answered just before the call went to voice mail.

"Uh, Mr. Conti? It's Adrian. Adrian Patras."

"Yes. Hi Adrian, how are you?"

I started to answer, but he continued.

"We were so relieved to hear that you were with Luca the

night that awful Russian terrorist went missing. It's ludicrous that they'd even bother charging anyone with this, but for them to try to pin it on Luca is even crazier."

I supposed that answered my question. "So you were aware that he said I was his alibi?"

"Sure. Why don't I have his lawyer call you now, just to make sure you don't have any questions?"

"Uh, okay," I said. I hung up and grabbed my car keys. The lawyer did call as I drove to the station, and he went over my story again. By the time I arrived at the station, I felt as prepared as I'd ever be.

The two officers offered me some coffee and led me into a private room then set up a recorder.

After they went over the basic events of that evening, they backpedaled

"Are you friends with Luca Marino?"

"No."

"But you're close?"

I shook my head. "He's quite possibly my least favorite person alive."

This seemed to genuinely surprise the detective. "And why is that?"

"You don't know?" I couldn't believe they hadn't looked into my history with Luca more before questioning me. "His girl-friend, er fiancée, er…" I winced at the still painful memory of what she'd told me the night before. "Whatever she is. Giada Conti. You know her?"

The men both nodded.

"Yeah, well, she was my girlfriend in college. She dumped me and then went out with Luca. And then she came back to me. And then she left me for him, again."

I paused to sip my coffee, and the Detective started to move on. I held up my hand to stop him.

"It gets even better," I said. "She then came back to me a third time and then while I was starting to think about marriage and kids, she was actually seeing Luca again, behind my back, the entire time. So, yeah. I wouldn't describe us as friends."

"When did you meet him initially?"

"The summer before I started law school. I was staying at Giada's family home while working with Jeremy, actually, and a couple of weeks into the summer, Luca waltzed in like a fucking prince. He stayed at the house too."

They exchanged glances. "Any particular reason you used that term, 'prince'?"

"Everyone treats him like royalty. It's a fitting word."

"Was anything promised to you in exchange for offering your alibi today?"

"No."

"Any reason to fear Luca or anyone else if you don't offer this alibi?"

"No."

"Are you familiar with the witness protection program?"

"The general concept, yeah. Someone testifies against a guy like Luca, and the government helps them disappear and stay safe."

"What do you mean 'a guy like Luca'?"

"I'm not an idiot. I see what kind of a man he is."

"And what kind of a man is that?"

"Not a good one."

"Can you be more specific?"

I considered this for a moment. "He's bossy and controlling, selfish, arrogant, manipulative."

"How do you think he would react if he heard you describe him in that way?"

"He already knows how I feel about him."

"Have you ever seen him engage in any illegal activity?"

I shook my head.

"That's a no?"

"Correct."

"Have you heard him discussing any illegal acts he's taken?"

"No. Look, I see what you're getting at here, but um, he's a cautious guy. If he was going to do something illegal, he sure wouldn't let me know about it."

The men exchanged notes for a minute, and I used the moment to catch my breath.

At the start of our conversation, I'd been nervous. My mouth was dry, my hands were shaking, and I was certain I'd vomit on the table if they asked me any specific questions. But now, I felt fine. It turned out to be easy to lie. Too easy, really.

The more they questioned, the easier the story flowed from me. The entire interrogation felt like a game, and I was winning.

The men then asked me a similar line of questions about Marco, Angelo, and Matteo. I kept my story consistent, offering some irrelevant details, but nothing concrete. The adrenaline coursed through my veins. I felt powerful and strong.

They said we were almost done, but then they took a lengthy break. On return, I was waiting for them to pick apart my story, but instead, they switched directions.

"Are you and Giada Conti still friends?"

I shrugged, trying to play it cool. "I think Luca prefers she not spend much time with me, and I understand. If she were mine, I wouldn't want her fraternizing with him."

"Do you still have feelings for her? I mean, with the back-and-forth nature of your relationship, it seems like there's a fair chance that if he were to go to prison, she'd come running back to you. Would you be open to that?"

I pondered that question, having asked myself the same thing several times over the course of the prior night. "I don't know," I finally said. "I'm pretty sure a part of me will always love her, but she's changed over the years. I don't think there's a future for us."

I realized they were both silent as I paused, and suddenly I felt the need to explain.

"I wouldn't lie for her, if that's what you're insinuating. And if we're being completely honest, yeah, my chances with Giada are greater if Luca stays behind bars." I paused. "But since I know he didn't do it, that means someone else did. I don't think I could live with myself knowing a killer went free just because I hated Luca too much to speak up."

The guys exchanged a glance again, and I knew I'd won my case. They started stacking their papers, and the redhead spoke. "Actually, I doubt there will be much of an investigation. Dmitry Petrov, the victim, let's just say nobody is going to miss him. He was wanted in thirteen countries and has been on the FBI's list for months. Whoever killed him did us all a favor."

They chuckled and then headed towards the door. "Hang on for one minute while we make sure there's nothing else."

I nodded and sipped my coffee.

They didn't close the door behind them as they stepped out into the hall. I heard muffled voices, then heard the familiar voice of my old boss Jeremy.

"Let me talk to him alone," he said.

I couldn't hear their answer, but a moment later, Jeremy and I were alone in the room.

"Long time, no see," he said, leaning in to shake my hand.

I smiled. "I'm sorry we're not getting together under better circumstances. I'm assuming you heard what I told the detectives," I said tentatively.

Jeremy nodded tersely.

"Look, I've been really impressed with how you've handled your career. You deserve a big break. I'm sorry this won't be it."

Now he frowned. "We can protect you, Adrian."

"I'm not afraid of Luca Marino," I said. For the first time in my life, it was the truth.

"He's not a good man, Adrian. We can put him away and keep a lot of people safe."

I shrugged and glanced to the wall, the sadness in Jeremy's

eyes piercing my conscience. "I don't disagree with your assessment of him. I think you'd be hard pressed to find a redeeming quality about him."

Jeremy slammed his fists into the table, shaking it so severely that some of my coffee splashed over the side of the mug. "So why aren't you helping us?"

I leaned closer. "I can't change the facts of when he was at my apartment. I don't question Luca's willingness to do this sort of thing, but in this case, it's just not possible. It had to be someone else."

Jeremy's jaw clenched so tightly together that I heard his teeth grinding.

"If it's any consolation, guys like him never change. He'll slip up soon, and you'll nail him."

Jeremy still didn't speak.

"Am I free to go? You know where to find me if you have more questions."

He nodded slowly. I stood and made my way to the door right as he spoke.

"You might be wrong," he said.

I turned, confused. He rose to his feet and stepped closer.

"A man like Luca might change," he said. "You sure did. I don't know what they promised you, but I sure as fuck hope it was worth it, because you can't come back from this. Once you cross this line..." His voice trailed off, but he didn't need to finish the thought aloud anyway. I knew what he meant, and he wasn't wrong.

But what I was just starting to realize was that I'd crossed that line long before.

"You take care, Jeremy," I said, patting him on the back then seeing myself out of the station.

CHAPTER 16

Giada

I couldn't shake the feeling that Alessio was wrong, that Luca wasn't really free and home, until I actually saw him with my own eyes. Even when I went into his mom and dad's house and heard the commotion, then saw the group of men gathered around something, I didn't let myself believe it until the crowd parted and revealed Luca standing right before me.

He was wearing the same clothes I'd last seen him in, and he had three days of beard growth. I watched as he embraced Alessio, saying something in Italian before releasing the man and patting him on the back jovially. Someone else called his name, but at that moment, my husband glanced up and saw me. His lips parted in a smile but he paused before stalking forward, broaching the distance between us.

My feet were glued to the floor, though it felt like an eternity passed while he approached.

"Amore," he purred as he reached me. "God, how I missed you."

I squeezed my eyes shut, not launching myself into his arms until I reopened my eyes and confirmed he wasn't an illusion. He held me so tightly that I couldn't catch my breath, but I didn't care. As long as I had Luca, I didn't need oxygen.

His grip loosened, too soon, as someone behind him cleared his throat.

"We should talk," the man said.

I frowned, instantly disliking that man. I recognized him as someone I'd seen with Luca's father many times, so he probably wasn't a person Luca could ignore without ramification.

Luca nodded, then glanced at me.

As Luca opened his mouth to speak, I fully prepared myself to accept that he was leaving me—already—for some unethical business meeting of sorts. Instead, he hesitated, then turned back to the man.

"It can wait an hour. I need to shower," Luca said, gripping my hand tightly and leading me down the back hall towards the bedroom.

He locked the door behind us then turned to me. He brushed my hair out of my face and ran his eyes over my body, as though conducting a cursory medical exam. "Are you okay? Did Alessio take care of you?"

I nodded. "He and Enzo and Thomas took me to some seedy hotel, but they were nice and kept me fed and whatever."

Luca cupped my chin in his hand then ducked to meet my eyes. "I'm so, so sorry Giada. You must have been terrified."

I thought I should be mad at him. Afterall, it wasn't like Luca was completely without blame in the whole scenario. He had, in fact, murdered someone. He'd also apparently bragged about it to the entire criminal underworld. And yes, we'd have to talk about all of that at some point.

But at the moment, all I felt was relief and gratitude. My husband was back home with me, and he chose me over his stupid business associates.

I leaned in and kissed him.

His kiss in return was tentative, and then he quickly broke it off. "Give me two minutes?"

I nodded, and Luca hurried into the bathroom. I heard the distinct sounds of tooth brushing, so I followed, not eager to let him out of my sight. He reached for his razor next, but I stopped him, placing my hand over his.

"I'll scratch you," he said, rubbing his chin.

"I don't care," I said. It was the truth, although at this point, his beard was past the prickly stubble stage anyway.

"I haven't showered in days."

"I'll wait," I promised.

He grinned appreciatively then slowly undressed while the water heated up. As I watched the muscles in his shoulders and back contract as he shampooed his hair, I decided I'd rather join him than wait.

I slipped my shirt over my head before lowering my pants to my feet. Luca turned to face me, his smile widening as I reached to unfasten my bra. I stepped out of my panties then joined him.

"Miss me already?" he teased, rinsing his head.

He kissed me before I could answer, and this time, there was nothing tentative about his kiss. I moaned into his mouth, letting the relief wash over me. Luca was safe and back in my arms, right where he belonged. His kisses devoured my lips, leaving no question that he had missed me as much, if not more, as I had him. His arms wrapped so tightly around me that I couldn't have wriggled away if I'd wanted to.

There was only one way we could've gotten any closer, and it was clear we both wanted that. I reached down between us, stroking the head of his cock as it pressed against my abdomen. Luca growled and released me quickly, swiveling me away from him so quickly that I would've slipped had he not been holding me so tightly. He nudged my legs apart with his knee then rubbed his fingers along my slit.

Luca entered me quickly, filling me fully on the first thrust and then stilling, both of us enjoying the connection. After a moment, I grew restless and pulled away, moving myself back and forth along him. I braced myself against the shower wall with one hand, my other hand clutching Luca's hand at my waist. He quickly took over for me, holding me in place while he thrust faster and faster, all the while trailing his lips across the side of my neck.

My orgasm took me by surprise, coming out of nowhere and sweeping me up like a rogue wave that I was powerless to stop. I cried out loudly, biting softly on the fingers he thrust into my mouth to muffle the noise. Then I ground my hips harder against him until a moment later when he found his release, moaning my name then gradually loosening his grip on my waist.

"I love you," he whispered into my ear.

I turned quickly, rising to my toes so I could kiss his lips. "I missed you so much," I said as I flattened my feet. I reached my finger up and traced the ring on his necklace, slipping my finger in and pulling him close.

Luca waited until I released him to reach for the soap, then he quickly finished washing. It hadn't even occurred to me to clean anything while I was in the shower, so I just stood there until he finished, afraid he'd disappear again if I so much as blinked. He shut off the faucet, gently wrung out my hair, then tugged me out of the shower.

Luca wrapped a towel around me before grabbing a second one for himself. He tied his around his waist before picking me up, carrying me into the bedroom, and gently depositing me on the bed. My towel fell open as I hit the duvet, but Luca quickly covered me with his body, so I didn't mind the draft.

We kissed for several minutes before he began to work his way down my body. His lips scorched my skin, with the fire spreading as he neared his destination. By the time his tongue brushed across my sensitive folds, I was panting.

No man knew his way around my body like Luca, and no man had ever turned me into a quivering begging mess of sensations so quickly as him. Within minutes, my hips bucked wildly towards his mouth, spurring him to grip my thighs and hold me in place while I rode out the last waves of my orgasm.

As I caught my breath, the intensity of it all overwhelmed me, and I was sobbing by the time he stretched out beside me.

"Baby, what's wrong?"

I shook my head, embarrassed to cry after he pleasured me so completely not once, but twice, all in a matter of minutes.

"I'm so sorry," he murmured, pressing his lips against my head.

"I just didn't know if we'd ever get to do that again. I wasn't sure I'd ever get to touch you or feel like that without you, and—"

"Shhh, I know, tesoro, I know."

He spent the next several minutes comforting me until, finally, I couldn't deny it was time for him to get dressed and rejoin the real world, at least for a little while.

"I have to go talk with my guys," he said. "We need to, uh, debrief, and so forth. I want you to stay right here, though. I won't leave the house, and I'll be back here beside you for bed. Okay?"

I nodded.

Luca tucked his shirt into his pants before tightening his belt. He dragged a hand through his hair, and I couldn't help but notice how he already resembled the old Luca. Looking at him, I couldn't even tell he'd missed nearly a week of sleep, that he'd undergone enormous stress. He didn't look like he had spent time in jail. He didn't look like a murderer.

I knew Luca was a master at concealing his emotions. His poker face was flawless. So just because he didn't appear to still be distraught over the events of the last week didn't mean he wasn't. Except…well, what if in his mind, it had all been resolved?

"Luca!" More desperation filled my voice than I'd intended.

He swiveled towards me, cocking his head to the side as he approached the bed.

"We still need to talk," I said.

Luca frowned, but nodded.

"You owe me an explanation," I continued.

Relief relaxed his facial features. "We're going to figure out what happened tonight. As soon as we identify the rat, I'll let you know."

It took me a moment to understand what he meant, and once I did, I felt silly. Of course, that was Luca's priority now, figuring out who betrayed him and went to the police. But that hadn't been what I wanted to discuss.

"Was it all a lie?" I asked. "When we were together in Italy, and you told me you would change? You made it seem like there was hope, like some day we could have a normal future. You said you'd try to be a better person."

My husband gazed at me, his expression equally unreadable and pitiable.

"You promised to do better, and then you—"

"I did what had to be done," he interrupted. "And I'd do it again in a heartbeat."

He dropped to the edge of the bed and gripped my hands before continuing. "I meant what I told you. I want to be the type of man you deserve. I want us to be able to get away from this life, someday. But you're not the only one with a moral code. I have to face myself in the mirror every day too, and I have zero regrets about ridding the world of that monster. Just because something breaks man's law doesn't mean it's immoral."

"But Luca—" I began.

He pressed a finger to my lips, shushing me. "I have to go. I'm sorry. You have every right to be angry with me, and you deserve more explanation than I can give you now. I promise we'll talk later."

I blew out a sigh. "Okay."

He tugged me close, hugging me so tightly that I could barely breathe, then he abruptly released me and started towards the door.

"Tomorrow I'll have to go into work. I've missed too much and everything's gotten off schedule. But I want you to come meet me for lunch, in the office. Will you do that for me?"

"Yes." I nearly added that he was dumb for asking, that I'd do anything for him. Except I didn't, because he already knew.

"I love you."

I blew a kiss and watched him leave.

❧

Luca

I'd been behind closed doors in my papà's office meeting with my guys until late into the night, but we hadn't affirmatively identified the snitch. I argued that it didn't matter. We already knew the Marinos had enemies, and as news of my hit had traveled, one of those enemies seized the opportunity and went to the cops. I assumed that was why Alessio hadn't wanted me to do it myself, but now that I was off the hook, I had no regrets. Yes, jail was awful, but I figured it was important for everyone—my guys and others—to know that I was willing to do myself what needed to be done.

Alessio had warned me that Giada knew what I'd done, but by the time I returned to bed, she was sound asleep. She'd stirred and snuggled against me when I'd climbed in bed, then once again in the morning when I'd roused to head into the office, but so far, we hadn't had a chance to discuss. I knew she must be disappointed in me, but hoped she'd understand.

The morning flew by in the office, and it was almost time for my lunch with Giada. I'd asked Alessio to pick her up, certain she was still too upset over the events of the past few days to drive herself.

I had just disconnected a call when there was a knock at my door. I glanced up to see Jordan.

"Sorry to interrupt, but there's a guy at the door. He says he knows you."

I shrugged impatiently. How the fuck was I supposed to tell him if I wanted to speak with the man or not if I didn't know his name?

"He says his name is Adrian."

"Ask his last name. If it's Patras, send him on in."

"Alone?"

"Sure." I rolled my eyes as soon as the pinhead left.

A moment later, he returned with Adrian. He held tightly to the back of Adrian's elbow.

"Let go of him," I said, noting Adrian's scowl. I motioned for my minion to leave then turned to Adrian. "Sorry about that."

I leaned forward and extended my hand. He accepted warily.

"Have a seat," I said. "I'm glad you came by. I was going to drive out to see you tonight to thank you, so I guess you've saved me a trip."

"To thank me?"

I frowned. Was this a trick? "Yeah, for cooperating with the police."

"You didn't give me much choice."

"You always have a choice, Adrian," I said pointedly. "Anyway, in light of our history, I wasn't sure you'd feel so cooperative."

"Water under the bridge," he replied.

I leaned back in my chair, trying to gauge what his game was. Then it hit me. He'd been "cooperating" with Marco for years. He expected something in return. "Well, I'd love to show you my appreciation. What can I do for you?"

Adrian raised an eyebrow, then chuckled. "I don't know. I

guess you can just owe me one for the time being. I actually came here to talk with you about Giada."

My stomach tightened.

"She told me your news."

"News?"

"That you eloped."

He said it so casually that I almost thought I'd misheard him. Giada hadn't mentioned telling him that information. I had thought we were keeping it between the two of us.

"Anyway, so um, congratulations, I guess. I just wanted to tell you in person that you win. I mean, obviously she chose you, but I figured you should know I'm taking myself out of the equation anyway, and that even if she hadn't made her choice, I'm done playing the game."

I really didn't know what to say to any of that, either. It definitely wasn't what I'd expected him to say.

Adrian stood. "And don't worry, I won't tell anyone your news, any of it."

I didn't dwell too long on what he meant by that last part. "Well, thanks again, and uh, glad there's no hard feelings about Giada."

Adrian nodded, and I sighed, relieved to have apparently said the right thing.

"Oh, and congratulations, too, on the other news. I can't say I think any of this is good for Giada, but that is not my business."

I smiled then paused. "Which other news do you mean?" It had been a busy few days.

Adrian cocked his head to the side, a quizzical expression on his face. "About the baby."

"What baby?" I asked, suddenly feeling winded.

There was a thump by the door. We both turned to the doorway as Giada appeared. Her purse lay by her feet, its contents splayed out across the floor. Her face blanched, and I realized then that she'd heard my question.

My words still hung in the air like an invisible fog, but no one made any attempt to answer me.

Instead, Adrian turned to Giada, my Giada.

"You still haven't told him?" he asked, his voice filled with accusation.

I faced my wife who, for once in her life, was speechless.

"I'm sorry," Adrian mumbled, brushing past her.

~

Giada

I'd never seen Luca look more hurt than he did at that moment. I half expected him to lash out, so I didn't approach immediately. But after a moment, it was too painful to see the look in his eyes and not comfort him.

I rushed forward right as he sunk into his chair as though pulled down by a string. I dropped to my knees in front of him.

"Luca, I'm so sorry. I didn't want to stress you out more when you were arrested, and…" I stopped, unsure how to explain why I told Adrian.

"You're pregnant?" he looked genuinely confused.

I opened and closed my mouth twice before finding the right words. "I think so. I'm late, and I haven't been feeling quite right. I'm not positive yet. I was going to tell you once I knew for sure, but…"

Luca still gazed at me, slack-jawed and bewildered.

"I'm so sorry, babe," I repeated.

"That's why you wanted to marry so quickly," he finally said.

He spoke so softly that it took me a minute to piece together his words.

"No," I said, leaning forward and tugging on his hands until he looked me in the eyes. "I didn't know anything about it then. I couldn't even be that far along. I wanted to marry you because I love you."

"But you told Adrian first."

"I didn't mean to. I wanted to tell you at lunch that day, when you were arrested. When I went to talk to Adrian about you, I got lightheaded. He figured it out. But I think that's what made him decide to testify, or whatever it's called."

"You're pregnant?" Luca asked again.

I started to repeat that I wasn't sure yet, but he abruptly stood, lifting me as he did. He set me on the desk and stared at me a moment longer as his expression transformed into a childlike smile.

He leaned in and kissed me firmly on the mouth, his hands steadying my head as though he feared I'd pull away. When he finally ended the kiss, he shook his head again.

"You're pregnant with my baby," he said.

"Maybe," I clarified.

His eyes widened, and I instantly realized my mistake.

"No, I mean, I'm not positive I'm pregnant, but if I am, of course, it's your baby. I'm one hundred percent sure on that."

Luca smiled and squatted down, nudging me backwards and lifting my shirt to kiss my stomach.

I giggled and squirmed, his breath tickling my abdomen while he peppered dozens of kisses around my belly. Just as I started to panic about the intimacy of this moment with the door wide open, he kissed his way back up my body, smoothing my shirt down as he went.

"Luca, we should find out for certain before we get too excited," I cautioned.

He nodded. "I'm surprised you didn't already. I had no idea you could be so patient about surprises."

"I always pictured us finding out together. Besides…I couldn't have handled finding out on my own with you behind bars."

Luca paled as though he'd already forgotten that less than twenty-four hours prior, he was a warden of the state.

"Jesus, if Adrian hadn't stepped up, if I was still there…"

"But you're not," I reminded him. "There's no need to ponder the what ifs because you're home now, and we're together." I paused and looked him straight in the eye. "And you're never again going to put yourself in a position where you might be taken away from me. Promise?"

"Ti prometto, mio amore." Luca leaned forward and kissed me again.

I pulled away after a moment, all too aware that his door was still open.

"I owe you lunch," he said.

I was tempted to point out that he owed me a lot more than lunch. Less than sixty days before, he'd promised not to kill anyone, and as easy a promise as that seemed to keep, he hadn't. But telling Adrian about the pregnancy, about the marriage, even, well, that felt like an equally big betrayal. Maybe we were even,

"Could we swing by a drug store and pick up a test?" he asked.

I nodded and let him kiss me again.

CHAPTER 17

Adrian

My talk with Luca hadn't gone exactly as I'd planned, but it didn't matter. I'd wanted him to know he owed me and that I was over Giada. I'd achieved both those objectives.

As for the rest, well, that was less intentional. I'd wanted him to know Giada confided in me about their marriage and the baby, even if she'd only done so to help him. I liked seeing the hurt in his eyes when he realized she still trusted me that much.

But I hadn't meant to blow her news about the baby. It honestly hadn't occurred to me that she wouldn't have told Luca by now.

Not wanting to lose my nerve, I called Marco as I left Luca's club, before I'd even reached my car in the parking lot. He answered quickly.

"It's Adrian," I began. "If you're not too busy today, I'd love to meet with you. It'll be quick."

Marco invited me over to the house, which left me close to a half hour to second guess myself.

When I arrived, Leo invited me into the house and walked me to Marco's office. Having spent a full month in that house in the not-so-distant past, I knew my way around, so I suspected the escort was more of a security measure than a hospitality thing. Still, we were soon alone.

Marco greeted me warmly and offered me a drink, which I declined. Then, he motioned for me to sit.

"I'm sure Luca expressed his gratitude already, but I'm glad you came by. I wanted to personally thank you for what you did, too. I wasn't sure if you'd go through with it, given your relationship with that prosecutor, but..." his voice trailed off and he smiled amicably.

"Well, you're welcome, but I did it for Gia, not you, and certainly not for Luca."

Marco raised his eyebrows and leaned closer. "Are you still interested in Giada?" He said it as though the possibility perplexed him, but he wasn't completely opposed to it.

I took a deep breath, then shook my head adamantly. "No. I'm done pining for Giada, and I'm done being your pushover errand boy. I've seen how this world works, and the good guys never come out on top."

"Adrian, I apologize if I've ever made you feel like a..."

I raised my hand to silence him. I needed to say my piece before I lost my nerve. "I don't need your gratitude, your sympathy, or your apologies, Sir. That's not why I'm here."

A bemused grin crossed his face. "Why are you here then?"

I braced myself, knowing that after my next breath, there was no going back. Once the words left my mouth, my fate would be sealed. I exhaled slowly, then stared straight into the unwavering hooded eyes of Marco Conti.

"I want in," I said.

The End

Thanks so much for reading! If you enjoyed this story, please take a moment to leave a review. If you're reading the digital version, this link here should take you directly to your retailer site to review. Review Mafiosa Princess-Omertà Here

You can also review on Goodreads and Bookbub.

Thanks so much!

https://www.LizaMalloy.com/registration

ACKNOWLEDGMENTS

I am so appreciative of everyone who has supported me and by writing career! Thank you to my family, my beta readers, and to the amazing community on BookTok. A huge thanks to my editor Sarah and to my cover designer J.D. Designs. Finally, thank you to everyone who reads and reviews my books!

ABOUT THE AUTHOR

Liza Malloy writes contemporary romance and women's fiction. She's a sucker for alpha males, bad boys, dimples, and muscles, and she can't resist a man in uniform. Liza loves creating worlds where her heroine discovers her own strength and finds her Happily Ever After. When Liza isn't reading or writing torrid love stories, she's a practicing attorney. Her other passions include gummy bears, jelly beans, and the occasional marathon. She lives in the Midwest with her four daughters and her own Prince Charming.

Visit her website at www.LizaMalloy.com

Join her email list at http://eepurl.com/gnuROD